Praise fo

Jea

TWICE UPON A W

"*Twice Upon a Wedding* is fun springtime reading."
—*Romantic Times*

ONCE UPON A BRIDE

"Delightful . . . Jean Stone provides a wonderful contemporary tale starring mature characters looking to regain the magic." —TheBestReviews.com

BEACH ROSES

"Rich in both humorous moments and sobering turns, Stone's novel shows that true friendship knows no bounds." —*Booklist*

"*Beach Roses* is a poignant story of relationships and camaraderie. The characterization is flawless, and the pages turn easily to the end."
—*Romance Reviews Today*

TRUST FUND BABIES

"If you like a good tale with strong women characters, in which love and loyalty battle grim reality and win . . . *Trust Fund Babies* fits the bill!"
—America Online's *Romance Fiction Forum*

"Witnessing these three women maintain their composures in the midst of such great tribulations was fascinating to read. Just when you think their bonds are subject to being broken, each woman surprises you by becoming a better friend."
—*Romantic Times*

"The characters earn your compassion."
—*Rendezvous*

OFF SEASON

"A thought-provoking contemporary romance that explores relationships and leaves the reader satisfied."
—*Brazosport Facts*

"In this highly readable story, in a plausible ending, love heals." —*Romantic Times*

"Jean Stone has outdone herself this time. The emotion in this book left me wanting more. Ms. Stone has another winner." —*Rendezvous*

"Ms. Stone develops striking imagery and flawless dialogue through her unique writing style, which through its sheer simplicity manages to convey deep emotion and feeling. Her masterful storytelling explores themes of love, friendship, trust and loyalty in a thought-provoking tale you will not soon forget. Treat yourself to *Off Season*—you won't regret it!"
—*Romance Reviews Today*

THE SUMMER HOUSE

"Stone is a talented novelist whose elegant prose brings the Martha's Vineyard setting vividly to life. *The Summer House* is a very good read."
—*Milwaukee Journal Sentinel*

"Secrets, lies and sacrifices make up a boiling cauldron of intense emotions in Jean Stone's dramatic saga." —*Romantic Times*

"Ms. Stone gives her readers another romantic, heart-tugging gem." —*Rendezvous*

More Praise for

Jean Stone

"Stone's graceful prose, vivid imagery and compassionately drawn characters make this one a standout." —*Publishers Weekly* on *Tides of the Heart*

"You will always remember the characters. It's a sensational book." —*Rendezvous* on *Tides of the Heart*

"Jean Stone is a truly gifted writer. I wish I could claim her as a long-lost sister, but I can't. I can merely enjoy her wonderful talent." —Nationally bestselling author Katherine Stone

"Imagine a follow-up star vehicle to *The First Wives Club* for Diane Keaton and Bette Midler (Goldie Hawn loses out—replaced by Whitney Houston perhaps) . . . [an] engaging read."
—*Publishers Weekly* on *Birthday Girls*

"Jean Stone . . . again weaves magic in *Birthday Girls* . . . a fantastic ending . . . a story that touches the soul." —*Rendezvous*

"It's about time someone wrote a good book about women approaching fifty. Stone has her own voice in Women's Fiction." —Judy Spagnola from Book Trends

"Compelling." —*Orlando Sentinel* on *Places by the Sea*

"I loved *Ivy Secrets* . . . an intricate, enthralling and intensely emotional tapestry of secrets, passion and love—with characters so engaging, so compelling, you won't want to put it down. A terrific, don't-miss book! I'm on my way to the bookstore—right now—to find her previous two books." —Nationally bestselling author Katherine Stone

"This is one of the most compelling, evocative, heartrending tomes I've ever read and one I'll always remember. Kudos to the talented author."
—*Rendezvous* on *Sins of Innocence*

"Jean Stone tackled a very controversial subject and has written a story that beautifully illustrates the deep emotional scars such a loss can leave on the human psyche. *Sins of Innocence* is a wrenching and emotionally complex story. Sometimes, if you are very lucky, you can build a bridge across all obstacles. A very touching read." —*Romantic Times*

"This one is emotionally consuming. This one pulls you in and doesn't let you go as the splendid characters absorb you into their lives."
—*Rendezvous* on *Places by the Sea*

Other Books by Jean Stone

TWICE UPON A WEDDING

ONCE UPON A BRIDE

BEACH ROSES

TRUST FUND BABIES

OFF SEASON

THE SUMMER HOUSE

TIDES OF THE HEART

BIRTHDAY GIRLS

PLACES BY THE SEA

IVY SECRETS

FIRST LOVES

SINS OF INNOCENCE

Three Times a Charm

Jean Stone

Bantam Books

THREE TIMES A CHARM
A Bantam Book / June 2006

Published by
Bantam Dell
A Division of Random House, Inc.
New York, New York

Cover art by Alan Ayers
Cover design by Yook Louie

ISBN-13: 978-0-553-58852-1
ISBN-10: 0-553-58852-4

Printed in the United States of America
Published simultaneously in Canada

www.bantamdell.com

OPM 10 9 8 7 6 5 4 3 2 1

To Eric Natti,
long-time-ago Indian guide,
who shared his northern Minnesota
home when I attempted to write
my first novel.

Three Times a Charm

1

It was absurd, Sarah knew, that she, of all people, was caught up in the business of planning second weddings. She had turned forty-three last fall and had never had a wedding of her own (not even a first), had never wanted one. Not to mention that she'd just said good-bye to the man with whom she'd lived for many years.

It was absurd, this I-do, 'til-death-do-us-part stuff.

"Cream puff?" It was Lily, offering a miniconfection topped with frosty icing and silver sprinkles in keeping with the theme of the New Year's Eve glitzy wedding—white and silver, snow and ice.

Sarah shook her head. "I want to get home."

Lily didn't ask why on earth Sarah would want to; she didn't mention that no one was waiting there. Instead, she popped the cream puff into her mouth and said, "This was great. We really pulled it off."

Glancing around the ballroom of the eighteenth-century Stone Castle, hearing remnants of the last-to-leave people-chatter, catching sight of high-heeled shoes abandoned near the dance floor and midnight-buffet dishes scattered across the tabletops, Sarah had to agree that, yes, they'd pulled it off. The mismatched former college roommates had orchestrated quite a spectacle disguised as a second wedding for media mogul John Benson and his lovely wife, Irene. It hadn't mattered that the first time the Bensons were married it had been to each other. What mattered were the cameras and the coverage and the *bling* of it all. What mattered was that Second Chances, the wedding-planning business for second-time brides, had now made it to the big time, hip-hip-hooray for them.

"Our phones will ring nonstop," Lily giggled, waving her shimmering chiffon scarf as if it were a magic wand. "Oh, this is so divine. It's just as I imagined."

Divine? Sarah considered Lily's drama-queen description. Perhaps the wedding had been that for her. From the tiniest of cream puffs to the chorus of fireworks, they'd planned every detail together, sometimes working as a single, enmeshed unit, other times like clawing, mongrel cats. Their goal had been the same: to create an extravagant second wedding that the world would notice, an event that would put Second Chances on the wedding-planning map.

Perhaps, for Lily, that had been divine. For Jo, it had surely been a business deal. For Elaine, a minor miracle. For Sarah, it had been a job, a break from her silver-jewelry–making, from the free-form earrings and the shining hair clips and the thick cuff bracelets that accessorized her days, the company of her friends a welcome distraction from the recent unsettledness that now tarnished her life.

"Excuse me, are you a guest?" A group of wilted-haired, wrinkle-shirted cable-TV people had converged around them; a microphone was aimed at Sarah's mouth. The fact that she was the tallest of the former roommates often mistakenly conveyed that she was the one in charge.

She sighed. She hoped this was a final, annoying ploy for one last, delicious, Benson-wedding morsel for the late, late news. "Sorry," she said, "I'm just the hired help."

Lily stepped out from Sarah's shadow. A rush of media, after all, had also been part of the public-relations plan. "Lily Beckwith," Lily chirped, her delicate hand extended with the practiced elegance of a lady used to frenzied spin. "I was married to Reginald Beckwith—the Third—remember him?" She withdrew her hand and gently cupped the reporter's elbow. "Let me help you find a yummy story." With a quick, false-eyelashed wink at Sarah, Lily led the troupe of cameras and reporters through the maze of leftovers across the ballroom floor.

No, Sarah thought, she would not call this divine.

Divine would be if she went home tonight and found Jason and their twelve-year-old son, Burch, waiting for her by the fireplace, telling her they both decided they'd rather stay sequestered with her in the safety of West Hope in the Berkshires instead of living in New York City. They hadn't broken up—not exactly. But Jason's accelerated pursuit of the musical spotlight was not what Sarah wanted for herself. She didn't want her solitary happiness to give way to the kind of farcical existence that she'd witnessed that night at the Benson wedding.

Unfortunately, Jason did not feel the same. "I'm forty-five," he'd complained a month ago. "I'm tired of being on the road. But I need to be in the city, Sarah. Singing is my life."

They hadn't fought about it; they loved each other, didn't they? But they knew each other's truths: He would not survive in West Hope, and she would not survive the noise, the crowds, the clutter of the city, where she would not be free to wander in the forest and gather wild herbs, to sit outside at night and be one with the stars. She would not be at peace; she'd become one of them, an ordinary member of the urban flock of sheep. The remnants of her heritage would slowly dissipate.

So, after more than fifteen years together, they'd decided on a trial separation. She only wished that Burch had not chosen to live his father's life instead of hers. A true Cherokee would have stayed with his mother's clan, if she'd had a clan.

She plucked her truck keys from her purse and readjusted the handmade silver clip that held up her long black hair. She caught Lily's eye and waved. "Happy New Year," she called out. "See you tomorrow." The main event was over, but this was a weekend celebration; tomorrow the women of Second Chances would continue to feed and entertain the Bensons' famous guests.

"Happy New Year, my darling friend," Lily sang, her voice dancing across the room, the theatrics quite in keeping with the presence of the cameras. "Here's to a grand and glorious year."

Yes, Sarah thought, with another, halfhearted wave, *here's to a grand and glorious year that I'll be starting off alone.*

Two hundred miles away, in a sprawling co-op on the Upper West Side of Manhattan, Laura Carrington squinted at the television. She had been sipping tea, watching the ball drop in Times Square. But she was not tired, so after the raucous ritual she'd kept the picture on to watch the late, late news, the clips of revelers from New York to the West Coast, where it still was last year, as if L.A. were stuck in a time warp on an old Hollywood set.

Though her glamour days were over long ago, Laura watched with interest: The glitter, the gowns, the make-believe evoked the same nonsense today as it had back then.

And then, she saw her.

At first it didn't register. But as the dark-haired woman in the crowded image on the screen turned from the camera's lens, a silver hair clip flashed against the light. Laura blinked. She blinked again. The off-camera reporter mentioned something about a wedding, John Benson's New Year's wedding, somewhere in the Berkshires.

And then Laura knew. Her hand slow-motioned to her mouth. Her teacup slid down the handwoven blanket tucked around her legs and tumbled to the floor.

She had seen the silver hair clip. The clip that matched the one that sat atop her bureau in the other room.

2

♥

"I have a room upstairs," Andrew said to Jo, as they stood beneath the staircase at the far end of the ballroom.

She deflected her reluctance and accepted his embrace, felt his body working closer, felt his warmth press eagerly against her silver sheath. She'd known that it would come to this when she had gone to him, after the wedding vows were vowed and the fireworks had burst and the guests had danced and danced and drifted to quiet corners, then away. Jo had known that it would come to this and yet . . . and yet . . .

"I thought the rooms had been reserved for wedding guests," she said. Talking was a technique in procrastination, an art she'd mastered well over the years, an adverse side effect of too much history with Brian. *But Andrew isn't Brian,* she now whispered to herself. *Andrew isn't Brian. This time it will be different.*

"I know the wedding planners," Andrew softly said, his breath so close to hers that she could taste its sweetness.

"And so you pulled some strings. You're a very clever man, aren't you?"

He answered her with kisses, on her cheeks, her eyes, her forehead.

She smiled; how could she not? "Andrew," she said, "whatever will I do with you?"

With a single finger he outlined her lips. Then he leaned down and kissed her mouth, once, then twice, then once again.

"Andrew," she said again. The problem wasn't that she hadn't been with other men except for Brian. The problem was that with the others she hadn't felt the tingle that told her it was special, it was real. The problem was, she felt it now, and it felt strange and scary and exciting all at once.

Without a word he took her hand. His soft eyes lingered on her, then he led her up the stone stairs to a lone arched wooden door that had a long, wrought-iron handle.

"I feel like Cinderella," she said, and he just smiled.

He reached into the pocket of his white tuxedo and removed a black skeleton key. With one swift motion, he unlocked the door, then turned and scooped Jo from her feet.

She caught her breath. She wanted to laugh, to ask wasn't this silly, two middle-aged adults acting like teenagers in lusty love? She wanted to delay the possibilities again, but Andrew's feelings might be hurt. She swallowed back her fears and let him carry her into the room, close the door behind them, then lower her onto a high-backed velvet chair. The mate to the chair sat next to her, a small, round table in between. A crystal bowl was there, cupping strawberries that had been dipped in chocolate; beside the bowl were two wineglasses and an unopened bottle chilling in a golden bucket. The romantic, still-life set design faced a massive fireplace. The flames snapped and cracked and glowed, like the sparks inside her now.

She smiled.

While Andrew tended the fire, she glanced around the room at antique lace draperies tied back with thick gold cords, at the regal four-poster bed, which stood so high that footstools had been placed on either side.

"Andrew," she said, because it was so beautiful and he had gone to so much effort. "If John and Irene see this, they'll think we commandeered the bridal suite." She didn't think she was procrastinating now; she was merely nervous. Ordinary, first-time-with-this-man nervous.

With a large saber-looking poker, Andrew turned another log.

Was he nervous too?

And then he said, "I think John and Irene would be delighted."

That was when Jo realized how vulnerable both men and women were, that middle age did not provide a cushion for the nuances—for the *nuisances*—of emotion. She stood up and went to him, slipping her arms around his waist. He turned and held her close again, nuzzling his face into her hair.

Okay, she thought. *I am ready for this.* She was ready

to be loved again. To be loved by Andrew. There were no secrets between them now, no reason to be afraid, nothing to prevent them from being together.

Then she thought about his daughter.

"What about Cassie?" she asked. "Shouldn't you take her home?" Cassie was eleven, too young to be left on her own all night. John and Irene were her godparents, so Cassie had been at the wedding. She'd taken on the task of telling anyone who asked that her father was on assignment and that was why he wasn't there as John's best man. Most folks assumed that meant Andrew was out of the country, because traveling as a journalist was how he'd once made his living and his name. Cassie did not explain that he was really in the kitchen of the Stone Castle, hiding from the guests and the paparazzi who might recognize Andrew David Kennedy and might make a connection between the women of Second Chances and his anonymous "Real Women" column in John's *Buzz* magazine.

Even though Andrew had come clean to the women, he'd said that he should remain undercover to keep stray gossip to a dull, disinterested roar. The focus, after all, needed to be on the wedding and, most important, on the wedding planners and the first-class job they'd done.

Andrew kissed Jo's neck. "Mrs. Connor came to get her. I told her I'd be staying late."

"Did she ask why?" Cassie might only be eleven, but she was a precocious child, intuitive and sharp.

"She didn't ask. But I wouldn't have lied."

There had been enough lies, Jo agreed. But that was over now. She leaned back into Andrew. She watched the dancing fire, not wanting it to end.

"I love you, Jo," Andrew said quietly. "I've loved you from the day I first saw you at Second Chances."

She turned to him again. She smiled and studied his face, his dimpled cheek, his steady eyes, his tawny hair that always seemed in need of combing. "I need to do this slowly," she replied.

He bent down and lifted her from her feet again. He carried her to the high, four-poster bed, where he lay her among the lace-covered pillows. Then Jo watched as he unknotted the tie of his tuxedo and removed the studs of the pleated shirt. Then he was beside her, touching her with gentleness, sliding one strap off her shoulder, leaning down to kiss the swell of her aching breast.

And the strawberries dipped in chocolate and the wineglasses on the table sat in silence while Jo reminded herself that this was Andrew and the past was done and she could trust him, she could trust him.

Sarah had been raised in the hills of northern California, on a little-known reservation. The Cherokee Nation, after all, had mostly stayed in Oklahoma, where its people had been driven by the federal government in the 1800s. It had been a sad, ill-fated era from which a few—Sarah's ancestors included—had been lucky to escape. They had not embraced the treaty and its limitations; they had kept moving west.

Sarah's grandmother—*Glisi* was the word in Cherokee—said that same determined, renegade spirit ran deep through Sarah's blood.

She missed her grandmother, the mother of her father. She missed the folklore and traditions that Glisi always shared, that Sarah had passed along to Burch, that Burch might miss now too. She missed looking up at the stars with her grandmother and wondering which one held the spirit of her mother. *Vega*, Glisi had suggested, one of the brightest stars, a point of the famous summer triangle. When Sarah's father died, she decided that he must now be Deneb, the second point. Later, Glisi became Altair.

The triangle was complete, her loved ones were all there, not here on earth, but visible mostly in August and September. Not in January, not tonight, when Sarah could have used the comfort.

When she arrived home to her log cabin, the only one to greet her was Elton, her large, brown dog. She supposed she should be pleased; if she were gone too long, Elton was content to escape through his giant doggy door and traipse off to the neighbors' in search of food and water. He was a fickle male when survival was at stake.

"Happy New Year," she said, and Elton wagged his tail.

She made herself a mug of herbal tea, fixed a bowl of food for Elton from which he promptly turned away (he must have hit the Davios' tonight, Sarah thought, they always fed him well), then she sat on the plump, moss-colored cushion of the twisted-tree-branch chair. The enormous fireplace beckoned; she decided not to light it. New Year's Eve was over, the ambience could only add to her unrest.

She glanced around the rough-hewn walls of the cozy cabin. When Jo had come to visit, she'd said the wall hangings and blankets that Sarah had scattered here and there were in shades of "grass and berries and cloudless skies." She had loved the tribal drums, hand-painted with an eagle, a bear, a wolf. She said the house was "Sarah," which was meant as a compliment.

Jo had been right, of course. But perhaps the cabin had been too much Sarah, not enough Jason, not enough Burch. Too much her home, not theirs.

Her eyes fell to her watch. It was nearly one o'clock, too late to call Burch. Too late to wish her only child a Happy New Year. She wondered if, now that he was almost thirteen, he'd been able to stay awake long enough to watch the television coverage of the ball dropping in Times Square.

"Maybe next year, honey," she'd said for many years, when he woke up in the morning and realized he'd missed Dick Clark again.

Jason had never celebrated with them. He'd been singing in one club or another ever since he and Sarah met. New Year's Eve, after all, was a big night for live music and for tips. Jason always loved the tips.

When Burch was five or six, she'd decided to pretend they lived in London. Then, when the clock struck seven, she threw confetti and blew noisemakers and sang Auld Lang Syne. Burch joined in. They'd started their own tradition, which they had carried on long after Burch understood the meaning of time zones.

She looked back now at the charred ashes of warm fires once shared. She thought of New Year's celebrations when she'd been a girl: fireworks, in the white man's way, tempered by the knowing that their real celebration for a "new" year would come with the first new moon of spring, when the grass would start to grow and hopeful spirits would be renewed.

Tradition, Sarah thought, needed people to nurture it.

And then the phone rang.

"Mom?"

Her heartbeat skipped. "Are you okay, honey?"

"Mom! I'm in Times Square! I saw the ball drop!"

The white noise of real-time celebration jarred the reception on the phone. "You're in Times Square? Where is your father?"

"Dad's playing somewhere. I came with my friend Glen and his mother. It's a blast, Mom. It was so cool."

She toyed with the cord of her old-fashioned telephone, a symbol of her old-fashioned ways. Her son no longer needed to pretend he was in London. He no longer needed to try to stay up watching television. He was right there at the source of all the fun, right there, not needing her. "Hey, that's great, honey," she said. "I'm glad you had a good time."

"I gotta go, Mom. Happy New Year!"

He clicked off his end of the call and she sat, bewildered, staring into the hollow fireplace, listening to the solitude again, wondering what Glisi would have to say about it all.

3

Brunch.

Sleigh rides.

Snowshoeing.

Cross-country skiing lessons.

An early supper of chowders and crusty breads for the hangers-on, the wedding guests who had not gone home.

"Stay as long as you like," Irene had instructed the couple's friends, and John had added jokingly, "But after New Year's Day, you'll be footing your own bills."

The Second Chances team had been assigned to keep everyone pleasantly amused until then.

Sarah returned to the Stone Castle on New Year's morning. The media, thank God, had already left. As had John and Irene, for their wedding trip to Rio.

Though she was hardly needed—her job had been

the decor, the theme, the visual magic for the ceremony and reception—Sarah went into the kitchen, searching for a menial task or two. Something to keep busy, to stave off unwelcome demons of too much aloneness. She had never been one to languish in a world of sorrow and self-pity. Glisi had trained her otherwise.

Elaine was in the kitchen, slicing orange wedges. Lily would hardly be awake by now, and Jo—what had become of Jo last night, anyway?

"Hey, partner," Sarah said with forced but, she presumed, convincing cheer. "You're up and at 'em early."

"Brunch in twenty minutes," Elaine replied with a wide and happy grin. "Here," she said, handing over a colander of cranberries. "I'll cut the oranges, you arrange them with cranberries and a sprig of mint on every plate."

Sarah turned to the long stainless counter on which dozens of plates had been neatly aligned. "Well, this has sure put you in a good mood," she said. "You did a wonderful job yesterday, Elaine. You proved to everyone that you're a formidable caterer. And you proved it to yourself." The wedding had been Elaine's first attempt at showcasing her culinary talents, which had been passed down from her father.

Elaine smiled. "Three cranberries per plate, don't you think?"

Sarah set down the colander and washed her hands. "Most people might acknowledge such a compliment with a simple 'thank you.' "

Elaine adjusted the tie of her crisp new kitchen

apron. "I know," she said. "Thanks. But our success isn't the only reason why I feel great today."

Glisi's training notwithstanding, it was hard right now to think that Elaine or anyone might actually be happy, to think that Sarah might be required to act as if she were delighted for her friend's good mood, when what Sarah really wanted was to crawl into a deep, dark hole of misery and have her friends be down there too. She dried her hands, picked up the colander, and began to plunk three cranberries on every plate.

"Okay, I'll bite," she said. "Why the big fat smile?"

Elaine laughed. "Well, if you insist. I saw Martin last night after I left here."

Martin? Martin was the man Elaine was supposed to have married. Sarah, Lily, and Jo were supposed to have been her bridesmaids. The wedding-in-the-making had been the catalyst for them to open Second Chances, to create a specialty, one-stop shopping haven for advice and services for discerning, second-time brides. Elaine had broken her engagement after the business was under way, but by then they'd already done so much and spent so much of Lily's money that they'd said what the heck and plowed forward anyway, never dreaming of the success they'd reach in just a few short months.

"Martin, as in Martin-your-formerly-intended?"

Elaine chop-chopped another orange with Ginsu choreography. "The same," she said, and Sarah figured she should ask for details, but she really was too tired, too preoccupied with her own tenuous issues, so she just said, "Well."

Just then the kitchen door swung open and Jo was standing there.

Sarah remembered seeing Jo last night, standing beneath the stairs with Andrew. She had not seen her since. And now here she was, wearing last night's dress.

Oh, Sarah thought.

Jo and Andrew.

Well.

She counted out three more cranberries and wondered if she should have stayed home with her dog.

The world is changing faster than most of us can notice, Andrew typed onto his laptop later that night. *Real women are changing before my eyes; so, too, are real men. Second weddings (and third, I'm told) are becoming commonplace, causes for ostentatious celebration ("So divine!" my friend Olivia exclaims).*

My parents' generation would not have understood. He pushed away an image of his physician parents in their plain gray suits and gold wire-rimmed glasses and their predictable cheek kisses when one or the other came or went from the same apartment where they had lived since they'd been married and had died fifty-some years later. It wasn't that they loved or didn't love each other; divorce simply wouldn't have occurred to them unless adultery or violence or lying was involved.

His own divorce had come because of Patty's "indiscretions." He wasn't proud he'd known about them longer than he'd admitted.

Sitting up straight, he tried to focus on the laptop screen. His mind drifted a lot lately, since he'd fallen like a jerk, head over his Air Jordans in love with Jo. It was difficult sometimes not to compare the feelings with those that he'd once had for Patty. It was difficult not to be afraid.

He wondered if that was why his parents had stayed together, because the thought of going from one marriage to another had maybe been too frightening.

His fingers hung above the keyboard for another moment, then he resumed his task.

Second weddings stir up different feelings, richer stuff than first or "starter" (as I now hear people call them) weddings. The bride and groom, after all, are older. Wiser. More mature. Or at least they're supposed to be.

He smiled as he reread his words. It was a risk, he knew, to mention second weddings so blatantly. Surely some hotshot reader of *Buzz* magazine would make the connection between this column and the recent press about John Benson's extravaganza. John Benson, who just happened to be the editor and publisher of the upmarket rag.

Then Andrew laughed for thinking anyone might give a crap about his life or what he did or didn't do. Still, he might as well stick to the pseudonyms he'd created for the women: Jacquelin, Sadie, Eileen, and dear Olivia, aka Lily.

Not that any of it really mattered now, because the time had finally come.

With quick, sure fingers, Andrew added: *So the world has changed. I have too. When I first began this column, I did it almost on a dare. "How well do you think you understand women?" John Benson had asked. He'd been a friend for many years. He'd been my mentor once.*

John would enjoy seeing those words in print. In spite of being over sixty now and having spent several decades as a viable, visible contender in the industry, John (and his ego) still liked to ferret out his name in print, liked to hear it spoken in any of the broadcast media.

Well, Andrew continued, *whatever I thought I understood about women, I've realized I was wrong.*

I used to think we were so different, so Mars-and-Venus different, so yin and yang. I thought if we were too much the same that life would be too boring, that living would be dull.

I am happy to report that is not the case.

It may seem sometimes that we—men and women—are of a different species. But I have learned we want the same things—happiness, contentment, respect. Another person we can share our life and love with.

Then he sucked in a short breath and typed: *And so this is my final column.*

A slow grin crept around the corners of his mouth. He pictured Jo the first day she walked into Second Chances, her soft smile turning to surprise when she noticed a male receptionist. He pictured her when they'd rowed the boat across Laurel Lake and she'd dived into the water in her underwear. He pictured the way her green eyes sparked with laughter when the four women were together, laughing, joking, being friends.

The others, he knew, would always be part of Jo's life. And now they'd be part of his life too.

He was glad he had at last come forward with the truth.

It's been a fun adventure, he concluded, *this research into what women think, how they feel, what they want. My findings were unexpected. Especially when I fell in love.*

He smiled again.

In love? He typed.

Yes! With one of my subjects!

Disaster for a journalist!

I can't, however, help myself. And I won't say which of the women stole my heart. After all, what fun would there be in that?

Andrew smiled as he signed his now-famous *AK* to the end of the column. In the morning he would e-mail this farewell column to the editorial department at *Buzz* magazine. He had toyed with the idea of revealing his true identity to his readers, of letting them know that the undercover columnist was formerly Andrew David, television journalist who'd been seen around the world, who'd been married to the even more famous international cover girl Patty O'Shay, who'd traded everything for peace and quiet and a simple life in the Berkshire hills of Massachusetts with his terrific daughter, Cassie, who was fast asleep upstairs.

He could have said who he really was and bumped his credibility up a self-important notch. But there would have been no fun in that either.

He turned off his laptop, sat back in his chair, and

let his mind wander into thinking that he'd see Jo tomorrow, that he'd be having dinner with her—and with Cassie—over at Jo's house.

Suddenly the only problem Andrew seemed to have was where they'd live once he proposed. He sure would hate to leave his little cottage and the lumpy couches in the living room and the slanted timbered ceiling that he often whacked his head against and the scraggly vegetable garden out in the backyard that he'd come to love so much.

Andrew.

Jo lay awake in what had been her mother's bedroom, the home where first mother then daughter had been raised. She stared at the shadows that played across the ceiling, whispering his name into the empty night.

She pulled the comforter closer against her body, trying to feel his warmth again, trying to re-create the wonder she had felt while lying next to him, not sleeping, really, just lingering in that postlove place of heaven, where all things were euphoric and fear did not exist.

Andrew.

She tried not to think about what would happen next, about whether last night had been a fluke, a coming together because of the joy, the wonder, the excitement that had surrounded them, a glamorous *wedding*, of all things. A rewedding of two people for whom Andrew cared a great deal.

Had their encounter only been a result of the mood?

She hadn't seen him since he left their castle bed early in the morning. She'd regretfully gone home, showered, and changed into jeans and an old, comfortable sweater, then returned to the Stone Castle, where she helped the others get through the festivities of the day. Andrew wasn't there. He'd said he'd be staying home with Cassie, that they always watched the football games on New Year's Day, eating popcorn, drinking egg creams, the kind of egg creams he'd grown up on, the kind made in the city.

New York City.

She closed her eyes to the shadows.

They'd had such different upbringings. He was a city, penthouse boy; she, a small-town, clapboard-house girl. Though she'd lived in Boston many years, West Hope still was home for Jo. For Andrew, it was where he landed when he'd needed an escape.

He was the son of doctors.

She, the daughter of a clerk at the town hall and a construction-working man who'd left when Jo was nine.

He had tasted the sweet, beguiling fruit of being a celebrity, of being recognized, respected, always waited on.

She had scrambled for what few rewards she'd won then lost.

They were so different, weren't they?

Could anything between them really ever work?

She turned onto her side, pulling the comforter

too far from the bed. A cloud of cool air slapped her skin. She shuddered in the darkness, wrapped the comforter more tightly, and wondered if she'd ever sleep as peacefully as she had slept with Andrew by her side.

4

The second of January finally arrived. Sarah went into the shop early; there would be lots and lots to do, now that Second Chances was in demand. *Lots and lots*, she repeated to herself. The distraction would be as welcoming as hot tea in the afternoon.

She spent the morning in the backroom studio, cleaning and reorganizing in the Benson aftermath. The sounds of Jo and Andrew cloud-nine-ing through the morning (disguised as work-related noises—they didn't seem to want to unveil the obvious new path of their relationship) were somehow tolerable today; Lily's perky giggle and her frequent boyfriend (yes, she had one, too) chatter about Frank-this and Frank-that were not even annoying. Let them all be happy if that was what they wanted. As for Sarah, she didn't need that drivel. She had work to do!

At noon, the other happy one, Elaine, came into the backroom from next door where she'd been directing renovations. The Forbes Antiques Shop—"Frank's little workplace," Lily called it—was being transformed into McNulty's Catering, a division of Second Chances. In addition to being Lily's boyfriend, Frank was their landlord. He was now moving his wares though not his love life across the town common, into what had once been West Hope's town hall.

Elaine toted a large cooler. "Jo said we need to have a working lunch. I brought asparagus salad, corn chowder, and potatoes lyonnaise from the wedding."

A mismatched group of leftovers, Sarah deduced. Not unlike the women—and the man—of Second Chances.

"Sounds perfect," Sarah said, stacking the last of her Benson drawings of silver sleighs, twinkling trees, and giant snowballs of angel hair, and sliding them into one of the wide, shallow drawers in a tall oak cabinet. She would no doubt use and reuse the creations for other weddings, with variations here and there.

"Sarah," Elaine said, setting the cooler on the floor, "are you okay?"

She shrugged. "Sure." She shut the drawer, rearranged the carousel of Magic Markers and pastel crayons on top of the cabinet. She preferred the old ways to the computer drawings of today; she felt she was more creative when it was the movement of her hand, not an acrylic mouse, that relayed her concepts onto paper.

"I meant because of Jason being gone," Elaine continued. "And Burch."

Sarah made a conscious effort not to jam a Magic Marker into its slot on the carousel, not to yank open another drawer for the follow-up potential of slamming it shut. "I'm fine," she said. Long ago, she'd learned that the less anyone knew about what was inside your true heart, the easier it was to live from day to day, the easier to survive from year to year.

But Elaine's eyes lingered too long on her. She'd always been able to do that, to stare without expression, to pause without a blink, as if to read the other person's mind. Her conclusions weren't always right, but she seemed to like the effort to connect. "You never tell us what you're thinking or how you feel," Elaine finally said. "I guess it's one of your secretive Indian ways. No offense."

Sarah laughed and said, "None taken," grateful that was the only deduction her friend had made. Then she said, "Let's eat," before Elaine—armchair psychologist, mother of three, once homemaker and caretaker—forgot that she now was a career woman and should not be wasting time on things as mundane as emotions.

"We have seventeen requests for second weddings in April alone," Jo remarked. Her shoulders slumped. "Not to mention Valentine's Day. We have to figure out which ones we can handle."

Sarah surveyed the group that sat clustered in the navy chairs in the "conversation" area—the space that she'd designed to help make the brides and their grooms or their best friends or whomever as comfortable as possible during the second-wedding planning process. Instead of magazines and sketches, the cocktail table held lunch dishes and coffee mugs and files with Jo's notes. Jo was their organizer, their sensible, natural-born group leader, the CEO of their amalgamated friendship. Not that she'd ever asked for such a dubious position: No matter what the four women had done over the years, Jo ended up in charge. Even when Lily railroaded them into one of her silly schemes, Jo was the one who inevitably made sense of it all.

"Well, we certainly can't handle every request," Lily said. "We'll have to be selective."

"First come, first served," Sarah said.

"No!" Lily cried. "Let's only do the ones we'll have the most fun with."

"Or those that will return the greatest profit," Jo added.

Andrew had remained behind his desk and didn't say a word, even though he, their pseudo-receptionist, had been responsible for the business's glorious predicament of being overbooked.

Elaine stood up and passed a plate of silver-frosted macaroons. "I'm with Sarah," she said. "First come, first served. It's only fair." It was difficult to comprehend that Elaine, though always thoughtful, was now on the same side of the business world as them. She'd been such a fifties kind of girl, who clung to polyester pantsuits while the rest had moved on to natural fibers. She'd been born a generation too late for her style, or her lack of it—until now, as if her newfound confidence and independence had yielded sophistication too.

"Oh, pooh," Lily said, "my do-gooder friends." Unlike sensible Jo, thoughtful Elaine, or, yes, secretive Sarah, Lily was not in charge of anything that counted (didn't want to be), never bothered to try to read anyone's inner thoughts, never kept one single feeling a secret for very long. "Well, you'll soon be bored, and that's a promise."

Jo shook her head. "There's nothing boring ahead of us." She shuffled through some papers. "Valentine's Day is the first requested date. A couple from Pittsfield had asked right after Christmas. Before we made the news. They want sixty guests. They want the ceremony on the ski slopes at Southfield Mountain and the reception in the lodge."

Sarah envisioned a decor of white faux fur and plump, angelic cherubs romping in the snow.

"Next is a woman named Julie Pearl from Stockbridge. She says she can't afford our full-blown services but will pay for our advice. She has multiple sclerosis and is in a wheelchair and wants our expertise on how to make her wedding special."

Even Lily wouldn't suggest they should skip Julie Pearl.

"Next is Rhonda Blair."

Eyes flashed like LED lights in a child's toy.

"*The* Rhonda Blair?" Lily asked.

Rhonda Blair was the reigning queen of daytime soap operas—hers was called *Texas Truths*, an updated version of the eighties' *Dynasty*. One didn't need to be a fan to recognize the woman's face, which frequented tabloid covers at supermarket checkouts. Sarah stifled a groan. She supposed Rhonda would want a lot of glitz, a lot of bling, with very little taste.

"I think we'll be too busy," Sarah said, "what with the couple from Pittsfield and Julie Pearl."

"Not necessarily," Jo continued. "There will be no guests, just a private ceremony with a justice of the peace. She wants it in the bridal suite at the Stone Castle. But she wants it decorated, *lavishly* was her word. Apparently Rhonda is a friend of Irene Benson."

It was hard to picture Irene with the sultry maven of the at-home matinees. Perhaps *lavish* was the one thing they had in common.

"No reception?" Elaine asked. "No food?"

"Only for the two of them. A private supper, a private everything. Elegant. But just for two."

"What about the media?" Lily asked.

"None. In fact, that's a condition. We are not to divulge anything about the wedding—or that we even know about it—to the press or to anyone. Not before, not during, and maybe not even after."

"Well," Lily said, "that sounds easy enough."

But Sarah's jewelry-making years had taught her that the simplest requests often turned out to be the biggest pains.

"So those are the first-comers for Valentine's Day," Jo continued, looking once more at her notes. "Do we think we can handle all three?"

"Absolutely," Lily remarked.

"Sure," Elaine replied.

Sarah simply shrugged.

"Andrew?" Jo asked.

The man who had been quiet now smiled and said,

"Well, you're the bosses," he said. "I think I warned you to be careful what you wished for."

Lily tossed a macaroon at him.

He caught it with a laugh. "I do have one event I'd like to add to your list," he said. "Cassie will be twelve next week. Will you help me throw a birthday party that isn't too mature?"

Lily wanted Cassie's party to be held at Laurel Lake Spa, where the twelve-year-old guests ("only girls," she said. "Boys at that age are so tiresome") would be treated to facials and manicures and pedicures and maybe a session in mud therapy.

"They're little girls," Andrew protested. "They don't need beauty treatments yet."

Lily said that wasn't the point, that it was about helping young girls feel good about their bodies and themselves.

Elaine said they'd feel better at a house party with boys. She'd raised three children, hadn't she? And twelve was a perfect age. Young enough not to get into real parental nerve-racking, opposite-sex stuff; old enough, though, to like to feel that they were grown-up.

Sarah wondered if Cassie would like a party at her log cabin, where she could teach the preteens jewelry-making. If it were summer she could take them on a hike to look for healing herbs, blackberry root, or sumac. They'd done that when Burch turned twelve; his friends had loved learning the Cherokee traditions.

She didn't tell the others now what a perfect day it had been, or that her heart ached from its memory.

Jo suggested a party at the stables, where Cassie loved to ride.

Andrew laughed again and said this shouldn't take precedence over the weddings that needed planning.

Just then the small bell over the front door jingled. In unison, they turned to see a dark-haired, dark-eyed, bronze-skinned man. He was dressed in a long black coat that looked to be cashmere, one hundred percent. A white shirt and navy tie poked out from the neck.

"Hello," the man said, pulling off black leather gloves and sliding them into the pocket of his coat. He was cool and confident, not confident like Elaine had recently become, but the kind that floated on an aura of knowing everything. His eyes landed on Sarah, but it was Lily who jumped up.

"Welcome!" she called, directing him toward the seat she'd just vacated. "Can I interest you in tea? Or lunch? We have a fabulous selection from our catering division." Lily was a magnet, especially with men.

The man did not sit down but stood in the doorway looking more in charge than Jo, which might have been because, like Sarah, he was so tall. His legs were long, his arms were long, even his cheekbones were set high. It was hard to tell his age because his hair was devoid of gray.

"How about a cup of chowder?" Lily flirted.

The man held up his hand. "Thank you, no," he said. "But I see why you're successful, if you treat all your customers with such grace."

Lily laughed as if the two of them were the only

ones in the Second Chances showroom. "Lily Beckwith," she said, extending her fine-boned hand in an upward, slightly arced fashion, so that he could kiss it if he wanted.

He shook her hand instead. "Sutter Jones."

The name flicked through Sarah's mind as if it were familiar, a name she should recognize. Was he another celebrity come to book a wedding?

"Please," Lily persisted, "you really must sit down." She led him to her chair. Then she made quick introductions all around. "So," she remarked when the hellos ended, "when is your big day? And, please, don't say February fourteenth."

Sarah turned her head away, embarrassed by Lily's overt silliness.

"Actually," he said, "I don't have a wedding date." His voice was clear and strong.

"We have some openings in May," Jo quickly interjected.

"May's a nice time for a wedding," Elaine added, nodding assuredly.

"Are you looking for a venue in the Berkshires? The Mount, perhaps? Or the Stone Castle? You're not from West Hope, are you?"

His eyes traveled around the group, then landed on Sarah once again. She shifted in her chair. "No," he said. "I live in New York."

"City?" asked Elaine.

"Well, of course, dear," Lily said, "they don't have that kind of cashmere up in Albany." She pointed to his coat and gave a wide Crest Whitestrips smile.

Andrew stood up. "You'll have to excuse the ladies,"

he said. "We just finished a big wedding and they're a little giddy." He picked up his dirty dishes and deposited them in Elaine's carryall.

"You might say I'm here because of the Benson wedding," the man named Sutter said.

Lily's hand lightly touched her throat, as if protecting her triple strand of pearls. "Do you know John and Irene?"

Sutter shook his head. "The event had lots of television coverage. Thanks to all of you, no doubt."

"Well," Lily said, "yes, of course," though Sarah doubted that this man spent many evenings in front of a TV.

"And that's why you've come to Second Chances?" Jo asked.

"In a way." His smile seemed genuine. But there was something that disturbed Sarah . . .

She scanned his high cheekbones, his smooth forehead again. And then she sucked in a short breath. *Of course*, she thought. *Sutter Jones is Indian. He is one of . . . me.*

It was enough for Sarah. It was enough of how-de-dos and ain't-life-grands and cashmere from New York, wrapped around a bronze facade. She stood up. "If you'll excuse me, I must get back to work."

Sutter quickly rose as well. "But, Sarah," he said as if he knew her, "you're the reason that I've come."

5

♥

"You don't want a wedding?" Lily asked.

The sense of *knowing* that Glisi had believed everyone could tap into if only they listened to their head and to their heart surfaced in Sarah now. The knowing came from deep inside, from her place of stillness that she'd found long ago and lately didn't listen to as often as she should.

"He's here for me," Sarah replied, and gestured for Sutter Jones to follow her into her studio, while the others were left there in the showroom, not knowing what to do or say.

"So you're not a groom," Sarah said once they were in the back and she'd meandered to the long table that held her samples. She folded the last of the velvet and faux fur and wondered if Rhonda Blair's event would require satin. "Are you Cherokee?"

"Yes," he said.

She put the fabric into antique wooden bins that Frank Forbes had donated to Second Chances. Then she placed the bins with others that were stacked along one wall, giving the studio an old-fashioned general-store look. "A wealthy Cherokee, I expect. Those are mighty fine clothes you're wearing." She knew she sounded sarcastic. But it was a rare Cherokee who worshipped money, and it usually meant he cared for little else. Yet it surprised Sarah that the notions of her heritage could still evoke such feelings.

He leaned against her drawing table. "I knew your grandmother," he said. "My mother was Margaret Jones. Little Tree. Do you remember her?"

Sarah focused on Sutter's face, searching for recognition, remembering Little Tree with surprising clarity. She'd been a tiny, petite woman with a quiet nature and a gift for weaving colorful, detailed blankets. Her husband had gone north in the seventies to work the Alaskan pipeline. Like many of the men who left, he had not returned. He'd left Margaret with a son, older than Sarah, who had been gone, too, by the time Sarah had been old enough to understand.

Averting her eyes to the pads of layout paper on the table in front of Sutter, she wondered if she should order more for the rush of weddings that lay ahead. She wondered if Sutter Jones would leave if she suggested it, demanded it, pleaded that he leave her alone. "How did you find me?" she asked, then added, "And why?"

"You sell jewelry in Boston, don't you? In Quincy Market?"

"Not for a long time."

"I saw your name on a bracelet tag. It said you were a Cherokee, a Native American. I remembered you."

She smiled at the political correctness of the way he said "Native American," as if he were not an Indian too. "Did the tag say where I lived?"

"No. That's what the Internet is for."

Burch had set up a Web site for her jewelry business last year. She never dreamed the link would have retrieved her past. "So," she said, "here I am." She went to the storage cabinet, counted one pad of tissue layout paper, half a pad of vellum. Yes, she'd definitely need more paper for the onslaught ahead.

"I came to town on business," he said, brushing his silky hair back with his hand. "I thought I'd look you up. A clerk in the coffee shop said I could find you here. There aren't many of us left, you know. California Cherokee."

Sarah nodded. She went over to the desk and picked up the wool jacket that she had draped across the back. She realized that her head was aching now. "I have to run to the graphic-arts store for supplies. Did you want to ask me something?"

His smile was wide, his black eyes so much like hers. The fluorescent lights captured small leather-cracks at the edges of his eyes: He might be in his early fifties. "I thought I'd ask you out to dinner," Sutter said. "I thought that we could share some stories about the old days on the reservation."

She wasn't sure if he was trying to be humorous. "I don't think so," she said. "But thanks for looking me up."

She opened the back door, stepped outside into the winter sunshine, and wondered what had just happened and why she couldn't breathe.

6

I want my party at the stables," Cassie said as Andrew drove toward Jo's. He'd told his daughter of the options that the women had suggested. She'd only thought a second before she gave her reply.

"I thought you didn't much like riding anymore. You hardly went over Christmas vacation." More than once Cassie had informed him she was too old for that now, that riding was for little kids. He'd have bet she would prefer the idea Elaine had offered: a boy-girl party, where the most fun (for the adult chaperones) would be in watching the dynamics. If they still lived in the sophistication of the city, not the boondocks of the country, wouldn't Cassie already have had such a party? But the thought of Cassie entering the boy-girl scene gave him acid reflux. The longer she avoided that, or he avoided that for her, the way better with him.

He took a right onto Main Street. "Did you pick

the stables just because of Jo? Because she thought of it?"

Cassie laughed and shook her head. "Dad, you are so lame."

Well, he knew that. His daughter mentioned it often enough. "That's beside the point," he said. "Honey, I want you to have the party that you want. Not because you think it will make Jo happy and subsequently make me happy and we'll all live together happily ever after."

She rolled her eyes and turned her head toward the window, toward the string of shops that held the luncheonette, then Second Chances, then McNulty's Catering. "What difference does it make, Dad? I'll have the party. It will be fun."

"We could invite some boys," Andrew said, another lame comment, no doubt. "It's too bad Sarah's son is in New York now. He might have liked to ride."

"Burch is too old, Dad."

He knew she'd had a crush on Burch; Burch was, after all, an older (almost thirteen), wiser man. Andrew would admit to no one that he had been relieved when Sarah announced her son had moved away. Andrew cleared his throat. "Anyone else?" he asked. "Any boys in your class?"

"Sure. Scott Baines and Russ McGuire used to ride, I think." He sensed a furtive look from the corner of her eye. "And maybe Eddie Mindelelewski."

Andrew's eyebrows went up. "Who?"

Cassie lifted her chin toward the ceiling of the old Volvo. "Eddie Mindelelewski."

"Good grief, that's quite a name."

"Don't make fun of him, Dad. Everyone else does. I spend half my life telling people not to make fun of him."

He stopped at the red light in the center of town. He wondered if this would be one of those moments he'd later bookmark as the dreaded beginning of the end of Cassie's childhood. "I'm not making fun of him, honey. I don't even know him."

"Well, you will," she said. "His parents own the big farm off Bramble Road. We bought corn on the cob there last summer. And tomatoes and green beans."

He tried to recollect a sixth-grader at the farm stand, but no picture came to mind. "Sure," he said, "it was good corn."

Just then Cassie swiveled in her seat belt and looked him in the eye. "And I haven't known how to tell you this, but he's my boyfriend, Dad."

There weren't many closets in the place. Andrew guided Cassie from Jo's kitchen through the dining room toward the living room, so she could watch television while he pretended that she was still a little girl, too young to want a boyfriend. His denial might give him sixty peaceful seconds to spend alone with Jo.

On the way to the living room he took note of his surroundings: The kitchen was good size, but it could use an update, with extra cabinets. The dining room, which Jo seemed to be using as a place for storage boxes, had a built-in china cabinet that was mahogany like the woodwork. Through the archway that led into the living room was a nice wall of tall windows, next to that a fireplace that was flanked by more built-ins (this time, bookcases), then an open wall to the front door, the stairs, and back to the kitchen. There was only one small closet, and that was in the hall.

Cassie settled in front of the TV. Andrew assembled kindling and newspapers, opened the flue, and lit a fire. He watched the embers flicker, flicker, then quickly catch. The action made him smile: Andrew David Kennedy, who'd never learned to swim or row a boat or ride a horse (at least not very well) had, in his five years in West Hope, mastered the art of starting a warm and cozy fire.

That accomplished, he slipped from the living room and back into the kitchen, where Jo was peeling potatoes at the sink.

The perfect picture of domesticity, he thought, snapping a mental photo of the only woman worth savoring since Patty. It was a good thing, he supposed, now that Cassie was making plans (he was quite sure of it) to grow up and get married and leave him alone.

Jo turned to him with a smile. "I have a feeling I'm being watched."

He folded his arms and smiled.

She turned her attention back to the sink. "You could come here and kiss me if you wanted. On the back of my neck. That would be quite sexy."

He waited a few more seconds, then he quietly approached her from behind. Without his hands touching her, he leaned down and lightly kissed the back of her neck.

"Ah," she said.

He kissed again. He reached up and moved her taupe-colored hair from the top of her collar. He ran his tongue along her hairline. She dropped the potato peeler and turned to him. They held each other's eyes for just a moment, then Andrew leaned down and kissed her on the mouth, a long, lingering kiss. He held her shoulders; he wanted to explore her standing there, he wanted to take her standing there; he wanted to do so many things right there, but he could not because Cassie was in the other room.

When at last he stopped, Jo said, "Well. Remind me to invite you for dinner more often."

He smiled again, stepped back, and put his hands into the pockets of his jeans, hoping to ease down his erection, wishing he didn't have to. He redirected his attention out the kitchen window.

"Birds," he said. "You get many of them over here?" He was staring at the bird feeders, all of which seemed neatly filled.

"They came with the house," Jo said.

The backyard was sizable. Andrew wondered if Jo had a riding lawn mower, then realized her mother had probably paid someone to do the landscaping.

If he and Cassie lived here, at least until she married Eddie what's-his-name, he would maintain the yard.

And maybe he would oversee construction of an addition onto the house, a big family room—or, wait, a master bedroom suite! With a couple of walk-in closets and a generous bath. The toilet and small sink tucked under the stairs to the second floor would hardly be sufficient. Yes, it would be better for all of them to live here, not at the cottage. It would be better for them all once he and Cassie lived here.

"Penny for your thoughts," Jo said, as she plopped the last of the potatoes into the pot and set it on the old stove. He wondered if she'd like one of those new ones with the flat top for the burners. He wondered where the hell he'd get the money for all these things now that he had written his last column and the college probably wouldn't take him back, because John would be pissed and he had clout there too.

Maybe they'd end up living in the small cottage by default.

Andrew sort-of grinned and said, "I was wondering what's for dinner."

She smiled. "No you weren't," Jo said, then pulled down the oven door and a cloud of beef roasting with garlic wafted up from it.

He wondered how many years it had been since he'd wanted to touch a woman so much, so often, and in so many places.

"I know, but it's safe," he said, then added, "Is it too soon to put Cassie to bed?"

Jo laughed. She put her arms around him and kissed his cheek. "I love you," she said, "but you are such a man."

Then she turned back to her work, and Andrew stood there, watching, hearing her words *I love you* over and over in his mind, knowing that when—or if—Cassie chose to leave his nest had nothing to do with the way he felt about this woman, Jo.

The next morning, Sarah went to work early because she'd hardly slept. Three cups of chamomile did not soothe her the way tea from the mullein flower would, but it had been years since Sarah needed to think about the flower, her grandmother's favorite sedative.

Instead of sleeping, she had spent the night in Burch's room, trying to convince herself she was sorting through the clothes that he'd outgrown, the toys that he'd no longer bother with when he came home for a visit. In reality, she knew she was searching for something there, some connection to her present and her future that would make her past irrelevant. Something that would reinforce that her life was okay where it was, that she belonged right there.

At dawn she'd taken Elton for a run around the reservoir; even that had not calmed her nerves, had not enabled her to find her stillness.

Juggling her purse and a bag from the graphic-arts store, she let herself in the back door of Second Chances before seven o'clock, determined to immerse herself in the Pittsfield wedding-on-the-mountain, the nuptials of the woman with MS, and the odd request of the soap-opera diva who was friends with the grand dame Irene.

She set down the bag and purse and then flipped on the lights. She did not expect to see Lily sitting there.

"God," she said, "you scared me half to death. What are you doing here?"

"I live here," Lily said. She was dressed in a thick, navy cable-knit sweater, under which she wore a crisp white cotton shirt. She also had on jeans, which Sarah did not know the woman owned. With Lily's wispy blond curls tied back by a navy band, Sarah noted that she looked like a teenager, not a woman in her forties who'd been married three "lovely, unregrettable, unforgettable" (Lily's words) times.

"You live upstairs," Sarah said. When they'd first opened the business, Lily "closed" her New York City apartment and moved into the space above the shop. She had decorated it in storybook, ice-cream colors and added life-size dolls, who now enjoyed a perpetual Alice in Wonderland adventure, complete with a child-size table that was always set for tea. "Downstairs is reality," Sarah added. "Downstairs is where we work."

Lily ignored Sarah's remark. "I tried calling you at home," she said. "I figured you were on your way in. I'm going to an auction with Frank this morning. It's being held inside a barn." Her little, turned-up nose wrinkled, and tiny stress lines crept out from the corners of her mouth.

Sarah thought she should receive an Academy Award for not laughing out loud. She did not ask if Lily had ever been inside a barn in her entire life, or if she'd ever even been awake before eight A.M. Instead, she went directly to her drawing table without hanging up her coat.

"Sarah," Lily said, getting up and following her. "I know you think I'm frivolous. Airheaded. Well, maybe sometimes I am. But give me credit for a few things. Like understanding men."

With a short laugh, Sarah said she'd never doubted that. She sat down on the tall stool; she and Lily now were eye to eye.

"Then tell me what you're doing," Lily said.

"Don't try to be my keeper, Lily. Your feet are too small for my shoes."

"Oh, bull pucky."

Sarah laughed again. "Excuse me?"

"A perfectly nice man comes to see you and what do you do? You blow him off."

"If you're speaking about Sutter Jones, you don't know anything about him."

"I know I sometimes say things that are none of my damn business, but I'm worried about you, Sarah. I know you let Jason up and leave. I know he took your son. I know a very nice man came here yesterday for the sole purpose of seeing you."

Unbuttoning her coat, Sarah wondered how Lily truly would react if she'd lived Sarah's life. "Yes, well, you're right to say that these things are none of your damn business."

"But you're alone now, Sarah. I do know what that's like. And if I've learned anything, it's that when you are alone, you must look for ways to fill up the emptiness."

Lily's emptiness, Sarah knew, had always been "filled" by one man or another.

"Besides," Lily added, "it wouldn't surprise me to learn that your dead grandmother sent Sutter Jones to find you."

Sarah blinked a long, slow blink.

"Well," Lily added, "I've never said your Indian spiritual stuff was just a bunch of hooey."

Bull pucky. Hooey. Not to mention that Lily called

her an Indian instead of a Native American. Dear Lily honestly meant well, airhead that she was.

Lily checked her watch. "I've got to run. But think about it. Please." She pointed to a pile of drawings on Sarah's table, on top of which was a small brochure from the Hilltop Bed and Breakfast. "Sutter left this with me after you bolted yesterday. He'll be staying there until tomorrow."

7

Friday afternoon was the only time the stables would be able to accommodate a birthday party for seventeen: five boys, seven girls (one of the many gender inequities bound to wind up in their lives), the four women of Second Chances (eager chaperones), and, of course, Andrew.

"I'll make gourmet pizzas," Elaine volunteered later in the morning when they gathered in the Second Chances showroom for a wedding-planning break. "Shall I shape them into cowboy hats and the state of Texas?"

If Lily had been there, she surely would have commented on Elaine's idea.

"I think regular-shaped will be fine," Jo, the diplomat, suggested.

"They'll be too busy noticing one another to pay much attention to the food," Sarah added, then instantly wished she hadn't when Andrew leaped from his chair and said, "I can't do this. I'm way too young to have a daughter with a boyfriend." He ran his fingers through his hair, his face crunched up, perplexed.

It brought back memories of Red Elk, the first boy Sarah had a crush on. She, too, had been eleven. Her father had threatened to chain him to the sluice down at the gold mine and let the rocks tumble over him until he was sorely black and blue.

Glisi had been more understanding. With her help, Sarah and Craig (though he'd always be Red Elk to her) saw each other from time to time and shared innocent kisses when they could. By the time Sarah was twelve, they were into "making out." Perhaps she shouldn't mention that to Andrew now.

"Cassie will be fine," Jo said. "We'll keep a special eye on her, won't we, girls?"

Elaine said absolutely and Sarah nodded as expected, though her thoughts drifted to Sutter Jones. She wondered if he remembered Red Elk and if he'd ever looked him up too. Perhaps Red Elk had been one of the few who'd stayed in northern California.

A surprise longing for home tugged at Sarah's heart. She thought of the long, hot summer days when she and Red Elk explored the valleys and the canyons at the foothills of the Sierra Nevada mountain range; she remembered hiking with him through the forests, gathering seven woods for a sacred fire. Seven woods, symbolic of the seven Cherokee clans. Seven woods, seven annual festivals, seven everything. It was tradition, after all.

She hadn't seen Red Elk when she returned for

Glisi's funeral. She'd heard that he was dating a girl from a Miwok tribe down in Sausalito. Maybe Sutter Jones knew if they had ever married, if they'd had any children. Maybe Sutter Jones would know about the others too, members of the clan she'd once thought belonged to her.

"Sarah?" Jo interrupted. "A trail ride, then some games, followed by a campfire, don't you think?"

A campfire, Sarah thought. "Sure," she said, wondering if Jo had read her mind about the seven woods.

She half-listened to the chatter about lasso games (to be conducted by an "expert" cowboy on the premises) and rides on a mechanical bull (rounded up from a now-defunct seventies' disco down in Stockbridge). The birthday cake—according to Elaine—would feature horse replicas as decorations. She was certain she could find some among the memorabilia from her father's restaurant in Saratoga Springs, New York, though they might look like fine thoroughbreds, not the old plug horses at the stables. Everyone agreed that the kids probably wouldn't mind.

By noon, the birthday-party plans had been happily resolved, subject, of course, to revision once Lily learned the details. Also by noon, it had become increasingly difficult for Sarah to shake her thoughts free from the past, thanks to Sutter Jones.

"Lunch?" Jo asked when they were finished.

Elaine shook her head. "Too much to do next door," she said, then waved good-bye and left the showroom, leaving Sarah alone with Jo and Andrew, the newly consummated (or so it seemed) couple.

Sarah stood up. "I think I have somewhere to go,"

she said. She didn't need directions to the Hilltop Bed and Breakfast; she passed it every morning on her way into West Hope.

"So what's your story?" Sarah asked Sutter Jones as she pushed her spoon around a crock of roasted-vegetable stew at the Bear Claw Tavern. He wore a coral-color sweater and fine wool pants and was the first Cherokee she'd sat with in more than twenty years. It felt oddly comfortable, like sliding into old, familiar slippers on a wintry night.

For the first time in a long, long time, she wondered what it would be like to be with a man other than Jason, not that—despite their separation—she needed or wanted to.

Sutter smiled. "My story isn't so different from yours. I grew up the same way you did. We were the Long Hair Clan. You were the Paint, I think."

She scooped a piece of carrot onto her spoon. The Long Hair Clan were the peacemakers, the Paint, the medicine people. They were but two of the seven clans of Cherokee. Seven, like everything else.

Sarah shifted on her chair. "The Paint was my father's clan." She wondered if he knew that her mother died when Sarah was born.

"I used to love to climb the cliffs," he said. "I used to love to prowl through the mines. My mother always said I had my head up in the clouds and my butt below the earth, and that my biggest problem was I never had two feet on the ground."

Sarah chewed a carrot, unsure if she should laugh. Instead, she swallowed and asked, "How is your mother? Is she still alive?"

He shook his head. "She died last year. She lived on the reservation until the end. I tried to get her to move down to San Francisco. I wanted to buy her a nice condominium near where I was living. But she wanted to stay up there. It was her home, she said."

"It was their home," Sarah replied. "I think their generation was the last to cherish it. The rest of us couldn't wait to get away."

"The world changed," Sutter said.

"And we wanted to be part of it."

"You never returned?"

She shook her head. "Not since Glisi died."

"I have a son who lives there. His mother, my ex-wife, was a white woman. When we split up, he decided to follow his Cherokee roots."

"Does that please you?"

"Not completely. I think there are greater opportunities for him in the world."

"Sometimes the world isn't all that terrific." She took another spoonful of the stew. They ate in silence for a moment, caught up in separate memories, or maybe in the same.

And then he said, "I lied." He said it so abruptly Sarah wasn't sure she'd heard him right. "I didn't see your name on a tag on a bracelet in Boston. I'm an attorney, Sarah. I found you for a client."

She set down her spoon and lowered her eyes to her lap. "What?" she asked through closed teeth. Sarah could abide many things. She could handle all those years of Jason being on the road. She could handle him taking their son to live in the city. She could not handle lying. Not from family, not from a friend, and certainly not from a total stranger who'd made her feel off balance to begin with, despite these last few moments of languishing in the comfortable-slipper syndrome. She should have known better, for godssake.

Then, instead of waiting for an answer, Sarah pushed back her chair, grateful that she'd driven herself to the restaurant. "Look, Mr. Jones. It's been nice meeting you. But I'm going through a tough time myself right now. And I really don't have the patience for strangers and their crap, Cherokee or not."

He stood up too. Even with Sarah's substantial height, he had a good four inches on her. He placed a hand on her forearm. "Please," he said. "Don't go. I've done this all wrong."

She glanced down at his hand, at his large, strong fingers and his copper skin like hers.

"Please," he said, "sit down."

She sat because she didn't want to cause a scene right there in the restaurant. She sat because he was a peacemaker, after all.

"Sarah," he said, his hand still on her arm. "Your mother sent me."

She flinched. He must have meant *his* mother sent him. But he had said that Little Tree was dead, the same way her mother was. She forced a public smile. "I talk to the stars too," she said, "but they rarely converse with me."

He shook his head. "Your mother, Sarah. Your mother is alive and well. And she's looking for you."

This time, she stood up so fast she nearly knocked the table over. She flashed her eyes at him just once, then darted from the place.

8

♥

Of course, she didn't have a mother. The man calling himself Sutter Jones must be some sort of con man, someone who had seen the success of Second Chances, caught sight, perhaps, of Sarah, tagged her as an easy mark. A fellow Cherokee who might think that he'd get something—what? Money? Had his penchant for the finer things in life left him penniless?

If only that was a likely scenario.

She did not go back to work. Instead, Sarah drove and drove all afternoon, trying to forget about it, trying to drive away the images of Little Tree and her colorful blankets and the dancing shadows that the cliffs cast on the reservation. She tried to put it all behind her, but this time she could not lock her misery within, as she'd done for so long.

Late in the afternoon she drove past the lake, the

rising winter moon shimmering on black waters. She thought about the Lake of the Spotted Deer back home; she used to love to sit by it at night and listen to nature's harmony and dream about her life and what was waiting for her. In daylight, she'd study her reflection in the same deep waters, hoping this was the magic lake of Cherokee legend, where looking at her rippling image promised to bring inner harmony and balance.

Sarah wondered now when it had been that she was transformed from a contented, inquisitive child into a closed, cautious adult.

"Sometimes you are so vacant," Jason had said on more than one occasion.

She'd thought about the odd choice of his word. Vacant. As if she had somehow become empty, detached from emotion, zombielike.

It had, of course, happened when her grandmother died, long before she'd met Jason.

"Your mother was a white woman," her younger cousin, Douglas, had said. "You are a half-breed, Sarah. A white Indian. You have no ties to our clan. You really never did."

Sarah knew their traditions as well as Douglas did. The Cherokee society was a matriarchal one: The women owned the houses and the children belonged to them. If divorce occurred, the father left his children and his possessions and went back from where he came. It was the mother's, not the father's, side that determined the proper clan. Technically, Douglas had been right. The Paint Clan was the heritage of Sarah's father. Sarah, therefore, did not belong.

Her father had always said his sister's son was an imbecile: "Not born with the brains of a buffalo." Sarah's father had been her idol. But he died when Sarah was only sixteen, then Glisi when she was twenty-one. Douglas had a mother and a father. How could he have been so cruel?

Sarah had gone to Douglas's mother, her aunt Mae (Weeping Dove). Aunt Mae said, "Oh, your father would be angry if he knew Douglas had told."

Sarah had folded her arms. Her eyes darted around Aunt Mae's shop, a dark-wood-walled herbal emporium that smelled of sweetgrass and sage. It was owned by the Cherokee, patronized by white women in search of miracles. The irony had not been lost on Sarah.

"Who was my mother, Aunt Mae?" twenty-one-year-old Sarah had asked.

Mae had shaken her head. "A white woman, that's all your father said. But it doesn't matter. The woman is dead."

It had, however, mattered to Sarah. It mattered that she was not who she thought. It mattered that no one had told her the real reason she didn't belong.

Sarah had been a senior at Winston College then, on the other side of the continent from California. Her tuition had been paid through graduation. When she returned to school after Glisi's funeral, Sarah never went back. If anyone wondered what had happened to her, they didn't try too hard to find out.

Until now.

Until Sutter Jones, son of Margaret, Little Tree.

Perhaps it was because Sutter had a son who was a

white Indian too. A half-breed. Long ago, Sarah had thought that one day she might try to learn about her mother: where she was from, who her people were, if she had loved Sarah's father. But as the years passed, it had become easier to forget. Easier to close herself off in the obscure hills of Massachusetts.

Until this man dropped by and said her mother sent him.

He was wrong, of course.

He was just a misguided Indian who was a long, long way from home.

The red light on the answering machine beckoned her attention when Sarah walked into the log cabin. She gave Elton a quick pat, then went over to the phone. She hoped the message wasn't from the owner of the jewelry store in Boston looking for the silver bracelets she'd promised for February.

"Hi, Mom." Burch's not-quite-man voice plucked a heartstring that made Sarah smile. "It's almost seven o'clock. Where the heck are you? Dad let me sit in with the band last night. It was so cool. Tell Elton I miss him. I love you, Mom."

Click.

She sighed, took off her coat, and put the teakettle on the stove, moving with the weight of the Cherokee Nation on her shoulders. She fixed the dog's dinner, then studied the contents of the refrigerator to see if anything interested her, since she'd abandoned her lunch.

Carrots.

Three eggs.

Some shriveled mushrooms.

Two McIntosh apples left from October, when she and Burch had gone picking right down the road.

An old hunk of Asiago cheese, Jason's favorite.

She could make an omelet without milk. First, though, she would call Burch.

"He's across the hall at his new friend Glen's," Jason said. "How was the wedding? How are you?" He'd said he didn't want a separation from Sarah, only from the dullness of life in West Hope. His band had been playing more and more often in Manhattan. He'd wanted to feel part of the city, not just a visitor who only knew hotel rooms and doormen and which places had room service. Jason had worked hard for his success. He'd spent too many years in and out of unpleasant bars and lounges, he'd said; he worried about money all the time. Sarah had tried to tell him that money didn't matter, but it did to him. He was a product of an affluent upbringing, after all. Those values and those measures of what constituted success were never far from him, any more than her values were far from her. Still, she could not, would not hold him back.

"Everything's fine," she replied. "Quiet." She twisted the phone cord. "How did New Year's go?"

"Great. We did a gig in the Village, then went back last night."

"Burch went to Times Square."

Jason laughed. He had a wonderful, infectious laugh that sounded as if it should come from a fat, jolly man, not from someone who ate only vegan and worked out every day. "Yeah. He went with Glen and Glen's mother. Don't worry, she's a normal parent. She's a schoolteacher."

"I wasn't worried," Sarah lied. She worried about Burch every day, worried for his safety, worried about his health. When he was nine he'd had appendicitis. What if something like that happened again? Would Jason know enough to take him to a hospital?

Worried? Of course she worried. She worried that Burch would become more acclimated to life in New York and would never want to come home.

She squared her shoulders, sucked in a small breath. "And then last night you took him to the club?" She tried not to sound angry or too protective or any of those things Jason might accuse her of.

"I brought him with me last night because I knew it wouldn't be crowded. He had a good time. He's turning into a great drummer."

The teakettle whistled. Sarah went to it, poured the hot water into her mug. "Well, tell him I called. And that I'll see him soon." Jason had a short road trip to Cincinnati and Cleveland at the end of the month. They'd agreed that Burch would stay in West Hope while his father was away.

"Sarah?" Jason asked. "Are you doing okay?"

If only he hadn't asked her that. If only he hadn't asked her that, she might have been able to say goodbye and hang up and let the dog in and make her omelet and go to bed and sleep through the night. Instead, her eyes filled quickly and she tried to swallow but waited a beat too long. "Sure, I'm okay," she answered, but she knew that Jason had sensed otherwise, because he paused too long too, then he simply said, "Well, good." Then there was a silence so long and so heavy it couldn't be penetrated even with one of Elaine's new, professional-chef, never-needs-sharpening knives.

"I'm okay, Jason," Sarah said again. "Lonely, though. I miss you both."

"We miss you too."

In the silence that lingered, she wondered why on earth she hadn't gone with them. Was it really that important to stay inside herself, to be a lonely, long-suffering recluse?

Because she did not belong with the Cherokee.

Because she did not belong with anyone.

Except maybe with the mystery woman who was supposedly her mother.

Suddenly she laughed, because laughter was more acceptable than tears. "Give Burch a kiss for me."

"Oh, right, I'm sure he'd let me." Then Jason laughed and said good-bye, and Sarah hung up and took her tea to the empty fireplace. She knew she'd spend the night right there again, without a decent dinner, without any warmth, without her son or the only man she'd ever let herself love. With only her present and her past, which she didn't really even know.

9

Does John know about this?" It was Frannie Cassidy, John Benson's assistant at *Buzz* magazine.

Andrew looked out the kitchen window at his daughter, who was strutting gaily down the driveway toward the school bus stop. The air was quiet, the sky was pewter and foreboding; it was going to snow. He was surprised they hadn't closed the school, but, he reminded himself with a chuckle, New Englanders were heartier than New York City folks. He only hoped the white stuff would arrive early enough to be cleared out on Thursday and make traveling safe for the guests at the party Friday afternoon. "If you mean did I tell John it would be my last column, the answer's no," he said into his cell phone.

"Well, gosh," Frannie said, "he's in Rio, you know?"

Her mousy voice went up and down like a seesaw in Central Park.

"Ah, yes. I know. But what I've written is for real, Frannie."

"Can't you hold off until John gets back? I hate to call and upset him—and Irene. Gosh, Andrew, it's their second honeymoon."

Andrew didn't say that John and Irene had renewed their wedding vows only because Andrew saw it as an opportunity to help the women at Second Chances. It had not been a romantic urge on John's part, but rather a business proposition as payback for Andrew's "Real Women" column.

Outside the cottage now, the big yellow bus lumbered to a stop, and the folding door screeched open. Cassie turned and waved; Andrew sent back the gesture. "John will handle it," he said.

"But what about our revenues?" She laughed a frightened laugh, as if trying to convince him that without his column the magazine would go to hell. "Between you and me," she added, her voice changing to hush-hush, "you're the reason any of us here still have jobs."

Frannie, of course, should be able to get a job most anywhere with her Masters in finance from Princeton and her ten years of dedication as John's right hand and his left. Her appearance, however, did not enhance her résumé: She was small and twittery and always looked to be in pain.

"Are you trying to make me feel guilty?"

"Please, Andrew."

"I can't."

"Well, if you don't want to keep doing research, can't you just make it up?"

"I'm a journalist, Frannie. I write fact, not fiction."

"But how will you earn a living?"

So far, he hadn't let himself think too much about that, hadn't, until now, needed to lose sleep over his finances. He had a small portfolio that his parents left to him, but he'd vowed to save it for Cassie. Despite a hefty salary in his years of television, he hadn't accumulated very much—Patty's lifestyle had seen to that. His greatest remaining asset was his brain, though he wondered if that would now disintegrate as quickly as his bank account. He shook his head and said, "Thanks for your concern, Frannie, but I'll be fine. I won't write another 'Real Women' column. That's all I have to say."

"But we're having the editorial meeting this morning. I won't know what to say." He pictured her blinking quickly, leaning forward on her desk, tapping a nervous pencil.

It always amazed Andrew that such savvy, go-getting business people could so easily be rattled. "Tell them I am finished. That I fulfilled my verbal contract." The editorial meeting would most likely be held in the large conference room, where, against the row of tinted, floor-to-ceiling-length windows, the Manhattan high-rise skyline was pasted like wallpaper. The meeting would not go well. Around the long glass table, the self-important crowd of those in charge (mostly young, mostly gym-sculptured bodies, mostly in unironed clothes that were gray or black and either too baggy or extremely tight) would sip from water bottles and ruminate about the options: They could continue publishing the magazine as if the column never existed; they could hire a ghostwriter with half the talent at half the salary; they could sue the bastard Andrew Kennedy, how dare he do this while John Benson was away.

The tap-tapping continued. "I thought you were supposed to write the column for a year."

He was surprised Frannie knew that. The discussion, Andrew thought, had been between him and John, two old friends. "I counteroffered with six months. It's been seven." They'd shaken hands. Should he say that?

"But you're giving him no warning." Her tone took on more edge as the meeting time approached.

"Look, Frannie, the job is over. I can no longer be objective." He didn't need to elaborate; she'd read the column, so she knew about the new woman in his life.

For a moment Frannie said nothing. He wondered if they'd been disconnected or if his cell phone had run out of juice.

Then she said, "No, Andrew, you're not being fair. Just because you've *fallen in love*, why should you take it out on us?" She said "fallen in love" as if he'd contracted bird flu.

"Frannie, look. I'm sorry. This is nothing personal."

He heard what resembled a faint hiss over the line. Then Frannie said, "Andrew David, or Andrew Kennedy, or whatever your name is, I can only say that speaking on behalf of the entire editorial staff at *Buzz* magazine, I hope the woman dumps you." She slammed down the receiver, leaving Andrew standing in the kitchen, his eardrum reverberating.

"I have a moral dilemma," Andrew said to Jo. They were lying in her bed, naked flesh to naked flesh, bodies still getting to know each other. She was smiling, happy—glowing, she supposed. "John's assistant is furious that I resigned. She said I'm the reason they all have jobs at *Buzz*. Am I being too unfair?"

It was, of course, amusing that Andrew was asking Jo about the niceties of something that had been the great deceit of their relationship. She scooted closer, stroked his shoulder. She was glad he'd come for a prework visit after Cassie had gone to school, that he'd dodged the early specks of frozen precipitation for a chance to be with her. There was something softly sensual about sex in the morning, even though after-sleep meant knotted hair and tangled sheets and natural body scents, and the morning light—though muted now by the low ceiling of clouds—could be so unforgiving. Yet it didn't seem to matter, at least not to Andrew, the compassionate, passionate lover that Jo had once dreamed Brian would have been.

"Do you still feel you have something to contribute?" she asked. "About real women?"

He slung one leg across her hip and gently cupped her breasts. "I'm more confused than ever. The world hardly needs to hear that."

Jo laughed. She realized she had laughed more in the past few days than she had in years. Years! She had felt more content, more at peace, than she ever had imagined she was capable of feeling. *Love,* she supposed it was. *The real thing. At last.* "Well, I don't care what you do. As long as your readers don't think you're for sale. As long as you don't tell them"—she reached down and took his penis in her hand—"about this," she said, then kissed his throat, ". . . or this," she said, then wriggled her way below his waist and took him in her mouth, ". . . or this."

He let her bring him back to hardness. Then he pulled her up to him and wrapped himself around her. "She said she hopes you'll dump me."

Jo closed her eyes and laughed again. "Why? So she can have you?"

He kissed her. "No chance," he said, then entered her again.

And Jo thought about the weightless joy of true love and how this was definitely it.

When she'd finally gone to bed the night before, Sarah forgot to set the alarm clock. She awoke to the phone ringing at ten o'clock: It was Lily, telling her not to bother to come in if she had thought she might, that Andrew called to say the roads were already slippery and that they should all stay home.

Sarah peeked out the window at a nasty clash of snow and ice and wind, which Lily said had been building for the past hour or so. It was the kind of day meant for staying home bundled in wool blankets, reading books, and drinking steamy mugs of hot chocolate.

Sarah, however, might lose her mind if she had to stay inside today.

She quickly showered and dressed in leggings and a thick sweater and her lined boots from L.L. Bean. She donned her storm coat with the hood, piled her hair up under a knit hat, grabbed her big leather purse, and headed out the door. Elton had the sense to want to stay inside. Then again, Sarah mused as she shielded her face from the spitting, freezing-needle glaze and trundled through a quickly accumulating crust, Elton did not need to distract himself from Cherokees who lived or mothers who were dead, from men who were happier without her or sons who were as well. Elton did not need to try to keep his mind off his entire life.

She yanked open the nearly frozen driver's door, flung her purse across the seat, then climbed into the truck. She sat a moment, shivering, then turned over the ignition and cranked up the defrost; it would be easier to sit there than to sweep and scrape the windshield. She drummed her glove-covered fingers on the steering wheel, waited for warmth, and tried to focus on the weddings that were imminent. Which would require the most work? The most preplanning? And what if Valentine's Day turned out like this day? What would they need to prepare for the couple on the mountaintop? What special needs would the wheelchair bride—Julie Pearl—have?

Sarah turned on the windshield wipers, but they groaned under the frozen layer. She flicked off the switch and thought about what it might be like to be in a wheelchair, trapped in a world dependent on motion, where it was expected for everyone to move swiftly and with purpose and to stand up for oneself.

Sarah realized it would not be fair to Julie to have the groom standing at the altar while she was seated next to him. Not the groom, nor the wedding party, nor even, good grief, the priest himself should be standing up, looking down upon the bride.

She should make a note of that. She reached across the seat where the corner of a piece of paper stuck out from beneath her purse. Without another thought, she pulled out the paper, which turned out to be a brochure. *The* brochure from the Hilltop Bed and Breakfast, where Sutter Jones was staying.

She stared at it a moment, then said, "Damn," and threw it on the floor.

She pushed out a puff of frosty breath, turned on the wipers once again. Slowly, they arced across the windshield, moving melting snow and ice as if it were a wide-shouldered mountain in the Sierra Nevada range.

Sarah thought about the burnished skin, the sharp-angled nose, the square, straight shoulders of Sutter Jones. They were the features of her father too, and her male cousins, even unpleasant Douglas, and of Red Elk.

Damn.

She watched the windshield clear.

Could there be any truth to Sutter's claim?

Her gaze dropped to the floor, where the Hilltop brochure lay upside down.

And Sarah knew that she could not go to Second Chances until she saw Sutter again.

"Do you mean we'll have to stay inside all day?"

"I think it's for the best."

"The driving will be awful."

"The walking will be impossible."

"I was afraid of this."

"We could go downstairs and build a fire."

"Or we could stay here."

"Yes. We could stay here."

"But what about Cassie?"

"When I called Lily, I called Mrs. Connor too. She'll watch for the school bus. She'll call Cassie over to her house."

"And you'll have to stay here."

"It looks that way."

"All day."

"I'm afraid so."

"Hmm. Whatever shall we do?"

Andrew rolled on top of Jo again and could not believe how happy he was.

10

♥

Sarah wasn't sure she'd ever make it to the Hilltop Bed and Breakfast. She wasn't even sure she should.

Sitting rock-rigid on the seat, staring out at the growing whiteout that was covering the sky, the road, and all the air in between, she gripped the steering wheel more tightly and thought about the facts as she knew them, the facts that she would replay to Sutter Jones if she ever made it to the inn alive.

My grandmother said my mother died in childbirth, she would begin. *She gave me the same answer when I was five, seven, eight, every time I asked, pretending I hadn't asked before. Finally Glisi told me to stop asking, because the answer would always be the same. She said I would see my mother one day when the Great Spirit called me home.*

She wondered if Sutter would be understanding or if he would be obstinate and stick to his story.

She would tell him how she'd once asked her father if he had at least a picture of her mother, but that he'd said no and left the room. Her grandmother then said she should leave well enough alone.

Maybe she would tell Sutter how she'd wondered about her mother off and on: What had she liked, what had she disliked? Maybe she would say she'd always wanted to know how her parents met but that she hadn't wanted to upset anyone any more than she already had just by being born and killing her mother.

When I was told my mother was white, she might say to Sutter, *I wondered what that must have felt like.* She might not tell him that more than once she'd studied herself in the small hand mirror that had been Glisi's, looking for traces of the woman who had not been Cherokee.

She might say she'd thought about her mother when she was pregnant with Burch. She'd wondered if her mother had experienced the same unending glow that Sarah felt from the moment, it had seemed, that she conceived. Sarah wondered if she had been as welcome as Burch had been, if her mother had felt the maternal connection Sarah felt each time Burch moved within her womb, each time she closed her eyes and imagined she could feel his soft, small breath within her.

She'd wondered so many times if her mother had died before she'd seen Sarah, before she'd held her in her arms, before she'd seen the miracle she'd wrought.

But she couldn't say that to Sutter, because he said her mother wasn't dead.

Around one last corner, down one last slope, Sarah

carefully turned the steering wheel and the truck did a slow skid into the parking lot at the Hilltop Bed and Breakfast.

"He isn't here," Grace Koehler said when she hustled Sarah into the living room of the cozy inn. Grace and her husband, Paul, had owned the inn since the late eighties, when many corporate types had ditched their nine-to-five jobs for the promise of their own business. The room was country-comfortable; the Koehlers seemed to have made their business a success.

"He left?" Sarah asked, not wanting to remove her hat and drip snow-water on the gleaming hardwood floor.

Grace nodded. "Very early this morning. Before the weather turned."

Sarah was surprised at her disappointment. She introduced herself to Grace, whom she'd never really met but had known about through the talk around the butcher shop, the town hall, the post office. Grace nodded as if she, too, knew who Sarah was, having no doubt learned from the same venues.

"He left a card for you," Grace said, "in case you came around." She dug her hand into the pocket of her long red sweater and withdrew a business card. "If you'd like to call him, you're welcome to use my phone. His cell phone number is on it—he said you can reach him anytime." The woman smiled. Perhaps she thought Sutter Jones was Sarah's lover.

Sarah took the card. "Thank you," she said.

"Would you like to call now?" Grace asked. "From here?"

Sarah thought quickly. She wouldn't want to call from the shop; if she waited until she went home tonight she might change her mind. "Yes," she replied, "if you don't mind."

Grace produced a cordless phone, directed her to the dining room for privacy, and told her not to mind her wet boots. She also said, "Don't worry about toll charges. We have free long-distance minutes."

Sarah made a mental note to add the Hilltop to the list of good places to offer out-of-town wedding guests. Then Grace left Sarah alone, and she moved to a large bow window and looked at the card.

JONES AND ARCHAMBAULT, it read.

ATTORNEYS AT LAW.

It listed an address and phone on Madison Avenue in New York City. Someone had printed *Cell* with another number after that.

She dialed.

He answered.

"It's Sarah Duncan," she said.

He paused, then said, "I'm sorry. You took me by surprise."

"I thought we might have coffee, but I understand you've left town."

He paused again. "I'm headed for Los Angeles on business."

"I'd like to ask you some questions. I'd like to tell you some things too."

"Yes. Well. I'm in New York right now. At the airport." He gave a short laugh. "Actually I'm on the plane. We're waiting to push back from the gate."

It hadn't occurred to Sarah that he would have gone so far so fast. "Oh," she said. "You really have left the area then."

"Well. Yes."

Outside, the snow had not let up. The wind made it look as if it were coming down sideways, Old Mother West Wind blowing to the east. "Is this true?" she asked. "About my mother?"

In the silence that followed, Sarah heard a female voice. *"Please turn off all cellular phones at this time. You may turn them back on once we reach our destination."*

"I'm sorry," Sutter said again, "I have to hang up. I'll call you from L.A. I have your number."

The line went dead, and Sarah sat with the phone in her hand, trying to recall how long the flight was to the West Coast but knowing it had been too many years for her to remember.

11

The snowy, icy misery of Wednesday turned into a full-blown nor'easter that left twelve to fourteen inches on West Hope's January ground.

Jo and Andrew had spent the day together, rising out of bed only sometime in mid-afternoon for homemade beef vegetable soup that Andrew thought she'd skillfully concocted, underscoring his belief, he'd said, that she was the perfect woman. When he was on his second bowl, Jo admitted that the soup hadn't come from her stove but from her mother's, that she had never once made soup, that she had no clue where to begin. He looked so disappointed that she told him she'd be sure to get the recipe.

After lunch they'd gone back to bed and hadn't gotten up again until late in the evening, when the grinding crunch of snowplows passed by the house a second time, alerting Andrew to the fact he could safely traverse the roads back to his cottage, to his daughter.

As they stood at her back door, holding each other longer than was necessary, Jo had said, "Let's not tell the others just yet, okay? Not until we know where this is going."

"I know where it is going," Andrew had whispered in her ear.

But she shook her head. "Please." She hadn't said she wanted a little more blissful time before withstanding the inevitable questions from Lily, the knowing winks from Elaine. Not that any of them wouldn't guess by her smile. Or her happy walk. Or the glow that Andrew had said radiated from her cheeks as he kissed her face one last time and went out the door.

Still, as she walked into the shop the morning after the storm, when the sky was smugly bright with sunshine, as if it had never done the things it had done the day before, Jo was greeted by Elaine, who looked so happy too that she had to hold back from blurting out, *I'm in love with Andrew and he's in love with me.*

Instead, it was Elaine who did the blurting. "Ovens," she said. "I need them."

"Well," Jo said, hanging up her coat, "you go, girl."

Elaine put one hand on her hip. "I'm serious, Jo. I need a full restaurant kitchen next door. It's the only way we'll be able to cater multiple weddings. Lily already took another call from a prospective bride this morning. We have to get this business into gear, and we have to do it fast."

Jo walked through the studio, said good morning to Sarah, who answered with a short wave, then went into the showroom, where Lily busily chatted on the phone and Andrew sat, smiling—maybe glowing too.

It was difficult to look at him and not reveal her joy.

"A full kitchen sounds like a heavy investment," Jo said in a steady, even tone, as if the most wonderful man who'd ever come into her life wasn't sitting five feet from her. "Maybe you should wait until our revenues are more solid. Until we have more checks in hand. Or at least until the Bensons pay off their balance."

Elaine shook her head. "I'm going to do this on my own. I plan to remortgage my house."

Moving to her desk, Jo marveled at the changes in Elaine, at the confidence she'd gained in the last six months. She'd been at such a low point after her breakup with Martin. Perhaps it was true that sometimes people had to hit bottom before they could pull themselves back up, one leg of panty hose at a time. Had Jo done that with Brian? Was that why she was finally able to love a man again? She cleared her throat. "You managed the Benson wedding without a problem."

"Only because the Stone Castle has a kitchen. I don't want the Second Chances catering arm to be restricted to those venues. I want a full kitchen here and the equipment for a field kitchen off site. Off any site. It will give the business a great competitive edge."

"A coup de grâce," Andrew said with a chuckle. "Or would that be foie de gras?"

Jo quickly glanced at Andrew. He winked a sexy wink.

"It's foie gras," Lily said, hanging up the phone.

"No *de* involved." She looked at Jo, who peeled her eyes from Andrew with much reluctance. "We just had another call. A July wedding at Laurel Lake. I doubt that there's a kitchen there."

"I rest my case," Elaine said. "Which is why I need to steal Andrew for today. I need him to go to Springfield with me, to the restaurant supply outlet. I'd like to be up and running to serve our Valentine's Day events."

Andrew laughed. "Elaine, I don't know anything about restaurant equipment."

"You didn't know about wedding planning either," Lily chimed in. "Now you're a pro. Or something like that."

Everyone laughed, because it was pretty funny. Andrew David, internationally renowned television journalist, turned Andrew Kennedy, receptionist to wedding planners. None of them had mentioned that now that they knew who Andrew was, past and present, perhaps he might desire an alternative career to working for a bunch of women. Perhaps, like Jo, the others wanted him to stick around. That would change, Jo guessed, when they learned what had occurred between the two of them. That would change if they caught sight of the love sparks that now jumped from her to him and him to her. If nothing else, Jo would be distracted, Andrew would be distracted, nothing would get done, and their secret might leap from its safe yet still fragile cocoon, and everything would change too fast, too soon. She sighed a quiet sigh. "I suppose we can spare him," she said. "I want to work with Sarah on the Rhonda Blair wedding this morning. This afternoon the couple from Pittsfield is coming in for their initial consultation." She pulled her eyes from his again. "Unless you need him for something, Lily..."

Lily shook her head. "I want to work on the Rhonda Blair wedding too. I'm thinking about over-the-top tasteful... I'm thinking harps...."

Elaine signaled to Andrew, and Andrew stood up. "At your service, ma'am," he said. "Please. Anything to escape the harps." He turned to Jo. "So we'll see you later, I guess."

"I guess," Jo replied with a lopsided grin, though what she really wanted was to stand up and kiss him good-bye, a long, lingering kiss that he'd remember all the way east on the turnpike and all day and then back home again.

By noon, Sarah had a headache. She loved Lily, really she did, but sometimes the woman's enthusiasm was annoying as hell. It had been bad enough that the day before, Sarah had braved the storm and made it into the shop (once she'd made it to the Hilltop Bed and Breakfast, she was more than halfway there). She'd worked all day, then spent the night on Lily's couch upstairs ("There's no need for you to risk your life, Sarah," Lily had said. "What would we do without you? What would Burch do without his mother?"). She hadn't bothered to tell Lily that Burch, apparently, would do just fine. Instead, she'd stayed because she was exhausted from trying to distract herself. She was glad she'd left extra food out for Elton. Even he would know better than to venture too far beyond his doggy door in the howling storm.

She hadn't, however, expected Lily to treat their snow day as if it were a girls' sleepover, complete with a dinner of popcorn and Doritos and endless chatter, chatter, chatter about Frank Forbes, her ardent beau, and how wonderful he was.

"His wife left him after years and years. How could she have done such a hideous thing?

"His parents are ailing but still living, and he takes care of them. And he still runs the family antiques business as if it belonged to his father, always asking his advice, always including him in the big decisions.

"And that horrid brother of his, Brian! What he did to Jo was bad enough, but can you imagine how his parents feel?"

When Lily got off the subject of Frank Forbes and got onto Sarah and Jason and what did Sarah think was going to happen, Sarah promptly said good night. Lily told her she was a bore, though she at last turned off the light.

Sarah rubbed her temples now, amazed that they had accomplished anything that morning. Because Rhonda Blair's fiancé was from Spain, and Rhonda's Texas home was so close to Mexico, they decided to follow a color scheme of red satin and gold lamé. "Fat red roses," Sarah had said, "bundled into bouquets with wide, metallic gold ribbon. We can layer them along the fireplace mantel—not in vases. I can make gold pouches to hold just enough water to keep them moist."

"And let's add touches of black leather to the decor," Lily had chirped. "It would be rather erotic, don't you think? We could make the groom look like a conquistador."

"Or a moron," Sarah said, and that's when Jo suggested they take a lunch break, and Sarah said it was the best idea anyone had had that day.

"I'm going across the green to see how Frank is doing," Lily announced. Converting the old town hall to hold his antiques business was proving a challenge. (Sarah had heard all the yakkety-yak details the night before.) But Sarah recognized that being involved—going with Frank to auctions and offering her feminine opinion—was keeping always-in-motion Lily from getting weary of the sometimes tedious tasks at Second Chances.

"Sarah?" Jo asked. "Are you interested in a sandwich at the luncheonette?" The luncheonette was two doors down from Second Chances, and the women (and Andrew) had become its best customers. No doubt that would change once Elaine's catering kitchen was up and running. But for now the luncheonette offered a decent sandwich and a cup of soup.

"Sure," she said, then went to get her coat. As she stood by the back door buttoning it, she heard Jo's voice call out from the showroom, "Hello, how are you?"

A man replied, "Is Sarah here?"

She retraced her steps into the showroom. Sutter Jones was standing there.

"I decided this was more important than going to L.A.," he said. "I would have come back right away, but what with the storm..."

Jo didn't say a word. Sarah knew that Jo would be confused—she didn't know Sarah had talked to Sutter again. Jo hadn't asked, because she respected Sarah's privacy the way Sarah respected hers.

"Maybe you could bring me back a tomato soup and grilled cheese," Sarah said to Jo. "Are you hungry, Sutter?"

"Tomato soup and grilled cheese would be great," he said. He took off his leather gloves and unwound the cashmere scarf from the neckline of his coat. "I never thought a New England winter could equal the intensity of the Sierra Nevadas."

Jo smiled and, without another word, slipped quietly out the door.

"I haven't told my friends," Sarah said as soon as Jo was gone. "I've known that my mother was white since I was in college, but I never told them"—she stumbled for the word—

"That you're a white Indian," he said.

She blinked.

"I know your mother's white," he said in a clear, definitive voice. "I've known her for many years." He sat in one of the plump navy chairs across from the desk. After a moment he said, "You don't know anything about her, do you?"

Sarah didn't know what to say. She watched as this man, this stranger who, curiously, did not seem like a stranger, unbuttoned his coat, set his elbows on his knees, and looked at her as if waiting for an answer.

She could tell him to get out of their shop. She could tell him to stop bothering her, that her life was quite fine, thank you very much, that she liked living as a recluse from the Cherokee, the renegade spirit in her stronger than the will of the white woman who might or might not have been her mother. She could have said and done these things, but instead she shook her head. "I was told she died while giving birth to me. Only later did I learn that she was white."

Sutter nodded. "As I said earlier, I am an attorney. Your mother sent me to find you."

It grew warm in the showroom, though the afternoon sun had yet to stretch itself across the glossy wood floor. Sarah moved toward Andrew's desk. She sat there, across from Sutter. She did not want to sit in the navy chair beside him; she did not want to get that friendly. She did not trust him yet. "So this woman who you claim is my mother sent you to find me because..."

"Because she'd like to meet you."

Sarah stared at him and wondered how she should respond, how she *could* respond when suddenly her mouth was dry and her head began to throb. She tugged the silver clip from her hair and let the cascade float down her back. "Does she live in Los Angeles?" she asked in a voice that sounded too meek to be hers. "Is that why you were going there?"

He played with his leather gloves for a moment, as if trying to piece together his answer. Then he said, "Your mother lives in New York City. As I do."

Sarah scowled. "Please stop calling her 'my mother.' I don't even know the woman. I don't even know you."

He laughed a short, auspicious laugh. "You might not think you know me, but I remember you. When I left for college you were still a little girl. You had a little doll you carried with you everywhere."

He would not have known about the doll her father had named Duchess, would he? He would not have known the way she was made of buffalo grass, with button eyes and a button mouth and long black hair made of yarn, the doll who sported lots of "silver" jewelry that Glisi had made of aluminum foil. He would not have known about the doll if he hadn't really known her.

Would he?

"I was named after the gold mine," he said abruptly.

She nodded; she'd already figured that. Many of the Cherokee had earned a living wage at Sutter's Gold Mine.

"After I finished law school," he continued, "I went back to the reservation. But you were gone by then. You had left for college. And then I started working for your mother. I've worked for her all these years."

"You work for her? What does she do?" Sarah knew that each question might bring more information than she wanted to know. She knew this and yet she could not help herself.

"She's retired now. But she used to be in the film industry. She still has interests that I see to in L.A."

"But she lives in New York."

"Yes."

She drew in another breath, then the questions

came out as a string of accusations, hostile fire on the man, the messenger: How had her mother and her father met? Why had she abandoned her? Did she have other children?

All he said was that her mother never had married, never had other kids. "But she's an interesting woman, Sarah. All else aside, I think you'd like her."

She studied the black eyes. She looked for a lie but could not see one there. "What's her name?" Sarah asked.

In the flash of an instant, Sutter said, "Laura. Her name is Laura Carrington."

Sarah sat quietly, digesting his words. *Laura Carrington.* Surely he didn't mean Laura Carrington, the Hollywood movie star, the woman that every man in the fifties and sixties wanted as his own, the woman that every little girl dreamed she one day would be.

"Wouldn't you know," Jo said, as she came through the front door, juggling brown bags from the luncheonette. "They were out of grilled cheese, so I got veggie burgers with the soup. I hope that's all right."

Sarah looked at Jo, then back at Sutter. "I think we'll take ours outside to the park."

12

♥

"Your mother was filming on location in northern California," Sutter said, after Sarah had spread a wool blanket across the snowy bench in the gazebo and they'd sat down. "Your father was an extra in the movie. That was how they met."

His words became crystal clouds each time he spoke; Sarah could feel the cold and dampness seep through her wool coat. Still, she needed the crisp air to keep her thoughts clear. The soup had cooled off quickly, but sipping at it gave her purpose while Sutter continued.

"What was the movie?" she asked suddenly.

"*Gold Dust.*"

Sarah nodded as if she'd seen it, which she had not. She'd always avoided films that depicted Native Americans in stereotypical roles. She took a bite of her veggie burger and slowly chewed.

"She came to the reservation whenever she could," Sutter went on. "Sometimes she and your father met in San Francisco, though it was difficult to be in public because her face was so recognizable. When she learned she was pregnant, she and your father wanted to get married. When she told the studio heads, they were furious. 'Laura Carrington cannot marry an Indian,' they said. 'It would be box-office suicide. Millions will be lost.'"

Sarah had heard the stories of what society was like in the fifties and the sixties. She'd heard the stories, yet had always had a hard time grasping the rigid standards, the restrictions. Cherokee had always been so open about babies, so accepting of their births, and so welcoming of their spirits.

Sutter took a drink of soup, then slowly, carefully continued. "They demanded Laura have an abortion; she refused. They threatened to sue. They threatened to make her life, your father's life, and, most especially, your life a living hell."

The veggie burger, like the soup, took on the chill from the air. Sarah rewrapped the white deli paper around it, then put it back into the bag. She tucked her hands under her legs. She exhaled a long rush of air.

"The studio hid Laura out until you were born," he said. "The only concession they allowed her was to relinquish you to your father and his mother. They were sworn to secrecy. I expect that your father's sister asked if your mother was white. After all, if she'd been Cherokee, the others would have known who and where she was."

The secrecy might not have been easy, but Sarah

knew Cherokee always kept their promises, never went back on their word.

"So," she said, "it's true, I guess."

He nodded. "She's always known who you are, Sarah. She saw you in Boston once, back in the early nineties. In a shop in Quincy Market." He waited.

"That's how you knew about my jewelry," Sarah said. "Not because you saw a bracelet..."

"She saw you. She approached you."

And suddenly Sarah remembered a woman who wore large sunglasses and a floppy felt hat. She remembered she had spoken softly. "You're an artist," she'd said.

Sarah had said yes.

"I admire your work." Then the woman removed her glasses and stared into Sarah's eyes. "You are so beautiful, my Sarah."

Sarah had tried to smile but had not known what to say. The woman replaced her sunglasses but did not turn away, as if Sarah were a piece of jewelry in one of the glass cases in the store, as if she needed to examine her for perfection or for flaws. "Excuse me," Sarah had said uncomfortably, and slipped into the back room.

Later that day she'd seen the woman again, not once, not twice, but three more times, as Sarah darted in and out of Crate & Barrel, the jelly-bean store, the fine leather shop. She had thought about calling security. Instead, she'd left, gone home to western Massachusetts, deciding there was no need to show her face in Boston again. Confrontation had always been difficult for Sarah. She much preferred a passive life, a noncombative life, half-breed that she was, never good enough.

"Oh," she said again now. The sunglasses, the hat, had belonged to Laura Carrington, the woman who claimed to be her mother. Sarah struggled to recall a clear photo image of the woman, but she could not.

"Will you come to New York and meet her?" Sutter asked.

She looked at him and laughed. She didn't know why she laughed, but the sound had slipped out there, frozen in the air, before she could take it back. She shook her head. "Meet her?" she asked, then added, "No, I won't meet her, Sutter. No way."

She didn't know why she felt so strongly, only that she did. No explanation necessary, she decided.

She picked up the bag from the luncheonette. "I'll let you know if I ever change my mind." Then she crossed the town green back to Second Chances, thinking of the irony of how everyone wanted Sarah in New York City, when all she really wanted was to stay here in West Hope.

13

Jo was on the phone when Sarah went back into the shop. She had to talk about this to someone. Lily would be too giddy and Elaine would be too gaga and Jo was the reasonable alternative. Besides, Jo was the most likely, the most trustworthy, the one who wouldn't spill the news until Sarah said it was all right.

She sat down in a navy chair, waited for Jo to get off the phone, and tried not to dwell on how much better things would be if only Jason were at home. She could talk to him about it, couldn't she? He'd never known the details of her life, only that she was Cherokee, only that she was an orphan who'd decided not to return to the reservation because she'd found her place elsewhere, had rooted herself in New England, where she was at peace with the seasons, with herself.

Once he had asked if living on the reservation was

as awful as he'd learned in high-school history, if they'd been terribly poor. Jason, of course, had been raised with wealth, so his concept of a poverty level was much different than hers. She'd said the reservation was fine, that the white men did not understand they did not aspire to be like them. The Cherokee she'd grown up with often laughed among themselves when they saw how the white men felt so guilty and talked of how tough the Indians—Native Americans—had it, when in fact they were content. On the reservation, they knew that those white men and women of today were not the ones who had displaced the Cherokee, who had driven their Cherokee ancestors along their Trail of Tears. Their white ancestors, not they, had done it. Sarah, like most of those of her tribe, wanted no one's pity, let alone commiseration from those who could never truly understand. And Jason could never understand, any more than he—or any man—could know what it was like to bear a child.

Jo hung up and said, "Wow. That was the editor of a bridal magazine. She asked us to be contributing editors to their new spin-off edition for second-time brides. Do you think they've stolen our idea?"

Sarah laughed. "I think if they have, it can only help our business. Get this stuff out in the open. Applaud any bride and groom who want to try doing this again." She swept her hand around the room, waving at the yards and yards of satin and tulle that decorated the windows and the walls. "*Eleghhhance, my darlings, is where it totally is at.*" She was imitating Lily, though she didn't know what had ignited such a need to laugh.

Jo walked around her desk and sat down next to Sarah. "You say that so well," she said. "Have you been taking lessons?"

Sarah smiled and shook her head.

"So what's up?" Jo asked. "This guy Sutter Jones. Is everything okay?"

She picked at the hem of her wool coat. "Sure. He knows some of my people. Or he thinks he does." Why was it so hard to talk about this? Why was this cavalier-sounding attitude the best effort Sarah could muster?

"From California? From the reservation?"

Sarah laughed again. "From a long time ago. A very long time ago."

Then the phone rang again. Jo groaned, reached over, and answered it while Sarah wondered why she kept laughing, why she kept joking, and why it was so difficult to express her deepest-entrenched feelings, even to one of her best friends. Was it that she'd become too accustomed to holding things in, afraid that if she didn't... what? The world would end?

It wasn't as if she held on to secrets that might hurt other people, the way Andrew had done.

"Yes," Jo was saying. "Yes, certainly... Well, no, we don't ordinarily recommend that the groom's former in-laws attend the wedding.... They'd been married how long?... Well, whatever the bride and groom decide, we can accommodate their wishes.... No, I'm sorry, but we can't give out information on the weddings we're planning. We offer our customers total privacy." She looked at Sarah and gestured a thumbs-down.

Sarah was relieved that the subject would now change. When Jo hung up she said, "That sounded absurd."

"Supposedly it was the bride's sister. She said she'd get back to us."

"Sounds like it was an ex-wife." At least it wasn't Laura Carrington, Sarah suddenly thought. She fiddled with the button on her coat. Would the woman—her mother?—do that? Would she spy on Sarah again or call the shop and pretend she wanted a second wedding? If that were to happen, what would Sarah do?

"Sarah?" Jo asked. "Are you sure you're okay? You look kind of pale."

"Ha-ha," Sarah said. "Is this a paleface joke?" She stood up and unbuttoned her coat. It was definitely time to get back to work.

Jo laughed too, then the phone rang again. This time they both groaned.

Jo said hello, and Sarah started toward the studio. Then Jo raised her eyebrows and said, "I'm sorry. But Andrew is out for the day." She signaled to Sarah and mouthed, *It's a woman*, with a slight smile of concern. "May I take a message?" She paused.

Sarah paused.

Jo put her hand up to her throat. "Excuse me? Irene?" She frowned; she looked at Sarah. "Yes, this is Jo. How is Rio?" She listened. She began shaking her head. "Irene? Please, slow down. I can't understand you. . . ." More listening. More head-shaking. She glanced at Andrew's desk, where his small gray cell phone sat. "No," she said, "Andrew doesn't have his phone with him. . . ." She paused again. "What?" she asked. "What? Oh. No. Oh, Irene . . ." She stood up, ran her hand through her hair. "Irene? Irene?" She waited another moment, then hung up the phone. "It's John Benson," she said. "Apparently he's gone."

"Gone?" Sarah asked. "Gone as in, Elvis has left the building, or gone as in . . . deceased?"

Jo scowled. "I have no idea," she said. "I only know Irene is still in Rio, and she is quite hysterical."

Shopping with Elaine had been fun. Andrew was both amused and bemused by the changes in Elaine since she'd had her makeover. Beneath the woman's former layers of polyester and overgelled hair was a bright, energetic lady who had found a mission: a productive career, an enthusiastic player in the game of her own life.

He had watched as she'd ordered deep-pit grills and warming ovens and steam tables with knowledge that had seemed to surprise even her.

They decided on a late lunch in downtown Springfield. Elaine promised she only wanted to make two more stops before heading back to West Hope—a party store for decorations for Cassie's celebration the next afternoon, and a restaurant that Elaine had heard was going out of business. She thought it might be a good place to pick up some cutlery and glassware at a bargain.

"I'm proud of you, kid," Andrew said after he ordered a burger with a side Caesar salad. Elaine asked for a small, thin-crust cheese pizza.

"Me too," she said, not with ego but with innocence. "I love my life these days, Andrew. I actually look forward to getting up in the morning."

He nodded. "I know the feeling." Would it hurt anything if he told Elaine? She had, after all, been his confidante, kept his secrets, when he'd needed her to. Though he'd grown up an only child, Andrew felt he recognized a big sister when he saw one. It didn't matter that they were almost the same age. Elaine had practical experience with living from day to day. She had been raised in a home where everyone was present and involved with one another's lives. She'd provided the same life for her three kids, despite her divorce. Andrew hadn't had that kind of luck. His parents never were quite sure what to do with a kid; his ex-wife, Patty, hadn't bothered with him very much either. Cassie had been the focus, the purpose, the meaning of his life for so long now that he'd forgotten what little he'd ever thought he'd known about love. He rested his arms on the table and leaned forward. "Elaine," he asked, "can you keep a secret?"

"Very funny," she answered. "But I thought you were done with those."

"This is a new one. I think you might like it."

Her eyes brightened. "Jo?" she asked.

The burger arrived along with his disappointment. "She told you?"

Elaine laughed. "No one had to, Andrew. It's pretty obvious."

"Do the others know?"

"We haven't discussed it, but neither Sarah nor Lily are, well, blind."

He bit into his burger without cutting it in half. He chewed, swallowed, smiled. "And so?"

"And so what?" She lifted a pizza slice and grinned back at him. "And so do I think it's the neatest thing that's happened so far in this New Year?"

He nodded again.

"No," she replied, and continued eating.

Well, Andrew supposed he'd asked for it. What made him think any of them would be happy for him after all his deceit and the hurt feelings that he'd caused?

Then Elaine laughed again. "I think it's the second-neatest thing. I think the neatest thing is that I went to see Martin on New Year's Eve and we are sort of back together. Not engaged or anything like that. But we've decided to take it slow and see what develops. Of course, I'm busy now too, what with the new business."

At some point during Elaine's monologue, Andrew had raised his burger to his mouth again. He had not, however, taken another bite, and instead remained sitting still, holding the sandwich in midair, stopped by the shocker that she'd just divulged.

"Well," he said at last, "it looks as if both our New Years are more interesting than we thought they'd be."

Elaine raised her glass of iced tea. "To love and romance and prosperity and peace."

He raised his glass as well. "And to second chances,"

he added, "no matter how or when or why they come into our lives."

They didn't know whether or not John Benson was alive or dead. They didn't know if he'd been kidnapped or killed or if he'd left Irene of his own free will, not hers.

Jo said the whole thing seemed too painfully close to what she'd gone through with Brian the night that he'd gone off to the men's room in a restaurant and never returned. One difference, however, Sarah reminded Jo, was that Irene had called for help and Jo had suffered on her own.

Jo said something about the pot calling the kettle black, and Sarah picked up the faux white fur that she planned to show the Pittsfield couple and tossed it across the room at her. For two women who weren't sisters, Jo and Sarah had each perfected the same flaw of keeping the world at an emotional distance.

At three o'clock, with still no further word on John, the Pittsfield couple—Allison and Dave—arrived. Jo and Sarah tried to be gracious and excited, while keeping focused on the clock. Surely Andrew and Elaine would be back any minute. Surely Lily would return from her *whatever* with Frank. Until then, Sarah showed her designs for the wedding gown in white velvet trimmed in the faux fur. She reviewed her ideas for golden hearts (which Allison said she would prefer in red) and snowy Cupid decorations. Then Jo jotted down the menu—as requested by the bride—of buttered rum and burgers and a heart-shaped, red-frosted cake.

"And a tent," Dave said. "A big, white tent, with kerosene heaters if you can get them." He grinned a wide grin, pleased, perhaps, that he had contributed.

"I know our wedding might seem common to you," Allison said, "compared to the glamorous ones you do." Then she took Dave's hand and held it with love as yet unspoiled. "But we're ordinary people. With just ordinary friends."

Jo smiled and said that the women of Second Chances were ordinary too, though Sarah wondered if she still qualified with a mother like Laura Carrington.

As the couple rose to leave at five, their heads filled with details and decisions to be made, the bride-to-be touched the faux fur one last time. "This will be fabulous," she said. "I'll feel like a movie star. And we'll pick the perfect photographer to capture the whole thing forever on video. Then he can make it into a movie we'll watch when we're old."

It was an offhand comment but went right to Sarah's soul.

Movies.

On video.

Captured forever.

Sarah said a fast good-bye to the happy couple, then told Jo to keep her posted on John's disappearance. Without explanation, she threw on her coat and dashed out the back door.

Once inside her truck, Sarah said a quick prayer to the spirit of Glisi, asking for more courage than she'd ever known. Then she turned the ignition, clicked the shift to "Drive," and headed west toward Route 7, toward the strip mall where she'd often brought her son so he could rent Nintendo games and movie DVDs.

14

Laura Carrington never thought she would have done it. Over the years, Sutter had become like a son to her—a child she hadn't raised but had watched grow to a young man, then to an adult. She'd taken selfish pleasure from the ways he managed her endowment to the reservation, had cheered the day his own son was born, and wept with him the day his wife left, and the day his mother, Little Tree, died.

She'd thought their relationship helped to compensate for the child she'd been forced to give away. He might have been enough if she hadn't watched the late, late news that night, if she hadn't seen the silver hair clip holding up that shining hair. If Sutter hadn't been trying to convince her to do this, to find Sarah, for the past twenty years.

The truth was, Laura did not seek her out sooner because she did not want to interrupt Sarah's good life.

She did not want to try to undo what had been done, or hurt other people, or ignite a scandal, even though today few people might care. She did not think Sarah would want to bother with her.

Now, however, none of that seemed important.

Turning back the black construction-paper pages of an old picture album, she studied the small black-and-white photographs framed by narrow white borders with scalloped edges all around. The corners had been inserted into black paper triangles that she had moistened with a tiny sponge and affixed into the album over four decades ago.

The subjects of the photos were unvaried:

Joe Duncan standing by the entrance to an old gold mine.

Laura standing by the same.

Joe sitting on the ground under a sequoia, eating a picnic lunch.

Laura doing the same.

They were never in the same picture; they'd taken turns snapping each other. No one could have been along to witness their courtship or their love.

She turned the page, the pages.

Then she came to a photo of herself in a bathing suit, at the far side of Lake of the Spotted Deer. In the photo, Laura's pregnancy was apparent. But though Joe had noticed her weight gain, he hadn't yet known the reason why.

"All the more of you to love," he'd teased with his gentle laugh, then added, "But the studio won't like it."

"Good," she'd answered. "Then they will fire me

and we can run away and live happily, happily ever after."

With a gentle finger, she touched the belly in the picture.

Then she turned another page. It was blank and empty, the sheet brittle from unuse. The pages that followed were blank too.

She stared at the paper. A tear dropped from her eye and splattered on the place where her dreams and life and her world had simply stopped.

15

Jo's grandfather had died twelve, almost thirteen years ago. She had been living in Boston, already a successful public-relations specialist, mature and detached from her childhood home. Yet when her mother phoned to say that he was dead, Jo had crumpled onto her sofa, a weakened lump of sorrow, a little girl again who no longer would go fishing with her much-loved Grandpa Clarke.

She remembered the pain she'd felt; if John Benson were dead, she didn't want Cassie to find out from a news anchor on television. She didn't want the child to face that kind of loss alone with Andrew still in Springfield. If John were only missing, that, too, might make the six o'clock news and probably would frighten Cassie. Jo couldn't let either of those things happen to Andrew's daughter. Not when she could be there to help.

After Sarah was gone, Jo left a message for Lily, telling her what had happened. She dropped Andrew's cell phone into her purse, then went directly to the cottage where Andrew and Cassie lived. Hopefully she wasn't too late.

Cassie was in the kitchen, peeling potatoes.

"You must be the lady of the house," Jo said when the girl let her inside.

"That would be me," Cassie replied, picking up the potato peeler once again. "Unless you'd like to give it a whirl?"

There could be some difficulty in Jo and Andrew's relationship if the dynamics shifted. Which female, Jo or Cassie, would play a larger role in his life? Where would his attentions be dutifully diverted any minute, any hour, any day?

Jo knew she'd have to act slowly and always be aware of the trepidation there.

"No thanks," she said. "I hate to cook after working all day."

Cassie smiled and returned to her chore. "My dad's not home yet," she said.

"He went to Springfield with Elaine," Jo said. "She's buying all kinds of things for her catering business. Your dad went with her to help."

"I know," Cassie replied, plopping another potato into a pot. "He called from a restaurant where they stopped for lunch. He forgot his cell phone. He's always doing that."

Well, of course, Jo thought. With or without his cell phone, of course Andrew would have called Cassie to say he might be late. She wondered how long it would take to grasp the inner workings—and figure out the boundaries—of a relationship with someone else's child.

Taking the cell phone from her purse, Jo set it on the counter. "It's one of the reasons I dropped by," she said. "To return his property."

Cassie smiled and rolled her eyes.

Jo took a step closer to the girl. "Cassie?" she asked. "Have you had the TV on?"

The girl's eyes flicked to the clock over the sink. It was a black plastic clock shaped like a cat, with round white eyes that moved back and forth and a pendulum of a tail that swung in synchrony. The hands read five 'til six.

"I never turn it on until six," she said. "Dad maintains that before six the news is usually bogus. I guess he'd be the one to know."

Jo laughed and hoped the laugh didn't sound too forced.

Then Cassie set the pot on the stove and wiped her hands. "We can watch it now, though, if you want. I'll just get the remote."

Cassie moved so fast from the kitchen that Jo didn't have a chance to react the way she would have wanted. "*No!*" she snapped, her voice too sharp, too harsh.

Cassie stopped in the hallway. She turned back to Jo. Her eyes were questioning, her expression doubting.

Jo shook her head. "Come here," she said softly. "Please, come sit down with me."

The girl drew back. Her shoulders straightened. Her face tightened. She didn't look as childlike as she had before. "What's wrong?" she asked. "Is Dad okay?"

"Oh, honey, yes," Jo said. She went to Cassie and put her arm around her. "Your dad is fine." She knew the fear that flashed in Cassie's eyes, the kind of fear that had sliced Jo's heart when her mother said that her father was gone, that he had left them, run away. That he was never going to come back. Jo cleared her throat. "But we received some news today that will upset him, I'm afraid."

"Is that the real reason you're here?"

"Well, yes. I wanted to be here when he got home." Jo reasoned that if she were still eleven-almost-twelve, like Cassie, she wouldn't want to think that a grown-up thought she couldn't handle grown-up things.

"But why aren't you at Second Chances? Isn't that where he'd go first?" She was a clever girl, Cassie Kennedy. The same way Jo had been.

"I'm here because I wanted to see you. Because I was afraid you'd heard the news and might not want to be alone."

Her small brow wrinkled. Her freckles crunched together. "What news?"

Jo drew in a breath. "It's about John Benson, honey. Something has happened and he is . . . gone." She used the same word Irene had uttered, because it was the only one she knew was certain.

"Gone as in away?"

Her calm demeanor reminded Jo that kids knew how to cushion what they didn't want to hear. "I don't know," Jo said.

Cassie chewed on her lower lip. "He's dead?"

Jo brushed a lock of hair from Cassie's face. "We don't know anything for sure, honey. Irene only said that he's gone. Then we got disconnected." She did not add that the disconnection might have simply been because Irene hung up.

Cassie stood there in the hall. Her arms grew limp. Her head nodded. Her lower lip began to quiver.

Jo drew her closer. "Honey," she said, "I'm so sorry. But we don't know the whole truth yet. For all we know he could have gone out for a walk and couldn't find his way back to the hotel...." When Brian had left, no one but Jo had been around to wait, to wonder at his fate. No one but Jo, because he'd been disappearing in and out of people's lives for far too many years and Jo was the only one left—not counting his parents or his brother, who couldn't remember when they'd heard from him.

"Oh, John's dead, all right," Cassie replied. "Why else would he be gone? Unless...maybe he was kidnapped."

Kidnapped? Jo had thought—hoped—Brian had been kidnapped way back when. It would have been so much easier to blame someone else for the fact that he was no longer there. "When your dad gets home, maybe he'll know how we can find out."

Cassie nodded again, and then huge pools filled her turquoise eyes, and Jo wished with all her might that she'd not had to do this, that she'd not been the one to bring such upsetting news.

Sarah positioned herself in front of the television. She sat on one of her favorite woven blankets that she'd brought from California, a vibrantly colored one that depicted the wind among the trees with a sacred fire of seven woods detailed at the center. (Had Sutter's mother, Little Tree, woven this? she wondered, but could not remember. Should she mention it to him? Not that she would ever speak to him again. Not that she would have a need.) Spilling off the edges of the blanket were a dozen videos that she'd dumped onto the floor.

The Secret of San Mateo.

Midnight at Macy's.

Lavender and Lace.

Others, including *Gold Dust*. All on VHS; apparently Laura Carrington nostalgia had not yet warranted redubbing onto DVD.

She picked up the tape jacket. Could she really watch *Gold Dust*? She'd seen a few Laura Carrington films—who hadn't?—back in her college days, when West Hope was poised for cable and the most exciting entertainment was a dose of the late show. The movies had been mostly thrillers, mysteries that required a sensuous leading lady who, more often than not, met up with an equally sexy man who wanted to help with her problem, but who took a backseat while she resolved things herself.

Sarah supposed the movies were the primitive attempts to promote women's liberation.

Laura's earlier films had been westerns—good-guy bad-guy, cowboys and Indians, "them versus us," her father had often kidded. It had been his way of making light of the prejudicial situation. Back then Sarah had no idea how closely the poison arrow struck to home, their home.

She eyed the video of the film in which Laura and Sarah's father had supposedly met and fallen so much in love.

She studied the photo on the front, the image of the movie star staring up at a mountain, a look of longing in her big blue eyes, a thin cotton dress wrapped around her body. Her *voluptuous* body, Sarah supposed. Tall, but not as slender as Sarah's. Curvy. Soft. Not angular; not, well, Cherokee.

At first glance there was nothing the two shared, not the eyes, not the body, not the hair (like Sarah's, Laura's hair was abundant, but it was red). Still, there was something in the way she stood, something in the way she held her arms at her sides, as if giving herself over to the mountain before her, as if she were unafraid of life, if not the people in it.

Could a mother and daughter be recognized by posture?

DNA, Sarah thought. Of course. Today they could easily put this matter to rest by a few strands of hair or some spit in a cup. Then she'd know the truth once and for all.

She turned over the video jacket and read the copy on the back.

> Johnnie Landers (Laura Carrington) needs to solve a mystery. Her estranged father has died in a gold-mining accident. But Johnnie—a struggling, refined widow who runs a dry-goods store to support her three young children—has come from San Francisco to the California mountains to stake her father's claim and, more importantly,

to find out if the accident had been murder instead. Also starring Rick Daniels as Blake Ashworth, the wealthy, British-bred rancher determined to win Johnnie's heart; and Davis Peterson as Bounty McGee, the bungling guide hired by Ashworth to help him traverse the wilderness and keep track of Johnnie.

Sarah recognized the irony that Johnnie Landers's fictitious father had been killed in a gold-mining accident when Sarah's real father had too, though it had been sixteen years later.

She tossed down *Gold Dust*. She'd watch that one later, maybe after the others. Then she took a deep breath, said, "Here goes," to Elton, picked up *The Secret of San Mateo*, and shoved it into the machine, grateful that she'd kept the old VCR when Jason had tried to convince her to ditch it once they'd bought the DVD player.

Men, she thought, sometimes were so stupid.

She tucked the old, comfortable blanket warmly around her legs, clicked on the remote, and waited for the titles to appear.

16

♥

W*here were you when you heard blah blah blah?* Andrew supposed that later he might wonder why it was that human beings became so fixated on shocking moments, why it was that tragedy became so easily branded into memory. Why it was that he, for one, knew so clearly where he was when he heard John Lennon had been shot, the Challenger had exploded, the Twin Towers had been hit; how it was that he knew those things so readily yet he could so easily forget to bring his cell phone with him when he went anywhere.

He wasn't sure what John Lennon had to do with cell phones, the former perhaps not having lived long enough to enjoy the latter. Later he'd make time to sort through those thoughts. But right now his feet were glued to the hardwood floor in his wonderful cottage, and Cassie was crying and Jo was holding his hand and suggesting he sit down because of the news she'd just told him.

John Benson was gone.

Andrew's mentor.

Andrew's friend.

Andrew's boss from time to time, depending on where their careers had positioned them.

John Benson, the man who'd been Andrew's father when Andrew's father had not.

Dead or simply disappeared, the man was gone, and all Andrew could say was, "Oh, Christ," and know it was one of those moments he always would remember.

"Please, Andrew, come and sit down," Jo said for the second or the third or the tenth time. "I'll get some water."

He dismissed her with a wave, a wave that later he might worry had been too abrupt, as if Jo had caused John's demise, as if she'd been the one at fault.

Andrew turned to Cassie and tried to speak calmly. "Honey, where's the phone?"

Cassie blinked, tears spilling onto her shirt. She pointed to the coffee table in the living room.

"I have to find Irene," he said. "I have to find her now." But his sneakers remained epoxied to the floor.

"She was still in Rio when she called," Jo repeated.

"What time was that?"

"I don't know. Around one-thirty."

"Do we know what hotel they were staying at?"

"The Grande Corcovado. We made the arrangements for their honeymoon." She pulled a paper from the pocket of her sweater. "I brought the number with me. I tried to call her back, but the operator said she isn't accepting calls."

He took the paper, stared at it. "I'll call the New York penthouse first. Maybe someone is there. The housekeeper. The cook."

"They have no family?"

He shook his head. "Only me. And Cassie." Cassie whimpered. He knew he must go to her, comfort her, reassure her that everything would be all right. But his feet still wouldn't move.

Jo went over to Cassie, sat on the arm of the chair, put her arm around her. *Thank you*, Andrew knew that he should say.

But then the phone rang. His feet came unglued. He bolted toward the living room.

"Irene," he said when he heard her voice. He closed his eyes, trying to ease the throbbing in his head, trying not to think about where she was or what she was doing or what kind of pain she might be in. Trying not to picture her in another of those embedded-memory moments, standing in chiffon, a drink in one hand, a look of seduction just for him, the seventeen-year-old prep-school boy with an aching woman-need. He forced his eyes to open. "Irene," he said, "what's going on?"

Her words were clipped. "Forty years," she said. "The man has been one humiliation after another."

Oh. Her words answered the question without elaboration. John Benson wasn't dead. "God, Irene," he said. He looked at Cassie and at Jo. He gave a thumbs-up sign and mouthed the words *He's okay*.

Irene sighed a short, loud sigh. "I'm still in Rio.

Dan Jervis is trying to get me out of here. It seems the bastard took the suitcase that had my passport in it."

Dan Jervis was a New York senator. He'd been friends with John and Irene for many years and had just been at the wedding. He was one of the guests whom Andrew had dodged to keep his connection to the women at Second Chances a secret. It all seemed so stupid now.

"Are you at the hotel? Are you all right? I'll come down."

"By the time you could get here I might be gone. I hope I'll be gone."

There was silence for a moment. Andrew was suddenly aware that Cassie was watching him, that Jo was too. He turned slightly away from them.

"Irene, what happened?"

That's when she cried, when her look-at-me-I'm-a-tough-New-York-society-lady exterior crumbled and Irene Benson broke down.

God, he hated that.

He turned another quarter-turn from Cassie and Jo, as if to protect Irene's privacy.

"We had a wonderful dinner. We went dancing. We spent some time in the hot tub in our suite. The bathroom has a glorious, panoramic view of the city. Have you been to Rio, Andrew?"

Irene must be in shock, he thought. She's sitting down there all alone and John has left her and she is hurting and confused and she is in shock. "Yes," he replied, "I've been there." He did not add "with Patty" because he didn't want to mention his former wife to

Irene, or within hearing distance of Jo. Women, he thought, remained the greatest puzzle in his life.

Although John seemed now to have presented a puzzle of his own.

"In the middle of the night," Irene said suddenly, "I was awakened by a most definitive noise. It was the sound of sneaking footsteps. Sneaking. You know, furtive, irregular."

Well, yes, Andrew knew what sneaking meant.

"At first I thought it was a burglar."

Andrew wondered how long it had been since he'd heard that word. An old black-and-white TV show maybe, like *Perry Mason*. It reminded him that Irene was so much older than he was. Only half a generation older, he'd told himself over and over that spring when he'd gone back to school and left his virginity at home.

"'John?' I called out from the other side of the king-size bed. 'John, is that you?' 'Go back to sleep,' John said, so I knew it was him, it was no burglar." She pronounced the word as if it had an extra *u*, as if it were *burgular*. He wondered if that was an old-fashioned way of saying the old-fashioned word.

"I did as I was told," she said.

Andrew realized that he'd been holding his breath, though he didn't know for how long.

"When I woke up in the morning he was gone," she added. She sucked in air, she blew it out. Then she said, "He left a note. *Gone to Tahiti*, he wrote. *Or some other exotic island. Don't wait up*. Then he added a meek little *Sorry* on the bottom, as if that would make everything all right."

The words hung there in the space between the phone and Andrew's ear, having traveled five thousand miles with extraordinary velocity and clarity and, unfortunately, finality. John Benson had left his wife. The idea that he was sorry sounded debatable to Andrew.

"Do you think... do you think he went... alone?" Andrew didn't know why it was so hard to ask her that. Irene, after all, had been down the infidelity road before.

"Who knows," she said. "He's over sixty now. One would think that's too old for a midlife crisis. Though I suppose people are living longer these days."

Andrew stopped himself from saying that John had been having a midlife something most of his adult life, or at least as long as Andrew knew him. Irene surely wasn't perfect, but she didn't deserve this.

"I don't care if our planes cross in the air," he said. "I'll get to Rio. I can drive to New York tonight. While I'm on the road, maybe Jo can check for flights." He flicked his eyes to Jo, who remained with her arm protecting Cassie. He hoped she didn't think he was treating her like an assistant or, worse, a taken-for-granted wife.

"No," Irene said again. "I'll need you in New York. I can't face it alone. The media... the people..." He felt her shiver across the line. Despite her social should-and-should-nots, Irene had never really embraced the attention the way John always had. "Can you and Cassie meet me there tomorrow morning? Jensen will let you into the penthouse if I'm not back yet." Jensen was the doorman; his first name was Jack, his last was Jensen, but he preferred the latter. When Cassie was a little girl, she'd said *Jensen* was more doorman-sounding anyway. They'd laughed at the wisdom of a four-year-old: John, Irene, Andrew, and even Patty.

That's when Andrew remembered. "Oh, God, Irene, I'm sorry, but we can't get there until tomorrow night." He might be inclined to forget his cell phone, but at least he had the paternal sense to recall that tomorrow was Cassie's boy–girl birthday party, and he wouldn't—good grief, couldn't—miss that for anything, not even Irene.

"Despicable, this is despicable," Lily said, flitting from one corner of Jo's kitchen to the other, voicing the word Jo needed to hear to remind her that Irene had been the woman scorned, not her.

After leaving Andrew's, Jo had stopped by her mother's looking for some conversation and . . . well, she wasn't sure what else. Mothering, perhaps. The emotional upheaval had left her exhausted, spent.

However, Marion and her husband had gone out.

So she'd driven home, where she tried calling Sarah, but there was no answer. She couldn't talk to Elaine—she'd be busy creating the menu for Cassie's birthday party. Which left Lily, of course, who Jo thought probably was out with Frank, but she tried her anyway.

Within half an hour there was Lily in Jo's kitchen, with Frank Forbes sitting at the table, commiserating as best he could or would, she guessed, because he was a man, after all. She wondered if he had any idea how hard it was for her sometimes to be in the same room with him, not because he looked very much like his brother, because he didn't, but because he had Brian's voice, the same low voice as her old lover who had scammed her, dumped her, and pretty much wrecked the first half of her life. Frank, however, had been awfully good to Lily, and Lily seemed to like him, so Jo just kept grinning and bearing it.

"Lily's right," he said, "what a rotten thing to do."

Neither of them acknowledged the similarity to Brian's stunt last year.

"So?" Lily asked. "What are the details?"

"Details?"

"You know, the gossip. Why did he leave, what about their money, did he take a young bimbo with him?"

"All I know is Andrew said John left a note that said something about Tahiti."

"Andrew is such a man. So lousy at conveying this sort of information."

"Well," Jo said, sitting across from Frank, toying with the silk tulips that she'd bought to make the winter less dreary, "I'm sure he'll at least help Irene feel better. He and Cassie are going to New York after the party tomorrow." She wondered what either Lily or Frank would think if they knew about her new relationship with Andrew. She wondered if they would think she'd be upset that he was going to Irene. It wasn't as if she should be jealous, after all. It wasn't as if he were leaving her the way John had left Irene.

"We'll go too," Lily said as she stopped abruptly in

the middle of the floor and planted both her hands on her tiny hips.

"What?" Jo asked.

"We'll go too. We'll be there for Irene."

"No. Absolutely not."

"Not? Why not?"

"Because we hardly know her, Lily. We hardly know John."

She tossed her scarf around her neck. "Well, we know Andrew. And we know Cassie. And we know a thing or two about what it takes to be a friend."

Jo stood up. "No," she said again. "We have too much to do here."

"We'll see," Lily said, with that sparkle in her eyes, that sparkle Jo had seen over the years just before Lily was about to launch into something really dumb.

17

Sarah hadn't eaten supper. She hadn't answered the telephone, which had rung on five or six different occasions throughout the evening until way past midnight. She hadn't answered the phone for the same reasons she hadn't eaten. The only movement she could manage was to change one VHS tape for another, after the credits rolled.

Laura Carrington had been beautiful—well, Sarah already knew that. But beyond the woman's beauty, Sarah scrutinized every close-up (Was that sorrow in her eyes? Was it self-centered arrogance?) and examined every turn (Did she walk in the same long strides as Sarah? Did she cross her feet as Sarah did every time she sat down?).

Nothing seemed obvious, nothing seemed apparent. Then, halfway into the Hitchcockesque thriller, *Lavender and Lace*, Laura tipped her head.

"Excuse me?" the woman on the small screen was asking a handsome stranger, who said he'd come to fix her telephone, who claimed there were reports of problems with the phone lines in the neighborhood because of a car accident at the intersection of State and Main.

People in the audience no doubt would have been cringing in their seats, wanting to cry out *Don't let him in!* to the unsuspecting beauty on the screen. None of them would have paid attention to the way she tipped her head slightly to the right, a motion that was a mirror image to the way Sarah tipped hers when someone asked her a question she needed to think about.

She hit the pause button, then rewind, then stop, then play.

"Excuse me?"

Pause. Rewind. Stop. Play.

"Excuse me?"

Pause.

Except for the red hair and the blue eyes, the woman might have been Sarah questioning a stranger.

"Excuse me?" The slight tip of the head. It seemed so insignificant, and yet it was so huge.

Sarah stared at the frozen image. And then she recognized the tiny birthmark on Laura Carrington's left cheek. It was a dainty, diamond-shaped image that had given her distinction. On the other hand, Burch, Sarah's son, had hated his since he was old enough to be teased by other boys.

He'd tried Clearasil and Erase. On the advice of his best friend, he'd once tried to bleach it out. At twelve now, almost thirteen, he seemed to have accepted that, short of laser surgery, the birthmark would be his for life.

She studied the woman's image.

A gentle tip of a head.

A tiny, diamond-shaped birthmark.

Were they evidence enough that she was Sarah's mother? That she'd been the one who had loved Sarah's father?

Only three words came into her mind: *How could you?*

Then she remembered *Gold Dust*. The film that Sutter Jones said Laura was making when she met Joe Duncan, when he'd been working as an extra, when they'd fallen in love.

She quickly ejected the VHS, scrambled through the others on the floor, and popped in the next.

He was so young, so handsome, that Sarah barely recognized her father, his sleek black hair, his high, jutting cheekbones, his copper skin, his black eyes shot with silver like Sarah's were. She barely recognized him—not that he'd been much older, almost seventeen years later, when he died. She barely recognized him because he was dressed-up Hollywood: deerskin pants and shirt and moccasins, not the denim and rugged work boots that Sarah's father wore to work every day.

He was so young, so handsome, as he sat among a crowd in a makeshift saloon. With all the times that Sarah missed him, had yearned to see his face again, she hadn't known that all she needed to do was rent a video.

He was an extra, one of the miners who witnessed the murder of the father of Laura's character. He'd been a witness but said, "No, ma'am," when Laura asked him if he'd seen anything.

"No, ma'am." Her father's voice startled her. She hit the pause again, her pulse beating softly in her throat, her facial features motionless, her eyes fixed on the screen.

Then, and only then, did Sarah allow herself to stretch out on the floor, to lean against poor Elton, who hadn't had dinner either, to stay there with Joe Duncan's face paused on the screen until dawn began to leak into the room and her wet tears finally went dry.

18

Dad, this is Eddie."

"Mr. Mindelelewski, I presume," Andrew said, shaking the boy's hand and hoping his grin would not reveal that he'd have preferred Eddie to be a scrawny kid with glasses instead of the tall, good-looking, blond-haired boy he was. "It's very nice to meet you." He thought he was being very cool for a dad. He thought he was being very cool for not shouting, *You lay one finger on my daughter, Mr. Mindelelewski, and you're a dead man. Got it?* He thought he was very cool for having spent most of the morning practicing the pronunciation of the kid's last name. Deep inside, though, Andrew knew he was not cool at all. He simply had his mind (for once) on other things. On John, Irene, the present situation, not on all the awful things that could happen to his daughter in the weeks and months and years to come.

"Mount up!" Mary Delaney, the West Hope Stables instructor, hollered to the group of twelve sixth-graders and two remaining adults, Andrew and Jo. Elaine had said she needed to be sure the food would be ready for their return; Lily had looked at the short, plump horse originally assigned to her and said, "I don't think so, thank you"; and Sarah had not arrived yet.

Andrew helped hoist the kids up onto their mounts as if he'd done this more than twice: once at Cassie's first horse show at the "Big E" in West Springfield, when her trainer had the flu and Andrew volunteered to be the substitute because he couldn't bear to see his daughter's disappointment; a second time two summers ago at a party just like this (except it was all girls) for Cassie's friend Marilla. He'd ridden for the first time, though he wouldn't have really called that "riding," more like walking, because the horse they'd picked for him was an old gray nag.

He was grateful that he could at least get up on the damn thing and not embarrass himself more than he already had in his earlier athletic endeavors in front of Jo.

He glanced at his watch: The trail ride was supposed to last forty-five minutes, which would bring them back to the barn just before dark. They'd watch a few rope tricks and take turns trying to ride the mechanical bull, have pizza in the mess hall, then Cassie would open the mountain of gifts already on the table, right next to the cake. A short campfire, a few ghost stories, and if all went off without a hitch, they'd be out of there by eight, eight-thirty at the latest and in Manhattan before midnight.

This morning he'd packed suitcases for both of them, putting in enough to last a week. Cassie had said that being out of school that long would be okay except she was worried about French. He'd left room in her suitcase for her French book. Irene spoke the language fluently and might enjoy tutoring her goddaughter for fun as much as for distraction.

He wondered what John was doing right now and if he would have left Irene if they'd ever had kids. Not that kids could keep a marriage glued—hell, he certainly knew that—but they at least gave couples something in common, something to have to pay attention to beyond their often too ego-driven selves.

"Andrew? Mary is waiting."

He hadn't heard Jo gallop up next to him. He gripped his reins. "Sorry. I was lost in thought."

Jo smiled. "Thinking about me, I'm sure."

"Sure," he lied, and smiled back, then fell into line behind her and headed up the trail.

"I tried calling you a million times last night," Lily announced when Sarah at last made it to the party later that afternoon. Before she'd finally gone to bed Sarah left a message at the shop saying she wanted to sleep late and she'd meet them at the stables. She woke up at noon, her thoughts quite clear, her "next step" apparent to her. Thankfully she hadn't had to think about a birthday gift for Cassie. To Andrew's chagrin, Lily had convinced the women to chip in and give Cassie a spa day for her and a friend.

"Andrew is going to New York after the party," Lily was saying while Sarah perused the food table, rearranging the peach and tan and turquoise napkins that featured motifs of the southwest. "John Benson has taken off. Left Irene. Andrew and Cassie are going to visit her. God knows when he'll be back."

Sarah shook her head and began straightening the plates. "How awful," she said, "about John and Irene. But I'm sure Andrew will be back as soon as possible."

Lily dropped onto a bench and began wiping sawdust off her Donald Pliner red suede boots. "That's all you can say? 'How awful'? If it weren't for the Bensons we never would have had our success." Success, of course, to Lily meant the media exposure caused by the Benson wedding, meant the long list of as-yet-unanswered phone calls from hopeful brides-to-be, meant the enormous checks that would be made out to Second Chances.

To a Cherokee, success meant satisfaction of a spiritual kind. She thought of Sutter Jones, made a mental note to ask about his fancy clothes—if they ever spoke again.

She looked at Lily, who awaited a comment. "We hardly know the Bensons, Lily. Breakups are hard, but most people survive." She did not want Lily to know that she had more important things on her mind right now, that while Andrew and Cassie would be en route to New York, Sarah would be traveling too, on a plane to San Francisco.

Sometime between falling asleep and finally waking

up, somewhere in that dreamlike, blissful state that crept in after dawn and seemed so important and so very real, Sarah had decided to go see her aunt Mae. She was going to learn everything her aunt had known, once and for all, about the woman who claimed to be her mother.

Sarah was going to do those things, but she was not going to tell Lily. She wasn't ready for her friends' opinions, well-meaning or not.

"It won't hurt," Lily continued, "for all of us to be just a tad supportive. I was thinking about granting an interview to a few of the media. Let them know what a wonderful person Irene Benson is."

Sarah moved toward the makeshift kitchen to check up on Elaine. "What? And be the one to tell the press what John's done to Irene? Surely you know that kind of gossip—coming from us—would kill Second Chances."

Lily scurried along behind her. "Well, of course, I'm not stupid. But if they find out first..."

"No, Lily," Sarah said. "It could be suicide. You might think Irene would appreciate it, but you never know. Besides, don't they still owe us money?"

"Yes," Lily whined, "almost eighty thousand."

"Then I rest my case."

Sarah walked over to where Elaine was busy placing pepperoni on top of the pizza, shaping the thin meat slices into a giant ten-gallon hat. She and Lily both stopped and stared at the concoction. Neither of them spoke.

"It's a cowboy hat!" Elaine said proudly. "Or a cow-girl hat! The kids will love it, don't you think?"

Sarah nodded and asked when they'd be back from the trail ride, and Elaine said in fifteen or twenty minutes. Sarah asked what she could do to help. Elaine suggested she fill the dishes shaped like Texas (she'd picked them up in Springfield) with nachos and her homemade salsa.

Without another word to Lily, Sarah did as she was told.

Lily moved to her elbow. "Well, I think the whole thing is awful. Irene's not the only one hurting. Andrew is too. John Benson is like a father to him. If it were my father or Jo's father or Elaine's father or your father, we wouldn't pretend nothing happened."

Sarah wished Lily hadn't said the words *your father*. Her father, who'd spent long days beneath the earth, then found eternal darkness there. "No, ma'am," he'd said. She swallowed back a mother lode of tears, opened another bag, dumped more nachos in another bowl. "Lily," she said, "stop it."

Lily made a small guffaw. "Well, it doesn't seem fair that John Benson can get away with this. Pardon me for thinking we should be there for Irene. And for Andrew."

"Before we can be there for anyone, she needs to pay off her bill."

"She'll pay the bill, Sarah. She is Irene Benson. She'd never risk that kind of indignity. Besides, she knows Andrew is like family to us too."

Lily, no doubt, had a skewed image of families, not having one herself. She mistakenly thought they were loving and kind and always there for one another.

Sarah carried the bowls of chips and salsa into the mess hall. Lily stuck behind her like salt on a Dorito.

"Is Lily trying to convince you to 'help out' Irene?" Elaine asked as she walked toward the table, carrying a large tray of cheese chunks shaped like horseshoes and pickles reconfigured to look like saguaro cacti.

"All of you!" Lily countered with quick, angry eyes. "All of you are insensitive bores." With that she spun on her Donald Pliner heels and flitted from the hall, sawdust leaving little puffs of anger in her wake.

"Are we insensitive?" Sarah asked Jo after the trail riders had returned and the kids were eating pizza and Andrew seemed preoccupied looking at his watch. She already knew they were "bores"; Lily had used the word often enough.

"Sure," Jo said.

Sarah sat beside her on a rough-hewn bench. "Lily is angry because we won't dance on the grave of John Benson's disappearance."

Jo shrugged. "Lily overreacts."

She thought about the movies still spread across her living-room floor and wondered how Lily would overreact if she knew the identity of Sarah's long-lost mother. She would no doubt romanticize the relationship between Laura and Sarah's father, spin a web of noble tragedy around the reality that the beautiful starlet had relinquished her first—and apparently only—born.

Yes, Lily would overreact. The term *drama queen*, after all, had been coined with her in mind.

"The truth is," Sarah admitted, "I have other things going on in my life to worry about rather than the demise of a relationship between two people I hardly know."

Jo looked at her quizzically but didn't pry. She was not like Lily, after all, not one to think that other people's business was also hers.

Sarah sighed. She picked off a piece of pepperoni that was on the corner of her pizza slice. It must have been part of the wide brim of the hat. "I need to go to San Francisco, Jo. Something's come up."

"Because of Sutter Jones?"

Sarah wasn't surprised at Jo's quick-thinking question. She nodded. "I have to straighten out some paperwork. Something to do with my mother."

"Your mother?"

"I mean my grandmother. Oh," she said, dropping the pepperoni on the side of her desert-colored plate. "I'm not sure what I mean about most things these days." She stared around the hall, looking at the kids, who were laughing and singing and making faces at one another, doing the kinds of things that kids did when they lived in a real town, not a city like New York, not the kind of place Glisi had called the big, bad world. Perhaps Glisi had tried to shield Sarah from the world for other reasons. Maybe she had died when Sarah went to college because she was so afraid Sarah would not come back to California, would not come back to being one of them, would learn that she was not.

If that had been Glisi's fear, she was right, for Sarah

had quickly learned that the big, bad world was everywhere.

She closed her eyes now. "I'm leaving right after Cassie opens her gifts. I don't know when I'm coming back." Maybe by then she'd be able to tell Jo what had happened. Or maybe she'd tell Jason. Maybe by then she'd be able to finally solve the puzzle of her life.

19

She'd been lucky to get on a flight out of Albany that had only one change in Philadelphia. But an hour and fifty minutes between planes in Philly left her too much time wondering what she was doing.

Maneuvering through the jumble of people who had one hand attached to rolling luggage, the other to a cell phone, Sarah sorted through her options. She didn't owe Laura Carrington anything. She could demand a DNA test before this went any further, before she returned to the reservation, before she faced Aunt Mae, cousin Douglas, any of them.

She located Concourse B, Gate 17. She wished she'd called Jason before she left. What if the plane crashed? Burch would have no idea that his mother was on it. She'd only told Jo she was going to San Francisco. Would they figure out the rest?

Eagles have wings for a reason, Glisi had often said. *Man does not because God does not want him to fly.*

With a small smile, Sarah sat down. She looked at the monitor: The flight to San Francisco was on time. She closed her eyes and listened to the white noise of the airport: the beep-beep of the transport, a small child fussing, the hurried footfalls that would be repeated by thousands of feet today, tomorrow, the next day.

She wondered how many of the passersby were familiar with the name Laura Carrington and if any of them cared that her supposed daughter was right there among them.

"Is this seat taken?"

Sarah blinked, then looked up. It was Sutter Jones.

"It's you," she said.

"Rest assured, I'm not following you. I've been here on business. Now I'm headed west."

"San Francisco?"

He shook his head. "L.A. The trip I canceled the other day."

Right, she thought. His "business" for Laura Carrington.

"My gate's across the way," he said. "I saw you sitting here and—"

"—and you decided you hadn't bothered me enough." She sounded flip, she knew. Flip, tired, irritable.

"Sarah . . ." he said, sitting down next to her. "Are you going to the coast to find out more about your mother?"

She supposed she could say she was going to visit an

old friend from college, but he'd already met the sum of her old college friends in West Hope, and he probably knew that. She looked down at her boarding pass, wishing the plane would get here, wishing she could leave.

"Sarah," he said again, "I want to help. What can I do to make this easier for you?"

She sensed the softness of his cashmere next to the roughness of her wool. She sensed the high gloss of his shoes, his teeth, his fingernails, next to her plain, unpolished self. She thought about Jason, about how much money meant to him, about how he'd been so willing to leave Sarah not only for his dream to play wonderful music but also to strike it magically rich. Her eyes moved toward the gate, then to the window. "How much is she paying you?" she asked. "How much is Laura paying you to get me to meet her?"

He laughed, which was not what Sarah expected. "Not that it matters, but I handle her business deals. I'm doing this as a favor. Let's just say I owe her."

A small flare of anger ignited in her heart; she cast a sharp look in his direction. "Since when does an Indian allow himself to be indebted to anyone? Are you that Americanized? Look at your expensive clothes. I'll bet you make a lot of money. Are you sure you're not white?" There it was, the real reason that his presence bothered her. He had left the reservation and found wealth. He betrayed the earth, the wind, the stars. In Sarah's eyes he was no longer Cherokee at all. He might as well have been Jason camouflaged by a suit.

His black eyes narrowed, his forehead scrunched. "I

have nice clothes because I like them. I earn a good salary because I enjoy working hard. But one thing is true, Sarah: If it weren't for Laura Carrington, God knows where I'd be. God knows where any of us would be. She didn't want me to tell you, but under the circumstances you leave me little choice. Since you were born—since she turned you over to your father and your grandmother—Laura Carrington has been paying for the education of the children on the reservation. She felt that only through education would we be free from the limitations of our past. She felt that education was the key to the future for us all." He stood up then, picked up his briefcase. "For what it's worth, Laura Carrington set up a fund that I manage for her today, at no charge, I might add. The money in that fund is what sent me to college and sent me to law school. It enables all the children of our tribe to get higher education. For your information, it sent you to college too. Because your mother wanted you—and all our children—to have every possible chance for a good, meaningful life."

Just then a voice over the speaker announced United flight 2215 to Los Angeles was boarding at Gate 16.

"I should be back in my New York office by the end of next week," he said with one more expectant look. Then he turned and crossed the concourse, leaving her feeling foolish, feeling numb.

20

The penthouse had two floors now.

Andrew had grown up in the unit across the hall, when both apartments had only one floor, which had been plenty big enough, with a living room, dining room, kitchen, study, and three bedrooms and three baths. In the early nineties, when the stock market took a tumble and most New Yorkers whispered the word *recession* as if it were a secret, John and Irene cashed in on their downstairs neighbors' misfortune and scooped up their equally sprawling apartment for half what it was worth. Within six months Irene had transformed it into guest quarters and a small theater and had renovated the upstairs master bedroom into a full-blown suite, featuring an ostentatious bathroom that once had been a bedroom.

The Bensons, of course, by that time could have afforded any number of the gargantuan residences that came onto the market, but Irene maintained that in New York location was everything, and they loved where they were situated, right on Park Avenue, so easy to get from there to anywhere, with a view of the East River that most of their friends envied.

The top floor of the Benson place was where the elevator brought you (after you'd been cleared by Jensen), depositing you at the front door that opened into the foyer. "It's called a *gallery* today," Irene had once corrected Andrew. He supposed that was society's way of designating a special place for whatever artist one was patron-ing that month or year. Irene most lately favored someone from Santiago named Pietro, whose cubist creations were too orange for Andrew's taste.

Sunday morning Andrew sat in John's study (to the left of the *gallery*), trying to decide if he should be angry at John or at Irene, who had left a message on Friday night before he and Cassie got there—while he was speeding down the parkway to rescue Irene from . . . well, he wasn't sure from what, listening to three hours of Cassie loading thank-yous on Andrew (well, that part wasn't so bad) because he'd let her have the party and he'd given her her own private cell phone as a birthday gift. He'd also endured the three hours of noticing from the corner of his eye that his daughter kept touching the small pink and silver teardrop earrings that Eddie what's-his-name had given her wrapped up in a bow.

When they'd arrived at the penthouse, Elsa, the cook and housekeeper, announced to Andrew and

Cassie that Irene wouldn't arrive until Sunday after all, that she'd decided to stop in Dallas.

No excuse. No explanation. Just Irene being Irene, always the one in charge.

So they'd settled into the guest suite for the night. The next day was Saturday, so they went to the museum and to the zoo, even though it was cold. Then they plundered John's videos and watched a bunch of movies and ate too much popcorn and stayed up too late.

And now it was Sunday. Cassie had gone to the market with Elsa, leaving Andrew to wait for Irene, if she ever decided to show the hell up. If she didn't come soon, they were leaving. Forget staying a week—he decided they would leave by dark, whether or not Irene arrived. He had a life—Cassie had a life—in West Hope, and Irene was obviously strong enough to survive without them.

He thought those things while sitting in a deep leather chair, aimlessly thumbing through an annual report of one of John's biggest ventures: a consortium of radio and TV stations known as the Benson Group. John had once wanted Andrew to join him as a partner; he'd said he looked upon Andrew as a son, the child he and Irene never had. Irene had laughed and told him to speak for himself, that she wasn't nearly old enough to have a son Andrew's age.

A partnership, a business deal, might have worked if John hadn't left Irene that one time, when Andrew was in his last year of prep school and Irene was lonely and Andrew was . . . well, there. There, and seventeen, and probably seeking a mother figure because his mother was always so busy as a physician or she was away. Or, more likely, just because he was so totally nuts over the first woman who had unveiled her breasts to him.

It had happened quite by accident.

Or had it?

Andrew had gone home on spring break. He'd gone across the hall from his parents' apartment and learned that John had moved out.

"A model from California," Irene had explained. "With a fake tan and no tits and too many teeth." It hadn't helped that the girl was only twenty.

The next day Irene made good on a promise John had offered, to line up a summer job for Andrew at NBC. After his interview, he went to thank her.

One of them (later he could never be sure which one it was) made the first move, touched the first touch, encouraged the first sweet, gentle kiss.

Irene's chiffon had slid from her shoulders.

She unzipped his jeans.

And he spent the rest of his vacation having sex.

He'd gone back to school no longer a virgin, but by the time the school year was over, John had moved back into the penthouse, the model apparently gone.

Andrew and Irene spoke about it only once, when Irene let him know she had not told John. It was best that way, she said. It was best for all of them.

Now, like then, and like the twenty-five-plus years in between, Irene was definitely the one in charge.

Andrew tossed down the annual report. He knew he didn't really have a right to be angry with her for stopping in Dallas, when he'd enabled her controlling behavior all this time by feeling so damn guilty about what they did way back when.

Jo didn't know if she should call him or not. She could give any number of excuses.

I wanted to be sure you and Cassie got there okay.

I was concerned that Irene made it home safely from Rio.

I was working on the wedding for the couple from Pittsfield and wondered if you had time to develop a contingency plan in case a nor'easter barrels over the mountain.

Or the more honest, *I was just sitting here missing you and I wondered if you think you'll ever come back and, if you do, if we'll be together again.* After all, once Andrew was among old friends that he knew in a place that had so much more to offer than West Hope, why on earth would he come back?

The first time she got up the nerve to call it was Saturday afternoon. Then Saturday night. Then three times on Sunday morning. But each time, Andrew's voice mail immediately kicked in, a signal that he'd either left his phone in West Hope or that something more exciting was happening that prevented him from taking—or wanting to take—his calls.

Andrew hadn't had a martini since that day in John's office when John challenged Andrew to write the column about real women for *Buzz*. It was a hundred years ago, he thought, as he stood in the Benson penthouse, looking out across the skyline of Manhattan, holding the thin, triangular glass Irene had thrust into his hand shortly after she blew in the front door half an hour ago, bravely issuing one order after another, setting her world—their worlds—into redirected motion.

Thankfully, Cassie and Elsa returned right after Irene's arrival. She immediately set them to work polishing the silver trays and coffee and tea services and the countless flatware they would need. Friends—only the closest—would be stopping by, according to Irene, offering condolences as if John were dead. They would not be told the details—only that John was not coming back—poor Irene! There would be one mini-wake after another, and it would help her process the pain, and heal the wounds. Andrew decided she must have stopped in Dallas to see a New Age guru who was based there, who catered to the stars, and who'd been featured recently in *Buzz*.

But behind her stoic posture, she seemed a little manic, even for Irene. It was obvious she really needed him. Them. It was equally obvious that Andrew must alter his resolve to be on the road by dark. Another night, another day, wouldn't kill him.

"I'm so glad you're here," Irene said when she finally took a breath. Her eyes were swollen and red, her face devoid of the makeup she rarely left home without. "I need you to keep the media away. They'll sniff around, of course. They'll hear that I returned to the States without John. I don't know how they get wind of such things, but they always do."

As a former television journalist, Andrew knew the press was invariably tipped off, often by the party who *doth protest too much*. He wouldn't mention that, however.

"You'll tell them that John is researching his next business endeavor, that he'll be home soon," Irene continued. "You must lie for me, dear Andrew. If the media learns what really has happened, it will be far too humiliating for someone like me."

Someone like her. Yes, he remembered how awful it had felt to see his name emblazoned in the tabloid headlines when Patty dumped him for the studly Australian cowboy.

Andrew sipped the gin now and tried to decide if he should serve as Irene's majordomo for the next few days. He supposed John would have expected that, would have wanted Andrew to be supportive, to be sympathetic.

And then he thought of Jo. What would she think if she knew he was being Irene's press secretary, a Dee Dee Myers to a Clinton, an Ari Fleischer to a Bush? And what would Jo think if she learned there was more to his and Irene's past than the fact that she was John's wife and Cassie's godmother?

He stared out at the city and told himself not to worry. The best part of being in the headlines was that they quickly changed, moved on to the next shocking event, the next person caught in or at or by something or someone else. Andrew would, after all, be back in West Hope soon enough, and this would all be over and Jo would never have to know. Until then, for the sake of old friends, he could, should, be Irene's front man.

"I'll help however I can," he said at last.

She smiled for the first time since she'd arrived. "Thank you. Now I'll phone Frannie." She rose from the chair behind John's desk. "I'll have her bring the wedding-guest list tomorrow. I'll decide from that which of our friends we contact."

He didn't comment that Irene needed Frannie—John's assistant—to tell her the names of her friends. She would have shaken her head and told him he was such a Pollyanna about the workings of society. He would have said it was because he'd never really bought into the crap of it all, for which he could thank his parents, who'd been too busy as philanthropic physicians, saving the cold and tired and hungry of the world, to be caught up in the pages of the social register.

He could have said those things, but why upset Irene more than she already was?

"Where's the phone?" she asked, roaming the room now, her eyes bouncing from one exquisite end table to another, all of which had been purchased by the workings of—and for—the society that she, not Andrew, coveted. "I must call Frannie right now." She waved her hand in front of her face as if the temperature in the penthouse had escalated. "Soldata is on her way to do my hair and nails. And Senator Jervis will be here for a late supper, did I mention that?"

Andrew spotted the cordless on the bar. He handed it to Irene. Yes, he would be her majordomo, and he would prop her up in case she fell, in case her stoic face collapsed under the weight of her mask. He owed the Bensons that much after all they'd done for him. After all they'd done for Cassie. Surely Jo would understand.

21

Sarah spent the weekend at home, not dwelling on mothers or fathers or lovers or sons, not spending time planning weddings for the dollars they would bring. Instead, she retreated to the comfort of her pieces of silver. She decorated a thick bracelet with the stars of the heavens; she created earrings in the tradition of a sacred fire, using seven "logs" of silver in place of the wood; she carved a man's face onto the oval of a belt buckle, then etched on hair. Long Hair, like Sutter Jones's Cherokee clan. By studying the pieces, maybe she would have a better sense of herself, a better sense of the man who had come to change her life.

She did not call Jo or Elaine or Lily over the weekend and apologized Monday morning when she learned that they'd spent Saturday and most of Sunday working.

"We're just glad you're here," Jo said to Sarah. "How did it go?"

Jo, of course, thought that Sarah had gone to San Francisco, had tended to business that had come up. Sarah saw no need to explain that she had changed her mind, that her unexpected encounter with Sutter had left her with a need to withdraw. "Everything is fine," she lied.

"Well, I certainly hope so," Lily said, "because our bride with MS will be here today."

"Could you please call her something other than 'our bride with MS'?" Sarah asked.

"Okay," Lily said, "how about Julie, 'our special bride,' because she really will be."

Sarah didn't question Lily's definition of "special." "I made some notes the other day," she said, "some suggestions for the ceremony."

"Oh, wonderful," Lily replied. "A tutorial for second weddings for the handicapped. A whole new niche market. A whole new specialty." She clapped her hands together the way she did whenever she was about to launch into a scheme, or maybe Sarah was imagining things.

"Will her future husband be with her?"

"She didn't say. But I'm sure she'll do absolutely anything to help us out."

"I thought we were the ones who were supposed to help her," Elaine said.

"Well, yes. Actually we'll be helping one another." Lily then adopted her sweetest of smiles, and Sarah knew something Lily-like was on the wedding-planning horizon. "Call me a silly goose, but I just happened to think over the weekend that it would be nice if Julie's wedding received some publicity. It would help create such a positive public service for handicapped people, don't you think?"

Sarah's eyes moved from Lily to Jo to Elaine.

"And so you contacted a few of the media folks who were here for the Benson event?" Jo asked the question they all surely were thinking.

Lily jumped from her chair and flitted from one lovely window display to another, from clouds of white tulle to cascades of satin. Her secret, at last, was out in the open; she was free to garner their praise. "The timing couldn't be better. With or without saying anything about the Bensons—oh, all right, I won't—right now the media thinks our business is pretty neat. And now we can keep them interested while the PR iron is still hot." She toe-danced back to the group as if she were as innocent as she was not.

"You mean you're going to tell the media about how we even plan weddings for people with special needs?" the question came from Elaine.

Jo said, "If I'd had Lily back in Boston, I might not have closed my business."

Lily waved away the sarcasm. "Julie will be here at one o'clock. The media, at one-thirty. I'm dying to know what she—and her new hubby—will look like, but we know we can make anyone look wonderful, wheelchair or not."

"I can't believe you're leaving it up to chance that the couple will be photogenic," Elaine said.

"And I can't believe you're exploiting the woman's handicap," Sarah added.

Then Lily said, "Oh, pooh, all of you. If you must know, this was Julie's idea, not mine. She sees it as an opportunity to show that even people in wheelchairs can have normal lives."

Sarah shook her head and Jo made no comment and Elaine looked bewildered.

Then Lily twinkled and sparkled and toe-danced some more over to the doorway to "run upstairs" and prowl through her closets for an outfit for herself that would be "better suited" to cameras than the plain, boring wool she had on.

To everyone's pleasant surprise, Julie-the-bride turned out to be gorgeous, with heaps of blond hair and taupe-colored eyes and a body that could wear an elegant sheath and look deliciously seductive even while sitting down.

To everyone's additional surprise, Julie's spouse-to-be was a tall, plain woman named Helen.

Sarah decided it was worth every second of Lily's prior nonsense to see the shock on her face when she finally "got it." As far as Sarah knew, Lily was not biased against any race, religion, or sexual preference. As far as Sarah knew, however, Lily had not expected Julie to marry a girl.

"Isn't it wonderful that we live in Massachusetts?" Julie said with a lighthearted smile. "We both had first weddings—to men, wouldn't you know—but mine was in Virginia and Helen's in Nevada, and look where they got us! Here!"

Sarah would have loved to ask where Helen was

from in Nevada and if it was close to the California border, close, maybe, to the Sierra Nevadas, close to where she'd been raised. But it was more fun right now to study dear Lily, whose facial expression hadn't yet changed since the couple arrived.

"We've been together eight years," Helen said. "Now I'll finally get to be included in the management of Julie's care." She was perhaps in her early fifties—Julie, not much younger—and when she looked at her partner, her eyes radiated love.

"Let's all get comfortable," Jo said, gesturing to the cluster of seats in the showroom. Julie guided her motorized chair to where the others were beginning to sit—the others except Lily, who remained standing by the door.

"Lily?" Sarah asked. "Aren't you going to join us?"

Lily put a hand up to her throat. "Absolutely! In a moment!" Then she spun around and offered a giddy, childlike grin. "But first, if you'll excuse me, I believe I left something upstairs!"

"What are you doing?" Sarah asked Lily twenty minutes later. She hadn't come back down, but the television reporters had arrived.

Lily was leaning against the wall in the room that she used as a living room, the one that overlooked the town common. Her hand was still poised at her throat.

"I have no idea," she said. "I simply don't know what to do."

Sarah laughed. "Because of Julie? And Helen?"

Lily, poor Lily, honestly looked pale. "How could

this have happened? How can we do this? What will the media say if we get involved?"

Sarah sat down on a lemon-lollipop–colored chair, her knees far too close to her face, and decided not to remind Lily that it was too late, that the press was already in the showroom. Instead, she said, "You're upset because Julie and Helen are gay."

Raising her chin, Lily tried not to look nonplussed. "Well, it's not that they're not entitled—I mean, I know it's legal and everything—but, gosh, Sarah, they want to get married! And they want us to help!"

"And I believe you made them a wonderfully generous offer to pay for our services in return for publicity." After Lily had flitted upstairs, Julie had told the others of Lily's magnanimous deal: the gowns, the tuxedoes, the reception, even the limos would be paid for by Second Chances in exchange for press coverage and unlimited use of photos.

Lily had made the deal but had failed to inform her partners.

Lily wilted. "I was going to surprise everyone. I was going to show you what a smart businesswoman I've become for recognizing a publicity coup."

"But you proposed the offer before you knew about Helen."

Silence answered Sarah's comment.

"Lily," Sarah said, "not everyone in this world is the same. Take you and me, for example."

Her eyes widened. "Sarah Duncan, are you one of them?"

"A lesbian? No. But it's okay to say the word, Lily."

Lily sighed. "I just can't picture it," she said.

"You don't have to. It's not about you. It's about them."

The "oh" Lily uttered came out like a whimper.

"You're our resident romantic," Sarah continued. "You're the one who believes that everything is better when people are in love. Remember how miserable you were after Reginald died and before you met Frank?"

"That's different."

"Why? Because Frank is a man?"

"Well," Lily answered, "of course."

Sarah shook her head and stood up. "Well, I would think you're old enough by now to know that relationships between men and women together aren't always the be-all, end-all. In fact, sometimes they're quite painful and fairly stupid." She supposed she was speaking for herself and for Jason, though Sarah would never admit that to Lily.

Staring down onto Main Street, Lily said, "They have bride-and-bride cake toppers now. Groom-and-groom too. I saw them when Frank and I went shopping in Northampton. I think they're very tacky."

"You think bride-and-groom statues are tacky too."

"Well, yes, that's true."

"Lily, please. Give them a chance."

She toyed with the beads that encircled her neck. "Well," she said quietly, "Julie certainly seemed nice enough on the phone."

"She is nice, Lily. And so is Helen. They're entitled to a wedding, just like you and me. Well, if I wanted one."

Lily pulled back the curtain. "Here comes cable news."

"You know," Sarah said, "for once, you actually have come up with a good idea. The press already knows us through John and Irene; I think they'll like this story. I think they'll run it."

Stepping from the window, Lily said, "Do you really think so?"

"Yes," Sarah said, as she stood up. "And we'll get the publicity for reasons more worthwhile than the Bensons' falderal. In the meantime, let's just be happy for Julie and Helen, okay?"

Lily bit her lower lip for only a second. "Okay," she said. "But I think a small nosegay of flowers would be better suited for the top of the cake."

And more exposure it was. By the time a dozen reporters and their various entourages left Second Chances after seven o'clock that night, they had the angle of the wheelchair, the angle of the same-sex marriage, and a few self-serving, yet unrevealing, sound bites regarding Irene. ("She called from Rio just the other day," Lily remarked. "She thanked us once again for the wonderful work we did for their affair." Sarah had cringed at Lily's choice of the word *affair*, but fortunately the press was oblivious.)

Lucky for Lily, she managed not to drop even the barest of hints that all was not well in Bensonville, or that Rhonda Blair's impending drama would be next.

Best of all, Julie and Helen seemed to delight in the

antics of it all. ("What the heck," Helen said, "I never liked living in that stuffy old closet anyway.")

So silly Lily had not only survived but had come out a winner after all, hugging the two brides after the media left, saying she was so glad that they had made their deal, explaining to her partners that the necessary cash would come from the profits the Bensons had afforded, once the final payment was received.

"And what's more," Lily announced the next morning, after no doubt spending half the night hatching her next scheme, "we are going to New York. That's where we'll find the most appropriate fashions and catering ideas and everything wonderful. We have three weddings within a matter of weeks, and we must get down to business once and for all."

She then announced that she had already phoned Antonia (her poor, dead Reginald's "beastly old sister") to have the Manhattan apartment opened and cleaned up for their arrival, that they would leave Wednesday morning, that she would arrange for a limo.

She did not have to add that Andrew was in New York, that they damn well knew Irene was there too. She did not have to ask Jo if she wanted to go. Nor did she act surprised when Sarah said yes, she would go too, though Lily had no way of knowing Sarah's real intentions.

22

♥

Tuesday night Jo picked out an ivy-colored Ellen Tracy suit and stretch silk jersey T to wear to New York. When she was in the city, there might be a chance for her to meet some of Andrew's friends. He'd dodged them at the wedding, but this time it would be different. This time they'd be on his turf, where he no longer had to hide. This time she was the woman who was sleeping with him, if one all-nighter and a snow day counted as sleeping together. As having a relationship. As wanting to be with each other. She wondered if he would let that fact be known or if he would keep her a secret from his city life, the way he'd kept that life a secret from her for so long.

She folded the silk T and told herself to stop being paranoid.

"Lily said I should tell everyone who calls that

you're in New York on business," Jo's mother, Marion, said from the rocking chair across the bedroom that once had been hers but now was Jo's because Marion's new husband had bought them a fancy condominium out by Tanglewood, and Jo had moved back into her childhood home. Rather than leave the answering machine on, Lily had deemed it best to have a real live person pick up the phone. She'd railroaded Marion with promises of assistance to decorate the condo, not that Marion needed to be coerced. "I think it would be better to say there's been a death in the family."

"That's awful," Jo said, layering another top, a pair of pants, a neat black dress in case Andrew wanted her to join him and Irene and Cassie and anyone else for dinner. She supposed she should tell the girls of Second Chances about their relationship now. Otherwise they might be hurt or confused if Andrew included Jo but not them in any plans. Not that Lily would have allowed such a thing, if Lily had anything to say about it. "We really are going on business, Mother. We have three weddings to plan very quickly."

"But we both know the real reason is so you can check up on Irene Benson. And Andrew."

"John isn't dead, Mother. Neither is Andrew."

"When a man leaves, he's gone. It doesn't matter how or why he goes."

Jo wasn't sure if her mother was talking about John Benson or Andrew. She pushed down the sting, the string, of memories of Brian. She looked into the suitcase, wrung her hands, and wondered what she was forgetting.

"You're only going to New York, Josephine," her mother said, "not to Princess Grace's wedding."

In spite of her nervousness, Jo laughed. Since she was a little girl, Marion had used the Princess Grace analogy to bring her daughter back to earth when she was getting too obsessed with how she looked or what she wore. Poor Grace had been gone more than two decades now, but her legacy remained alive and well in West Hope.

"I want to make a good impression," Jo told her mother. "In case I meet anyone."

"Anyone special?"

She smiled. "Yes, Mother. Any of Andrew's friends. Or his former colleagues."

Marion rocked once, then twice. "I knew it," she said. "I knew the two of you would finally get together."

"We're not 'together,' Mother. We've just decided to go out once in a while and see if anything, you know, clicks."

Marion nodded. "Oh, I know exactly what you mean, Jo. I'm a newlywed, remember?"

Jo looked back into her suitcase, embarrassed to be having this conversation with her mother. Sometimes she thought she belonged in her mother's generation more than her mother did. "Something casual," she said. "What about my navy sweater and pants—you know, the Dolce and Gabbana ones?"

Marion lifted an eyebrow.

"All right," Jo said, "don't say it." She took the pants from her closet, the sweater from her drawer, while Marion rocked some more.

"He means a lot to you, doesn't he?"

"He isn't Brian, Mom. Andrew is a good man."

"I know. I believe I'm the one who told you to give him a chance."

If she brought the pale green sweater and her Calvin jeans, she could do something with Cassie—maybe take her shopping or to a museum to help give her a break from the monotony of adults.

"Does Andrew know you're coming?"

Jo realized she had enough clothes now to stay a week or two. "I don't think so," she said. "Lily thought it would be best for him to be surprised."

"You mean, you'll just drop in?"

"Drop in?" she laughed. "Mother, for one thing, we'll be staying at Lily's apartment. For another, there are no more secrets between Andrew and me. You sound as if he has a wife and another family stowed away in New York City."

"Well, he did have another life there, that's all. What if his ex-wife shows up again? Won't that make you uncomfortable?"

The only things making Jo uncomfortable were Marion's presence and her comments. "Mother, to use two of your favorite terms, you're being both a worry-wart and a spoilsport. For one thing, we'll get a lot of business done while we're there. We'll check out some bridal shops, maybe even a couple of wedding planners. And Andrew will be delighted that we've come. Cassie will be too. Everything will be fine. Just you wait and see." She had no reason to doubt anything. Did she?

She zipped her suitcase closed before she could add

another outfit, another option for a date that might or might not happen. The phone rang; it was Lily.

"I can't get the limo! Can you imagine! The only limo in town is booked. Booked! So here we are—*us*, of all people, having to take the train into the city for what might be John Benson's funeral if only he were dead!"

Yes, Jo thought with a smile, *us* of all people. She did not mention it was also a pity that they'd all been born long after Princess Grace had wed.

"There's an eight-fifteen train," Lily moaned. "We might as well take that one."

Jo hung up the phone and it rang again. This time it was Sarah.

"Lily is hysterical about not getting a limo. I'm still going with you, but I'll stay at Jason's. While you girls are doing whatever Lily has planned, I'll spend time with my son. Or Lily will drive me insane."

Jo agreed that Lily sounded rather wired.

As soon as Jo clicked off, the phone rang: Elaine. "What are you wearing? How long will we be there? Do you think we can pick up my father and Mrs. Tuttle at the airport on Saturday when they fly back from their cruise?"

When Jo hung up that time, Marion laughed and reminded Jo how lonely she'd been when she first returned to West Hope and how she'd worried about whether or not she'd ever have a new life.

They sat in the two-and-two seats, Sarah and Jo facing Lily and Elaine. Sarah and Jo rode backward; Lily said if she could not face the direction in which they traveled, she might throw up. She had the same problem in limos.

The train clickety-clacked out of the Berkshires and wove its way along the Hudson River that shimmered in the morning sun, past the little islands of snow and ice that floated slowly downstream, toward the city too. Sarah sat by the window, her knees not quite touching Lily's, her ears not quite listening to Lily's description of the layout of Frank's new store. She had a far greater matter pressing on her thoughts, though she doubted she'd ever have the courage to share the details of her quandary.

"I told him the Duncan Phyfe collection should be in front," Lily went on. "I said, 'Tourists expect things like that up here in the Berkshires.' "

After a brief silence, Elaine asked why, and Lily went on to say that though he ended up in New York City, Duncan Phyfe's family emigrated in the late eighteenth century from Scotland to Albany, "practically across the street from us."

Sarah mused at the way Lily referred to "us," as if she'd lived in West Hope all along, not in places like New York and Milan and even Copenhagen. "Those are just cities," she'd said once with a quick wave of her hand. "West Hope—where you girls are—will always feel most like home."

It was too bad, Sarah thought, that Jason didn't feel the same way.

A tiny flutter squirmed inside her stomach as she thought of Jason and Burch and *her* in New York—*her*, Laura Carrington.

Jason had said, "Great," when Sarah called yesterday and told him she'd be coming into town, staying until Saturday. "I'm pretty busy at the studio now, laying the tracks for the new album, but we'll make time in between. And I won't tell Burch. You can surprise him when he comes home from school."

It was hard to hear Jason refer to their son as coming home to a new home that was not hers, home from a school that was new too. Burch had said that school was "cool," but they'd moved into the city during Christmas vacation, so he'd only gone a few days so far.

She wondered if she'd be able to tell Jason about Laura.

"Among so many other things," Lily's voice chirped over Sarah's thoughts, "Frank has a special fondness for antique mechanical banks. Do we all know what they are?" She posed the question as if this were a classroom, not a train, and they were students, not passengers.

They all nodded, because what else could they do?

"Well, I had this stupendous idea. In what used to be the tax collector's office, there's a big, beautiful, walk-in safe. Imagine! Who'd have thought West Hope had so much cash they needed to put it in a safe?"

Elaine laughed, Jo politely smiled, and Sarah looked out the window again.

"The thing is painted black and has magnificent stenciling on the inside. The inside! Anyway, I convinced Frank to set it up as a display area for his mechanical banks. It's too perfect, don't you think?"

Yes, Jo and Elaine thought it was.

Sarah wished she could break the monotonous conversation. If she told them her mother was alive, that she was white, that she was Laura Carrington, that would certainly stop Lily in her Donald Pliner tracks. The looks on their faces might be well worth the effort.

"What's so funny?" Lily asked, and it took a few seconds before Sarah realized that the others had gone quiet and Lily was talking to her.

"Funny?" she asked.

"You laughed. You laughed out loud. What's so funny about Frank's mechanical banks?"

Sarah shook her head. "Nothing. I was thinking about something else."

"What?" Lily asked.

"Nothing important."

"Well, it was important enough to make you laugh."

Sarah looked at her watch. She suddenly thought of Glisi, who'd always said the Cherokee believed the best healer in nature—for heart and spirit—was laughter. "Find something to laugh about every day," her grandmother had said. "If you can't find something funny, make something up." In this case, Sarah wouldn't have to pretend, because despite its seeming serious ramifications, the fact that at age forty-three Sarah discovered that she had a mother was a little absurd, worth a chortle or two.

She glanced at darling Lily, who waited for an answer. "I was thinking about my mother," Sarah said. The words popped from her mouth before she'd reconsidered, but the silence that dropped over the two-and-two seats made her want to laugh all over again.

"You've never spoken about her," Jo said. "Other than to say she died before you knew her."

Sarah smiled, the veil of boredom now lifted, the cloak of depression gone. Glisi—and the Cherokee—had, as usual, been right. She turned to Jo. "I thought she died, but I guess I was wrong."

Blinks and scowls and appropriate "*What?*"s blinked and scowled and were uttered all around.

"My mother is alive and well and living in New York City," she said, then laughed again. "Isn't that a hoot? She's in the same city as my lover and my son. I might meet her while we're here. For me it will be more interesting than visiting Irene." She stood up. "I'm going to the café car. Can I get anyone anything?"

23

It was childishly amusing that for the first time since Sarah had known them, for the first time in over two decades, she had rendered Lily, Jo, and Elaine—all of them—thunderstruck, flabbergasted, speechless, all at the same time.

It was childishly amusing, and yet it had been fun.

She walked away with a grin, thinking it would be good for the others to take a few minutes to discuss her revelation with one another. Of course, she would have loved to be a fly on the window of the railcar. She chuckled all the way to the café car, which was empty because it was past morning rush hour and there were few commuters this far north, anyway.

"Good morning," the attendant behind the counter said with a smile. "You look happy this morning." He was young (well, maybe in his thirties), with bright blue eyes and blond hair and a notable physique outlined beneath his standard-issue white shirt and black vest. It was also interesting that he had a tan in January on a train that ran along the Hudson.

"Oh, I am happy," she said. "It's a beautiful day." She ordered tea. He poured hot water into a cardboard cup and pointed at the small tray of various tea bags.

"Help yourself," he said, and when she picked green tea he said that was his favorite.

She started to pay, but he said, "My treat."

She said thank you, then dunked the bag, and he said, "Nice skirt."

Her eyes fell to the long, dark skirt that she'd tie-dyed a few years ago. "Oh," she said, "thanks." Then she glanced back at him and said, "Nice tan."

His smile flashed more widely, the tip of his tongue resting between his healthy, straight teeth, and he said, "Oh, thanks. I've been working the Auto Train from D.C. to Orlando."

She had one of those quick, unexpected, sex-with-a-stranger fantasies, where they were both naked and he was on her and she was on him and he was in her and she was breathless.

She caught her short, happy breath and turned back to her tea, gently squeezing the bag until it no longer dripped, tucking it into the flap in the counter that read TRASH, and hoping he wasn't as psychic as he was good-looking.

Something to laugh about, Glisi's words echoed.

"You're with those other women," he said, nodding toward the back car. "I saw you get on."

She grinned. In her fantasy he was all sweaty and

she was now spent. "Yes," she replied. "They're my friends." She wondered if he was thinking about her the way she was thinking about him. She wondered why life was so full of subtext and moments not captured, moments not acted on. She suddenly wondered how many of these moments Jason had been exposed to on buses, on trains, on planes. Then she pushed thoughts of Jason from her picture, because it was more fun doing this on her own, laughing at her life, laughing at herself, not dwelling on lovers and on mothers and on other things that she could not control.

He leaned on the counter. "Did you make it?" he asked, gesturing back to her skirt.

"Ah. Yes. Yes, I did."

He nodded approvingly. Was he flirting with her?

She supposed she should pick up her cup and return to her seat, return to the questions, return to explain the contents of the imaginary box (perhaps Pandora's) that she had opened. But then the young man smiled again and asked if she was going into the city to go shopping. "That's what usually happens," he said, "when four women travel together."

Sarah laughed again. "Oh, not these women," she said. "Our adventures are much greater than that."

"Sounds intriguing. I'd love to hear the outcome. Are you coming back on the nine-thirty train?"

Yes, he was definitely flirting with her.

"She absolutely is not." Lily must have tiptoed up to Sarah's side. Unlike Sarah, she was not laughing. "Sarah will be spending three days in the city with her son and her son's father," she remarked. "Not that it's any of your business."

The young man laughed and saluted. "Just being friendly."

Sarah shook her head. "Lily . . ." she said.

"Don't you dare 'Lily' me. You get back to your seat right this instant and tell us what the hell is going on." She placed a hand on Sarah's elbow and steered her away from the young man with the tan.

Sarah looked back to him and shrugged. "Thanks for the tea," she said, and knew the time had come to trade in her laughter for some serious talk; the time had come to let her friends in on the great mystery of her life.

24

The Yellow Cab dropped Sarah off in front of Jason's building while the others went on to Lily's. She rode the elevator to the twenty-first floor, feeling lighter now that she'd unburdened her secret—well, part of it, anyway.

She hadn't told them that her mother was who she was. She'd only said that she existed, that she lived in New York, that she was white. She'd decided to share the woman's identity with Jason first. It seemed only right; it seemed like the kind of intimacy that partners should share first.

And she and Jason were still partners, weren't they?

"Make yourself at home," Jason said now, gesturing to a dark brown sofa that Sarah had never seen. "Would you like some tea?"

"No," she said. "I'd like a big hug."

He quickly obliged. She closed her eyes and succumbed to the strength of his arms wrapped tightly around her. "I miss you," she said.

"Me too," he replied.

They stood quietly, Sarah feeling his heartbeat, offering hers. It was a scenario they'd played out many times over the years, when they'd been so often separated by time and by distance, when Jason had been on the road touring and she'd stayed home. She pulled back from him and grinned. "Can I see Burch's room?"

Jason smiled that crooked smile she always loved so much. "I'm not sure that's allowed. Not by me but by our son."

He'd always been more lenient than Sarah. She'd thought that was because he was a part-time father. She wondered if she'd become the lenient one now, giving in to Burch's every whim so there would be no disagreements in the few hours they'd have to visit. She sat down on the sofa and smoothed the long skirt that the young man on the train had liked but that Jason had seen too many times over the years. She wished she'd worn something else, something prettier, more citylike.

She looked around the room. It had changed since she'd first helped settle them in. It had things now; it had life. A grand piano sat by the window; bookcases lined one wall. A music stand was there, and a tall acoustic bass. It was a small apartment, but it was filled with things that were important in Jason's life and would become important to Burch because he lived there too.

"Well, if you won't show me his room, we'll have to talk about something else. My mother, for example."

He sat beside her on the sofa. He put his elbows on his knees and cupped his hands under his chin. "I haven't seen you in weeks, and you want to talk about your deceased mother?" He probably thought this was a joke.

She touched his arm. "It's not as simple as that." It felt good to touch him, to sense his flesh and blood, even though it lay beneath the fabric of a shirt she didn't know, that she'd never laundered, that she'd never seen hanging on the back of the twig chair in the bedroom of the log cabin.

Her longing, her loneliness, melded together; she did not feel like laughing now.

Taking a slow breath, Sarah told him the story that Sutter Jones had told her, the story she'd told her friends on the train. Still, she kept Laura Carrington's identity hidden; she didn't know why. Perhaps she was trying to protect her father. Or the woman she didn't even know. Perhaps Sarah had simply spent too many years keeping too much within. *Let stillness be your friend*, Glisi had instructed. Most times, it had worked.

"Wow, Sarah," Jason said when she was finished. "Are you sure it's true?"

He was voicing the same reaction she'd first had. It seemed so unbelievable, and yet...

"I told you I knew I was a white Indian. Of course, by the time I knew it, no one was alive to corroborate the story—at least, no one I trusted for the truth." She remembered when she'd told Jason, back when she first learned she was pregnant. "I'm only half Native

American," she'd said, as if it might have mattered to him, which, apparently, thankfully, it hadn't. "I don't care if you're from Mars," he had replied, and they'd hugged their naked bodies and lay together with their legs and arms entangled and their smiles becoming kisses and their hearts beating with the same rhythm, even back then.

"What do you suppose she wants?" he asked suddenly.

Sarah frowned. "What a horrid thing to ask."

"Not really. In these situations, don't people usually want something? Money? Housing? An organ transplant?" He smiled, but she couldn't tell if he was joking. He took hold of her hand.

The sweet gesture took her by surprise. She'd become so accustomed to their independent, separate lives, their one-beat-short-of-total-commitment. He was a musician, after all, not a vocation prone to permanence or availability—emotional or otherwise—when your partner had a problem and needed to talk. It occurred to her now that for all their years and their happiness together, they'd never really become one.

"I don't know if I'm ready to meet her," Sarah said. "I just wondered what you thought."

"I think you're in New York and your mother is here, but before you go see her, you should find out some more facts."

She almost told him then who her mother was. But Jason turned to her first, lifted her heavy hair and piled it on her head, leaned down and kissed her neck. "I also think that Burch won't be home from school for another hour," he said.

So instead of telling him about Laura Carrington, Sarah tipped her head back, settled into his kisses, and realized that everything else could wait, that everything would be fine, if only he'd stop calling this place Burch's home.

25

Irene had been back four days—Sunday, Monday, Tuesday, Wednesday—during which time Andrew had served as host to her select group of friends; fielded a few phone calls from the media, who vanished once Andrew convinced them there was no juicy story; and attended a few meetings with Irene and Barry Franklin, John's attorney, regarding how to keep John's business interests flourishing while he was on the lam. Each time Andrew hinted it might be time for Cassie and him to go home, Irene conjured another pretext to keep them in New York.

"I'm so nervous about the businesses. I need you to help me understand."

Or, "Cassie's presence simply calms me down. You're so lucky, Andrew, that you have a child."

Or, the worst, "Next to John, Andrew, you're the only one who ever understood me."

Not that he believed it. But the collective comments did their job of successful manipulation.

By Wednesday night, however, he was determined to tell her they would stay for the remainder of the week and then leave on the weekend. He waited until he and Irene were alone, when Cassie was in the kitchen helping Elsa prepare dinner and Irene had made cocktails in John's study.

Andrew, however, passed on the martini and poured himself club soda. "Irene," he said when she had settled on the sofa and he in the leather chair, "I'm so glad Cassie and I were able to come down and help you out. But you need to think about what else we can accomplish before the end of the week."

She plucked the olive from the gold pick that she'd balanced on the glass. Thankfully her mania had leveled off in the past few days. She was acting sensible again, less like a whimpering prima donna. "Is that your way of saying you'll be abandoning me too?"

So much for acting sensible.

"Irene," he said, "I'm not abandoning anything. I'll help you when I can. But only from West Hope."

She seemed to think a minute. Then she said, "Andrew, must we talk about this now?"

"Now or later. Not that there's much to say. West Hope is where I live," he said. "It's where Cassie goes to school."

Irene emitted what sounded like a reluctant sigh. Then she stood up and walked over to John's desk. She opened the center drawer and pulled out a piece of paper. "Andrew, dear," she said, "you've helped me keep the media at bay, you've helped me entertain my friends, but we've barely begun the work. The real reason that you're here."

Of course he didn't understand.

She crossed the room to him. She handed him the piece of paper. "John left this letter with his departure note. It outlines what he needs from you."

Andrew took the note but did not open it.

"Read it," she said, touching his chin with her long fingernails. "You'll find he has appointed you to administer his businesses—you know, the magazine interests, the broadcasting group. He's asked for you to do it until a buyer is found. It will no doubt take some time, several months, perhaps."

She went back to her position on the sofa. "Barry wanted me to tell you right away, but I thought it might be better to acclimate you first. Familiarize you with the businesses. Get you a little used to being back here in New York."

He didn't say a word; he just sat there, trying to absorb what he was hearing.

"It's a big job, Andrew. But you'll be compensated nicely. John is giving you your choice of TV or radio station for your trouble. Oh, yes, and managing interest in *Buzz* magazine." Then she smiled and raised her glass again and added, "Your work will keep you very busy in the city. But you and Cassie will be comfortable right here in the penthouse. Don't worry your sweet mind, I'll see to everything."

They knew the address of the Bensons' Park Avenue penthouse because that was where they'd sent the invoices for the wedding, including the last one that hadn't as yet been paid. Jo convinced Lily to wait until Thursday to show up at the door, to give Irene more time to breathe, to give Andrew more time to help her get situated in her new life alone.

In truth, Jo wanted to wait because she was so uncomfortable just "dropping in."

They spent Wednesday afternoon at Bergdorf's and Calvin's and Carolina Herrera's, because Lily had phoned ahead for appointments. Though they saw many things and got many ideas, Lily sputtered because Sarah hadn't joined them, because now she might be too caught up in this mother-thing to pay full attention to her duties. "The couple on the mountain and Julie and Helen are très simple, don't you see?" Lily bemoaned. "But we haven't begun to nail down the details for you-know-who!" She couldn't say "Rhonda Blair," because even on the streets of New York, Ms. Blair's name was recognizable.

After wearing out their feet and their energy too, Elaine suggested they go somewhere famous for dinner, like Sardi's or Tavern on the Green, both of which Lily loved because they meant being seen. She said, "Yes, it will be grand for our business," though Jo suspected it was more grand for Lily's ego, which had already endured the small blow of having to take the train into the city.

A nice dinner out might also help divert their conversation from Sarah and from speculation about what she might or might not do, and what might be her most effective approach.

"If the woman is her mother, she must meet her," Elaine, mother of three, proclaimed.

"She's been fine without her all these years," countered Lily, whose parents had both been killed in a car accident when Lily was seventeen. "Why change that now?"

Jo thought it should be totally up to Sarah, that none of them had any idea what it was like to be her, what it was like to have been raised on a reservation, how the Cherokee thought, what their beliefs were.

They all agreed, however, on having dinner out.

They ended up at Sardi's because Lily said Reginald had often invested in Broadway shows and his caricature was on the wall somewhere, did the girls know that?

They had their dinner and strolled through Times Square now, where Elaine had never been, where the lights glowed as if it were daytime and people crowded on the sidewalks as if it were rush hour. While they walked, Jo kept an eye out for Andrew, as if he'd suddenly appear amid the throng.

Elaine linked arms with Jo on one side, Lily on the other. "Dinner was fabulous," she said. "Sardi's is a good example of the philosophy my father adhered to: that the key to perfect food service is in knowing when to serve and when to let the guests breathe on their own. I need to follow that for catering too." For years Elaine's father's upscale restaurant—*the* upscale restaurant—had been where the tony people dined during Saratoga's "season." Drawing from his expertise (and his recipes!), Elaine hoped to turn the catering division of Second Chances into a much-sought-after business.

"Your father is a wonderful man," Lily interjected as she broke from the others, danced around a couple of young boys who were looking up instead of where they were going, then linked arms again. "After your mother died, I considered marrying him."

A taxi honked. Another echoed. Elaine dropped both her arms and her lower jaw as well.

They stopped at a crosswalk at Broadway and West 45th Street.

Lily shrugged. "Oh, don't be such a prude, Lainey. I wouldn't have done it without your approval."

Jo bit her lip and tried not to laugh out loud. The digitized icon of the little man on the lamppost changed from red to white. They crossed the street.

"You're joking, Lily," Elaine said as she darted around an oncoming pedestrian with the adroitness of a New Yorker. "Tell me you're joking."

Lily laughed. "Not at all. Your father is a good-looking man. And he is so kind. It was after my second husband went back to his mother, and before I met my dear Reginald. It's not as if I'd have harmed him or anything."

They kept walking. Jo thought back to Elaine's mother's funeral. They all had gone, of course. Sarah had brought a bouquet of herbs tied with a lovely ribbon. "The word *death* does not appear in the language of the Cherokee," she'd said. "When we are born we come into a body that we call a robe. When we depart this earth, we simply leave the robe behind."

She wondered how Sarah must feel now that she'd

been told that her mother had not departed, had not left her robe behind. The woman had not died, yet Sarah had lost her.

Loss of any kind did not feel good.

John Benson had not died, yet Irene had lost him.

Andrew had not died, yet he was not with Jo now.

A sudden chill invaded the night air. Jo turned up her coat collar and wondered what Andrew was doing right now and how he'd react when they showed up, unexpectedly, at the penthouse tomorrow.

"How does it feel to hang out with your dad, the celebrity?"

They sat in Jason's kitchen eating Chinese take-out—steamed vegetables, brown rice, and plump fried dumplings.

"He's not a celebrity, Mom," Burch said between bites. "He's only Dad."

Burch looked more like Sarah every day, with his dark hair and eyes, his high cheekbones that became more dominant as his face grew toward manhood, his lean, angular body that promised to be tall.

Well, Jason was tall and lean too, she supposed. But lately she preferred to think of Burch as being more a part of her than him.

She wondered how he'd feel if he knew he had a grandmother other than Jason's mother, who'd become stodgy over the years, living in the damp, overtaxed home on the New England shoreline, taking solace in the fact that the once merely middle-class abode was now worth well more than a million. She wondered how Burch would feel if he knew his other grandmother still needed to go about in sunglasses and a head scarf, not that he'd have an inkling who Laura Carrington was.

She looked at the tiny diamond-shaped birthmark on Burch's cheek and felt a sudden need to touch it, to connect with her son and her mother and her past. Instead, she smiled and said, "He's not 'just Dad.' He's *your* dad. And he's always been famous to us, right?"

Burch groaned and Jason laughed and scooped more brown rice onto his plate. For a moment Sarah felt they were a family once again.

"So tell me about your new friend Glen," she said. "What do you do together?"

With a boyish shrug, Burch said, "I don't know. Stuff. Nothing. You know."

Sarah looked at Jason, then back to their son. She forced a smile. "No, I really don't know, honey."

Jason maneuvered the chopsticks, stacking the brown rice into a pyramid with ridiculous precision, the way that always had annoyed Sarah, but she had never told him. He said, "Glen's going to teach you how to skateboard. I said I'd buy the gear."

"Yeah," Burch replied. "That'll be cool."

Skateboarding was not a sport that was conducive to the winding roads and dirt trails through the woods that surrounded the log cabin. Burch had watched it on TV from time to time, but he'd never said it was something he might like to try.

"It sounds like fun," she said with a smile she hoped would seem sincere. She wished, however, that Burch were five or six again, when she'd been able to tell if he liked something or not just by the way his forehead wrinkled or the way he squared his young-boy shoulders.

"I hope you don't mind, Sarah," Jason said, "but I promised Burch he could go to the studio tomorrow after school. It's the only chance he has to sit in on a session. You're welcome to come too."

Sarah never had enjoyed the dark, windowless confines of a recording studio, the thickly padded walls and ceilings that suffocated sounds of life outside. She supposed it represented another of those wedges in the floundering relationship with the man she loved.

So she said, "I need to do some work with the girls tomorrow, but I suppose I could come by when we're done."

"I'll be there at three-thirty," Burch said, his face more animated. She thought of the hours, days, years she'd spent wishing Jason was around to spend more time with Burch, wishing father and son could form the kind of bond that comes from shared experience, shared memories, creating a kind of inner harmony that can't be recorded in a studio.

"I'll leave you directions," Jason added. "Come by whenever you're finished with your business. My session starts at nine, and I'll be there all day." Unlike most musicians, Jason preferred to work during the day, when studio time was cheaper and the technicians were relatively alert.

"Hey, maybe I'll get a chance to play the drums, huh, Dad?" Burch might have his dad's proclivity toward music, but Sarah had always liked to think it was the spirit of the Cherokee that led him to the drums. Now she could also wonder if Jason's genes weren't the only ones that provided Burch with the yearning to simply perform.

She thought about the other part of Burch's heritage, how it might direct his life, once he knew about it, about her. "I'll be there by three-thirty, for sure," she said, then leaned across the table to touch the birthmark on his cheek. "Brown rice," she said, and smiled at the secret she now held.

26

It had seemed years, not weeks, since Sarah had seen Burch, since she'd slept next to Jason. At nine-fifteen she finally awoke, feeling weighted from the night, thinking she should instead be invigorated in spirit and in body after making love to the man she adored, even if she couldn't bring herself to live with him here.

She opened her eyes and listened to the quiet. Tonight she would tell him about Laura Carrington.

But for now, it was quiet. Her "boys" were gone: Jason at the studio, Burch off to school. Later they would do the things that boys did, bonding, she remembered. She tried to push away that jab of jealousy that Burch apparently was having such a great time in New York, such a great time without his mother, whom he no longer seemed to need.

"Argggh," she vocalized, then rolled onto her back

and looked around the room. The high white walls were stark except for two framed posters, an original from Woodstock '69 that Sarah had bought him for Christmas three years ago, and a black-and-white one of Jason's concert in Montreal back in July 1990, the time, the place, where they had met.

She'd been in Canada selling her jewelry. The weeklong international crafts show was being held in the old part of the city, which was attempting to be as European as Quebec. A young woman in the canvas-tented booth next to Sarah sold exquisite pottery. She told Sarah she dated a bass player in a band and they were having a concert that night at the arena. Would Sarah like to go?

Sometimes life changes just that fast, she thought now as she stared at the poster, at the memories of that meeting, which were as crisp and clear as if they'd happened in a dream last night.

"Sarah, this is Jason. Jason, Sarah."

She'd supposed Glisi would have said *Yolda*—that all things were as they should be, planned by the Great Spirit. At best, Sarah would have admitted perhaps it had been love at first sight.

They had so much in common: They were both still in their twenties(!) yet were on their own, Sarah by circumstance, Jason because his straitlaced father wanted his son to be a lawyer, not a singer, and his mother was terrified that her only child would start taking drugs.

"Sarah," he'd said. "Wow, you're beautiful." They stood eye-to-eye, his chocolate-brown ones lost somewhere in her coal-black ones, a tenderness revealed by the blush that rose in his Irish cheeks, a smile that displayed a secret emotion, something of a cross between euphoria and alarm.

She lost her ability to speak.

"If you think she's beautiful, you should see her jewelry," the young pottery-woman said, then drifted away, her arm linked through the drummer's.

"I'd like that," Jason said to no one but Sarah. "If you'd like to show me."

Other than Red Elk, Sarah had never had a real boyfriend, not the kind who lasted beyond a month or two, beyond the stage of getting-to-know-each-other that, once partially complete, left her feeling unfulfilled and untrusting and not wanting to spend another day or night in the company of the guy. It was not that way with Jason. They walked through the old city, then drove to Mount Royal, where they climbed up to the lookout and watched the lights of Montreal until the dawn arrived over the horizon of the famed St. Lawrence River. Soon after, he moved into the log cabin that she rented outside West Hope. A year later they bought the place from the landlord, and the next year Burch was born. They'd never gotten married, because there was that independence thing: a need, perhaps on his end, a barrier on hers, she knew, to avoid getting too close, in case he left her as the other people she'd loved had. When Burch was still an infant, Jason's upper-middle class, prim and proper parents had finally come around, having chosen to accept their lives instead of losing Jason completely.

Despite the lengthy time-and-travel separations, Sarah had thought that they'd grow cliché-ingly old together. She never thought that they'd be loving each other from separate homes. Then again, she never thought her mother was alive either.

The clock on Jason's nightstand, which, like the other furnishings, was new, said nine thirty-four. Sarah decided that between now and when she went to the studio, she would go to Lily's apartment—she knew the location from their many years of September "Girls' Weekends" in the city. They hadn't made concrete plans to get together. The others might be at the apartment, or they might be at Irene's, or they might be shopping for wedding-planning ideas. She didn't know the phone number of Lily's apartment; she didn't know any of their cell phone numbers because she'd never bothered to get one of her own. Being available 24/7 might be convenient, but it represented *stress* that Sarah felt the world simply didn't need. She closed her eyes and sighed. No matter what, she'd go to Lily's so she could at least say she had tried to connect.

Maybe Laura Carrington lived near Lily's in a brownstone next door or around the corner.

No. She laughed. *Too coincidental.*

And yet, maybe Lily knew, maybe Lily had heard, where the old film star lived. Sarah could ask. But did she want Lily involved?

She flipped from one side to the other. In Hollywood there were tour buses that drove the paying customers to see the mansions of one star after another. New York, however, would be way too refined for that.

Opening her eyes again, she tried to think of an

alternative. She could check the Internet, but she didn't really know how. Too many years living as a recluse. Too many years living with her hands in the earth and not in cyberspace.

And then Sarah thought about the library, the New York Public Library, whose main branch served as guardian of Fifth Avenue, whose regal lions and long flight of stone stairs promised all who entered vast access to knowledge.

The library. Of course.

Without a blink of hesitation, Sarah bolted from Jason's bed. She wondered how long it would take to shower, dry her hair, then get a cab from East Greenwich Village to Midtown.

They stepped into the elevator that led to the Benson penthouse after Lily told the doorman that she was Lily Beckwith, Andrew Kennedy's business partner. The doorman had called up to the thirty-seventh floor and Andrew said to send her up, because what else would he have said? He did not know Elaine and Jo were with her.

Lily pushed the button that read PH as if she went there every day. "This will be fine, you'll see," she said.

Jo was not as certain.

The elevator doors closed and the car began its quick ascent.

Jo looked over at Elaine, who gripped a glass ichibana vase that held three tiny yellow orchids. Lily had insisted that her favorite florist create it in time for them to bring it to Irene. "Just a small, thinking-of-you gift," Lily had said. She chose yellow, not white, because white would be too much like the flowers from the wedding.

For a reason Jo could not explain, she felt unsettled, an unexpected guest at a private party. Andrew had said he'd lived in this building as a boy—he must have ridden this same elevator countless times. Jo thought that the first time she went there, it should at least be at his request.

It was, however, too late to change her mind. The elevator slowed, rose up, then down, then stopped. The shiny brass doors opened, and Andrew was standing there.

"Lily," he said. Then he noticed them. "Elaine." His eyes moved over to her. "Jo." He laughed a small, short laugh. "Hey, what the heck are you guys doing here?"

"We've come to offer our condolences," Lily announced, stepping from the car and into the hall. "And our friendship. It's not as if at least one of us hasn't been through this kind of horror."

Jo—the one who everyone knew had been through the closest thing to "this kind of horror" and certainly most recently—lingered in the background as if she were no one special, as if she were merely another acquaintance. She pushed the elevator button that signaled the doors to stay ajar.

"I'm sorry I haven't called," he said to everyone, though his eyes were fixed on Jo. "I've been so busy. Tending to John's things."

Jo offered a half smile. She didn't want him to think she was pressuring him.

"Is she here?" Lily continued. "Irene?"

"Sorry. She's resting." He did not invite them into the penthouse, the door to which was open, less than twenty feet from them.

"How is she feeling?" Lily asked.

"All right. She's strong."

"And Cassie?"

"Cassie is good. Irene's been helping her with her French. Plus she's polished all the silver and is downstairs right now ironing linen napkins."

The word that was unspoken was, decidedly, *intrusion*. "Perhaps we should have called," Jo said.

"It wouldn't have mattered," he replied. "Irene really isn't up to seeing anyone."

Jo nodded. She remembered the feeling that crawled inside your belly when a man just up and left, the feeling that someone, indeed, had died. She remembered the feeling of wishing he had, because it would have been so much easier to rationalize, so much less embarrassing.

Lily remained in place.

Elaine held out the ichibana vase. "Please, Andrew. Give these to Irene. Tell her we were thinking of her."

He took the flowers.

"Perhaps we can help," Lily said. "At a time like this, a woman needs all the friends she can get."

He shook his head. "She's fine. Really."

"Well, we all know that friends of couples often wait a while to see whose side they should take. You know, should they feel sorry for her or stand by him?" Lily pressed on, oblivious to Andrew's obvious dilemma about what to say or do next.

Jo couldn't stand another minute of this ridiculous scene. "Lily," she said, "get back on the elevator. We have bridal shops to visit, remember?"

"Ah," Andrew said. "That sounds like a good idea. What with business booming..." He tried to smile a soft, Andrew smile, but Jo noticed that behind his eyes something was wrong.

Lily took a step back, as if finally understanding that they were not wanted.

Andrew examined the yellow blossoms. "I'm sorry. I never dreamed you'd come. Any of you. Not with the business so busy and all..."

"If it hadn't been for John and Irene, we wouldn't be busy, now, would we?" Lily said, then kiss-kissed his cheek and tucked one of her personal calling cards into his hand. "We'll be at my apartment if you need us. We're not going back until Saturday. We only came to the city to check out a few shops and pick up Elaine's father." She pointed to the card that she'd just given him, to the gold foil-embossed "B" for Beckwith, naturally. "That's my address and phone. Please don't hesitate." She blew another smiling kiss, stepped back onto the elevator, and pushed the CLOSE DOORS button as if leaving had been her idea.

"Was that a visitor?" Irene asked when Andrew went back inside the penthouse and closed the door behind him. She swished up to him in a lavender chiffon caftan, her eyes sparkling not from tears but from the champagne in the mimosas she'd insisted Elsa prepare for breakfast, though she'd hardly eaten. "Has Barry arrived so early?"

Barry Franklin had scheduled a full day with Andrew to review the duties that Andrew hadn't asked for and didn't think he wanted. So far he'd learned that selling the Benson Group was going to involve a dumpsterful of paper and more meetings than the pope gave blessings in any given year. He'd tried—to no avail so far—to let Barry and Irene know that he was a journalist at heart, that he was no Donald Trump.

"It was just a flower delivery," Andrew said, setting the vase on the sideboard in the foyer. "From the women at Second Chances."

She eyed the orchids, then quickly turned away. "Well, isn't that sweet," she said. "Alms for the bereaved."

"The women are in town," he said. "They're staying at Lily's apartment."

She went into the living room and poured another mimosa from the long bar by the windows. "Well, they'll have to get used to life without you now. But it isn't as if that wedding business was a real job for you."

They hadn't spoken about it further, about his life and Irene's life and what would or should happen next. He hadn't brought up the subject this morning, because he did not know what to do after reading the contents of John's letter that she'd dropped on him last night.

"I like working with the women, Irene. They're my friends."

One perfectly waxed eyebrow lifted. She could have

mentioned the great number of years that she and John had been his friends, but Irene was too much a lady to do that. All of which, of course, made him feel even more like crap.

She handed him a mimosa; he said no thanks and sat down on the sofa.

"Irene," he said. "I had no problem coming down here, even though you didn't show up when you said you would. I've had no problem playing dodge 'em for the press or being the official greeter for your friends. But as for me handling John's business affairs, well, you—or he—might have considered asking first."

Her forehead flattened. "I don't understand you, Andrew. You know how much he—*we* need you. You're the only one John trusts. He's giving you a broadcast station. He's giving you control of *Buzz*. Isn't that enough compensation for this one teeny favor?"

"It's not about compensation, Irene. And it's not a 'teeny favor.' It's an enormous responsibility to keep the Benson Group running well until John decides either to sell it or return to his mind." Irene began to pace. He wished he hadn't added the part about John's mind.

"But it's my future as well as John's. I don't know what I'll do. I can't do this without you, Andrew. I simply can't, that's all."

He wanted to provide a reassuring hand on her shoulder or her arm, but Irene was in motion now and seemingly not going to stop. "Irene, please," he said. "It isn't about you. I said I'd do what I can. But Cassie and I have a life we love. I have a woman I care about.

All of that is in West Hope. It isn't here." He felt tired, depressed, angry at himself for getting caught up in his guilt.

Irene said nothing but suddenly stopped pacing. She stared out at the cityscape, then turned to Andrew, her eyelids lowered, her voice emitting a new softness. "I'm sorry you feel that way, Andrew," she said. "Please understand it was not my idea for John to desert me. And you're right, he should not have entangled you in his business affairs, or in our personal matters, without asking in advance. It seems as if his stupidity has affected more than me." She went back to the bar and set down her glass. "Feel free to go back to your life. You'll understand if I don't say good-bye to Cassie."

She left the room, her footsteps slow, her sorrow trailing behind her.

Andrew tipped back his head and closed his eyes. Then, with an exasperated sigh, he stood up and followed her out of the room, calling, "Irene," until she stopped in the gallery and turned around and he said, "Irene, please, I'm sure we can work something out."

27

♥

The awning over the door was teal, not the deep maroon that Sarah had seen in a photo in an old *Movie Star* magazine, which had captured Laura Carrington emerging from her *newly acquired* Central Park West apartment. The issue was dated May 1983. The accompanying article Sarah had unearthed in the library did not mention that by 1983 Laura's stardom years had waned. Nor did it mention that the daughter she'd abandoned, who'd turned out to be her only child, was by then at college in New England, had lost her father, and had outgrown her buffalo-grass doll.

But if Glisi had taught Sarah anything, it was tolerance, patience for the mystical workings of the Circle of Life, where all is for a purpose, where all things—man, animals, plants, trees—are one in harmony and balance.

She did not feel particularly in balance as she crossed West 82nd Street for a better view. Instead, she felt wobbly, unsteady, and totally unsure as her heart thumped quickly in her throat.

From the opposite sidewalk, she felt a little safer, a little more calm.

It wasn't a tall building by the standards of New York. She tipped back her head, counting the floors, all of which had large, imposing windows that peered over the pavement and the concrete walks to the lushness of the park.

She wondered which windows were Laura's, and how often the woman looked out of them, and if she might be doing that right now.

Would she notice Sarah?

If Sarah were more confident, more *in balance*, she supposed, she might march up to the front door and have herself announced.

Sarah Duncan, she would say to the doorman. *Here to see Ms. Carrington.*

The doorman could say Ms. Carrington was not in, a probable bogus message used to pacify unwanted guests or old Hollywood hangers-on who'd learned her New York address the way Sarah had.

He could say that no one lived there by that name, because Laura might call herself something else now, a name she'd confided only to her closest friends.

Or he could say, *Just a moment, I'll call upstairs for you.*

No, Sarah thought, she was not that much in balance.

And then a drapery stirred at the front window up

on the fourth floor. Sarah held herself still, wondering if it had been her imagination, wondering why her gaze had landed there just as the motion had occurred. Was it a sign from Glisi? Was it where Sarah's mother lived?

"Move, lady!" a man's voice shouted at her.

She snapped around and saw a clean-shaven, middle-aged man who wore an old gray hooded sweatshirt and a knit cap pulled down around his ears. His cheeks were puffed and red; his thick, dark eyebrows were knitted into one. He clutched the handle of a large vending cart that he obviously wanted to steer around her. "Please," he added, with a weary testament to the new, people-friendly New York.

Sarah stepped aside.

A small gust of wind eddied around her. She clutched her long, cloth coat, wishing she'd worn something warmer. She checked her watch. It was just past noon. Maybe the others would be at Lily's apartment. Maybe she'd be better off to go there after all and stop standing on the sidewalk, where she was in the way.

It was a sunny, crisp January day, the weather no excuse for Laura to have skipped her morning walk in the park with Karl, the man who'd been "keeping her company" for ten or twelve years. But the best part of growing older, Laura reasoned, was that you didn't always have to explain why you wanted—or didn't want—what you wanted or didn't want, that you could just say, "No," without feeling remorse.

Besides, she didn't even know why she'd canceled their plans today. For some unknown, unexpected reason, it had seemed like a better idea to stay at home, to look out at the park that she loved so much, to watch the predictable, ceaseless motion of comings and goings of dog-walkers and nannies and bright Yellow Cabs.

With a last, cheerful look, Laura stepped from the draperies at her front window and decided a cup of tea would taste really good now.

28

It's insulting, that's what it is," Lily was saying to Elaine as Jo led Sarah into the living room. "After all we did for Irene, she can't even invite us in?"

Sarah laughed and Lily turned around. Her blond curls were slightly askew, her cheeks extra pink, as if she'd run a road race, which Lily never would have done because she didn't like to sweat. Perspire. It was so ungirlielike.

"Well," Lily declared, "look who's here. The fourth musketeer." *The Four Musketeers* was a label Elaine's father had bestowed upon them back when they were in college. "I would have called but I didn't have your number," Sarah said. "What's going on?"

Lily moved to an end table, opened a drawer, removed a calling card and thrust it at Sarah. "Here's my number," she said. "Someone might as well make use of it."

Sarah, of course, was puzzled. On the way to the apartment she'd decided to tell them that Laura Carrington was her mother, that Sarah had been—just then—to where Laura lived. But timing being everything for harmony and balance, Sarah knew that the timing was far from right now. Lily was showing signs of the greatest distress, the kind that might not even be cured by a spa trip or by lunch. She tucked the calling card into her pocket and waited for the next bit of information.

Lily pressed a hand against her forehead and sighed like Scarlett O'Hara. "I simply can't do this. We have a business to run now, and I can't let my emotions interfere with our work."

"Which is what I was saying before you got here, Sarah," Jo said.

Sarah couldn't guess at the conversation that had gone on before; she couldn't imagine what "emotions" had been "interfering" while she'd been standing outside the building on West 82nd.

Elaine motioned for Sarah to join her on an exquisite, slightly curved sofa that been upholstered in soft butter brocade. Sarah, however, chose to stand. She glanced around the commodious room, perusing the additional matching sofa that was complemented by five chairs in flowered Provençal fabrics, all of which were nicely accented by the dark woods of occasional tables, a long sideboard, and a tall étagère—pieces that might have similar mates in Laura Carrington's West Side apartment. The focal point in Lily's room was an ornately carved wood mantel above the wide fireplace, which snapped and crackled a warm January greeting.

Now, as in her previous visits to the apartment, Sarah was surprised that Lily had created such a grown-up, down-to-earth place. Lily had always seemed to prefer the childlike spaces like the one she'd created above Sarah's studio at Second Chances.

"Well, we do have weddings to plan," Elaine said. "Like Rhonda Blair's. You're right—what a challenge that one will be!"

Lily did not seem interested in weddings now, challenging or otherwise.

Sarah sat down. "What's going on? Did you see Irene? How is she? How's Andrew?"

"Don't get me started," Lily said, as she flitted to the sideboard and poured a glass of water from a tall decanter. "I feel positively insulted. I don't know why we're being snubbed." She downed the water.

"We're not being snubbed, Lily," Jo said. "She wants privacy, that's all."

"It's not about us," Elaine added.

"Well," Lily said, tiny bursts of steam nearly visible from her gently flaring nostrils. "This is so embarrassing. I've told everyone that we're her friends."

"Everyone?" Sarah asked. "Like who?"

Lily wrung her hands. Her agony was plain. "Well, Darlene and Dennis, for beginners."

Sarah looked to Jo and Jo said, "The cleaning people."

The cleaning people?

"Not just the cleaning people!" Lily replied. "*My* cleaning people, who also happen to clean the homes of the Stantons and the Percys and the William Hunt the Thirds."

"I thought you didn't care about those kind of people anymore," Sarah said. "Those society folks."

"This is different. This is John Benson."

"But no one will know that we were 'snubbed,'" Jo said. "We were the only ones there except for Andrew."

"Believe me," Lily said, "they'll know. Irene has servants. Servants have ears. And mouths."

"Oh for goodness' sake," Elaine cried. "Who cares?"

"Don't you get it?" Lily wailed. "People are watching. People are judging. Especially Reginald's friends. They're dying to see if I fall flat on my Botoxed face—yes, girls, it is Botoxed—or if I end up marrying the next man who comes along, so they can whisper among themselves that they knew I never loved poor Reginald all along, that I only wanted his money, that I can never amount to anything on my own. If they hear that Irene Benson has snubbed me... well, don't you see? They'll all laugh behind my back."

So, Sarah thought, this was about Lily, not about Irene.

Lily poured herself another glass of water.

Sarah stood up. "So what's your point? People have been laughing at me for years." Yes, now was definitely not the time to bring up her mother again or to ask their advice. It was better to leave, better to take her troubles back to Jason. She could get to the studio early enough, and watch Burch play too.

Jo ignored Sarah's comment. "Think about it, Lily. Didn't you say your New York friends are in Palm

Beach by now? That the season down there has just started?"

Sarah backed toward the foyer, positioning herself for a quick exit.

"No offense, my dear friends, but none of you can possibly understand," Lily whined.

Before any of them had another chance to try to "understand," the doorbell rang. Because Sarah was the closest, she quickly opened the door. Someday, she supposed, she'd be proud of herself for not showing surprise or uttering something sarcastic when she saw that the person on the other side was Irene Benson, the woman who, apparently for some unprovoked reason, had insulted the women of Second Chances.

Sarah asked her to come in. Irene said she would only stay a moment, that her driver was waiting, but she'd wanted to stop by with a few words for Jo.

"Is Andrew with you?" Sarah asked.

Irene shook her head and removed her gloves. "Andrew doesn't need to hear what I have to say."

The comment seemed odd, but Sarah was beginning to get used to odd things in her life.

The new guest walked into Lily's living room as if she and her husband owned it, along with the rest of Manhattan. "Ladies," she said. "Thank you for the orchids, though they were hardly necessary. I've come to pay my invoice for the wedding. I believe the balance comes to seventy-eight thousand?"

Lily hesitated before stepping forward. "And some

change," Lily said. "Seventy-eight thousand, one hundred forty-eight, to be exact."

It was odd to see Lily be so direct with a woman such as Irene, as if she, for once, gave no thought to trying to impress.

"So it is," Irene said, withdrawing a check from her handbag, then slowly filling out the amount while the others sat and stood there in silence. When she was finished, she handed the check to Lily. "I am paid in full now."

Lily examined the paper, then slipped it into her pocket. "Would you care for tea? A glass of wine?"

Sarah would have bet that even though Irene didn't really know Lily, she would have known that the offer was as thin as Irene's tightened lips.

"What I have to say won't take long," Irene said. "I'd appreciate it if there were no interruptions."

Sarah checked an impulse to return her to the door, to say, *Thanks for coming, but you're really not welcome here.*

Then Irene raised her chin and said, "This is about Jo, but from what I understand you're all so chummy it won't matter which of you hears." She spun on one heel so she squarely faced Jo.

"I know that Andrew's fond of you, which is why I decided to come and tell you this in person. He won't be going back to West Hope. He and Cassie belong here in New York now. With me. He has undertaken the enormous task of handling John's affairs. I've come to ask that you not interfere. I have known Andrew many years, and I know what's best for him. You've known him mere months, most of which, I should remind you, he spent lying to you."

Jo stood up. Like Elaine and Lily, Sarah remained motionless.

Jo smiled at Irene. "I understand this is a difficult time for you, Irene," she said. Her hands were surprisingly steady, her voice unwavering. "But I'm sure you'll agree that if Andrew chooses to live in New York, I expect it should be his decision and that he should be the one to tell me." Her eyes darted quickly around the room. "To tell us," she added.

Irene returned the smile, though hers was cool enough to chill the roaring fire in the room. "How shall I say this?" She crossed the room, lifted a finger to the mantel, swept it across the wood as if in search of dust. "This is not that droll little town where you all reside. This is the big time, darlings, and you are way out of your league."

The fire hissed and popped and spit.

"Mrs. Benson," Lily said, stepping forward, "I'm afraid I shall have to ask you to leave. I'm sorry about your husband, but you're in my house now, and Jo is my guest." She planted her hands on both her hips, her edges now visibly returned. "I'm sure in your big-time life, even you understand common courtesy."

Irene's tongue repositioned itself from one cheek to another. She checked the top button on her sable coat—real, smooth, inky sable, for women like Irene Benson did not care what others thought about animals or their rights. "I assure you I did not come here to offend anyone," she said. "I only wanted to let everyone know where Andrew's allegiance will be from here on out. As I said," she added, moving toward the door, "you've only known Andrew for a few, unsettled months." Her gaze fell back on Jo. "But the fact is, he was my lover long before he was yours."

With that, Irene went out the door, closing the latch quietly, as a true lady would.

29

We need to talk to Andrew," Lily said a few stunned seconds later—was it only seconds?—when the tsunami of Irene's visit slowly started to recede.

"I don't think he has his cell phone," Jo replied. She was standing in the same position that she'd been when Irene's words lashed.

Was it true? Sarah supposed she wasn't the only one wondering. Had Andrew really been Irene Benson's lover?

"She's a textbook case of a woman scorned," Sarah said. "She wants to strike out and hurt others the way that she's been hurt." She checked her watch. It was almost two-thirty; she really must leave soon to get to the studio, to think about how she was going to tell Jason about Laura.

"Andrew with Irene?" Elaine asked, then laughed.

"No offense, Lily, but I'd be more inclined to believe that you'd be with my father than that the two of them were... well..." She stopped speaking there, as if linking Andrew and Irene as lovers was too unfathomable to mention.

Lily walked to Jo and put her arm around her shoulder. "First, I want to say that we all know about you and Andrew, Jo, so don't be embarrassed." Jo did not respond. "Next, I want to add that we will get to the bottom of this tall tale of hers. And I will come up with a plan to subvert it. We are, after all, the four musketeers, aren't we?"

"We are," Elaine said.

Sarah added, "You bet." Just because she was preoccupied with her own problems didn't mean she wouldn't "be there" for Jo.

Lily paced to the mantel, rubbing her tiny hands together, invisible sparks shooting this way and that, her energy definitely back. She looked into the flames as if they were a crystal ball. "Now," she said, "where should we begin..."

Sarah braced herself for another of Lily's schemes. As much as she wanted to offer support to Jo, could she really fit one of Lily's brainstorms between Jason, Burch, Sutter Jones, and... well, the rest? "The only place to begin, and end," Sarah said, "is by talking to Andrew. And I think the only one who should talk to him is Jo."

With a small harrumph, Lily said, "Even if it means we lose him as an employee?"

Sarah averted her eyes to the étagère. She decided that Lily must have had a decorator. Surely she'd never quite matured enough to have such elegant taste. In West Hope, the little-girl furniture and the little-girl accoutrements in her apartment were certainly more "Lily" than butter brocade and sophisticated flowered Provençal.

"Sarah's right," Elaine said. "Lily, you'd be the first to say that love should come before all else. Certainly before something as tedious as work."

Lily did not seem to know how to argue with that.

"Besides," Elaine added, "I know that Andrew is in love with Jo."

Sarah stopped thinking of her watch and what time it said now. Her attention, instead, zoomed to Elaine.

"We talked about it," Elaine said. "We had a toast to second chances. And I don't mean the company."

Lily pursed her lips, perhaps a little miffed that Andrew had confided in Elaine and not in her. "Well, okay, then," she said. "It proves my point that Irene Benson is deranged. Imagine... the two of them together." She shook her head. She rubbed her hands again. "So unless we think of something better, we agree that Jo will talk to Andrew."

Sarah realized that during this conversation Jo hadn't shifted from her place. Her gaze had moved as Lily, Elaine, and Sarah spoke, but her stance had remained rigid, betrayed-woman rigid.

"Jo?" Lily asked.

She wet her lips; she turned her head. "I don't think Andrew has his cell phone," Jo said once again. "And, anyway, I'm going to bed now. I feel a migraine coming on."

Sarah supposed that, sooner or later, she'd lose Jason too. Irene had been right about one thing: New York was not West Hope, the droll little town, on whose fringes Sarah had been sequestered for so many years.

She stared out the cab window as it stopped and started down Seventh Avenue, headed toward Greenwich Village. Sarah wondered when the tingling would leave her arms and legs, the tingling that had given her a floating, out-of-body feeling since she stood in front of the apartment building on Central Park West.

If she lost Jason, she might lose Burch as well. The city had so much to offer a young boy, especially when his father was on the way to fame, to fortune, to hard-earned success. All that West Hope had to offer was her.

"We always get what we think we deserve," Glisi often said, though Sarah had not known whether or not it was another Cherokee belief or just the wise words of a caring grandmother.

Jason believed he would succeed. He believed his music would be loved by many beyond the small towns and out-of-the-way places where he so often performed. It had taken years, but he had grown from bars to lounges and now played in two of the hottest clubs. His new CD should be out in the spring, and he was hopeful that, by working hard enough, he would get what he deserved.

In the process, would he get another woman? A younger, hipper, city woman, who would take Burch to premieres and to openings and cool stuff at the museums?

Maybe Sarah could ask Laura Carrington to take him instead.

She stared out the window at the small, untidy shops that crowded one another for a plot of sidewalk space. Fashions, handbags, shoes, and souvenirs seemed almost animated, clawing for the attention of every passerby.

And then she saw the dress.

On a freestanding rack, almost on a corner, Sarah saw a deep, blood-red dress—a gown—the ideal wedding dress for Rhonda Blair.

"Stop!" she shouted at the cabbie.

Brakes squealed. She shoved a twenty at the driver, not bothering to check the fare. Then she bolted from the backseat and raced back to check out the dress.

The skirt was layered with petallike softness—rose-petallike softness. The bodice was crimped and fitted, strapless. With wide, gold-mesh-wire ribbon configured upright from the waist, Sarah could create an apparition, an unfolding of a blossom, a rose blossom. It was a vintage dress, vintage Rhonda Blair. The price was twenty-nine dollars and ninety-five cents.

She completed the transaction and hailed another cab, deciding to go back to Jason's apartment, drop off her purchase, and let Lily know before she continued on to the studio. No sense in the others wasting their time looking for a gown for Rhonda (if Irene had not completely distracted them from their work) when Sarah had the perfect one right here in the bag. She quickly checked her pocket, reassured that Lily's card was there, so at least this time she had the phone number.

It was quiet in the apartment. Sarah roamed from the foyer through the living room into the kitchen and rechecked the street address of the studio, which Burch, not Jason, had written on a Post-it and stuck on the refrigerator, right below a large magnet that advertised a pizza delivery shop on East Houston Street.

Next to the building number he had written *Fifth floor, which comes after four.*

She smiled because her son was so fresh and she loved him so much.

Returning to the living room, Sarah dropped the bag with the red gown on the sofa and picked up Jason's phone to call Lily. The women would be exuberant, especially when she told them the price. Lily would want to tell Rhonda it cost twenty-nine *hundred* and had been a great deal.

As Sarah began to dial, she noticed a red light on the phone base that was flashing the number *01*. A message from Jason, no doubt.

PLAY MESSAGES, read a small black button just below it.

She held the receiver to her ear and hit the small black button.

Thursday, two thirty-three.

"*Hi, it's Melissa,*" said a sweet, melodious voice. "*Am I going to see you later?*"

It could have been anyone. It could have been anyone, Sarah thought, trying to ignore that her free-floating feeling had abruptly stopped, as if someone snapped a light from on to off, as if someone had flipped a valve from hot to cold. Melissa could be a backup singer at the club or the girl at the dry cleaner's calling to say Jason's shirts were ready or a fat old lady who cooked dinner for him on Thursday nights.

She could be anyone. But anyone would probably not have said, "*I love you,*" as Melissa did before hanging up.

Sarah's first instinct was to run back to the safety net of West Hope, to forget that she'd heard Melissa's voice.

She might have done that if it weren't for Burch.

What was Jason subjecting their son to? Had another woman taken over already? Had another woman—Melissa or Margie or Maxine, it didn't matter—already assumed the position of taking Sarah's place as Jason's lover, as Burch's mom?

If Sarah were like Lily, she might march over to the studio, blast open the door, and demand answers. If she were like Jo, she might be able to appear stoic and unaffected, keeping her pain in perspective. If she were like Elaine, she would simply close the drapes and feel as if she deserved it.

But Sarah was Sarah, so she sat down on the sofa, her hands slightly trembling, her heart slowly breaking, each injustice she'd endured in all of her years rising to meet her once again. It was the kind of pain she'd never dared to share: not with her friends, nor with, most of all, Jason. If they knew she was hurting she would have to let them in, into her world, into her shame.

Her aching, after all, had little to do with Jason. Nor was it about Burch. It was about her.

Half-breed, ha-ha. White Indian girl.

She sank her teeth into her lower lip to stop it from quivering.

When the phone rang nearly an hour later, Sarah was still sitting, hands folded, the red petal dress still bundled at her feet. Her eyes jerked toward the phone, though her head did not move. After three rings, voice mail kicked on. Her body braced itself.

"Hey, Mom," a voice, Burch's, said. "Where the heck are you?"

She bolted from the couch, grabbed the receiver. "Burch? Hi, honey, I was just about to come to the studio." She didn't say she was late because she'd been distracted by shopping, or lie and say she'd been tied up in traffic. She didn't say she'd been sitting there sulking.

"Wait for us there. The coolest thing happened. Dad got us tickets to see *Wicked.*"

"Wicked what?" She pressed her fingers against the back of her neck. At some point in the last hour she'd developed a headache, a dull, I-hate-my-life kind of headache.

"It's only the coolest thing on Broadway," Burch said, with almost giddy excitement that she hadn't heard in a long time. "*Nobody* can get tickets for something like six months. But Dad got them for tonight. For four. He's a genius, Mom."

She might have responded about his comment on genius, but she was trying to process that Jason had tickets for four. He must be including one of Burch's new friends.

"Is that boy going?" she asked. "Your new friend Glen?"

Her son paused for a moment, then he nervous-laughed. "No, Mom, it's not Glen. I've met this girl. . . ."

"You have a girlfriend?" *So soon?* she thought. *So young?* She thought about Andrew. And Cassie. And all that.

"She's beautiful, Mom," Burch said over her thoughts. "She has big blue eyes, and long black hair just like you. Except she's not a Cherokee. Her name is Melissa."

30

Melissa was a quiet, shy girl with pale eyes and pale freckles who might be pretty one day but was now far from the "beautiful" that Burch had conveyed. She was, however, fourteen, older than Burch, and she dressed like a premature slut.

"Can't you do something to stop them?" Sarah whispered to Jason during intermission as they walked out to the lobby, leaving the two kids snuggled in their seats.

He laughed. "Why would I do that? Our son is in love."

"He's not in love, Jason. He's mesmerized by her breasts. Burch is too young to be mesmerized by breasts."

It had been an awkward evening so far—well, awkward for Sarah, who didn't keep her attention on the stage but on her son, who was rapidly maturing between the first and second acts in the Gershwin Theatre.

"Say something," Sarah said, leaning against a wall, trying to dodge the crowd.

"What?" Jason asked, his smile as enchanting as the night they'd first met, his body as long and lean as hers, the same as when they'd met. "You'll only accuse me of being a man."

She folded her arms. "It's a conspiracy."

He stepped closer to her. He bundled her hair into his hands, then leaned down and murmured in her ear. "You are a good mother. You are a good woman too. You know enough to know he's growing up, that's all."

Sarah closed her eyes. "I thought Melissa was in love with you."

Jason laughed again. "What?"

"Well, not *that* Melissa. I heard a phone message. She said, 'Am I going to see you later?' then added, 'I love you.' I thought it was a message for you."

His smile became a smirk. "Didn't she sound a little young?"

"Give me a break. I'm not used to women calling my son."

"Women?" Jason asked. "Oh, you are so very funny." He scrunched her hair again, then rubbed the back of her aching neck. "Tell me, dear Sarah, were you jealous?"

She could have said no, but it would not have been true. "Yes," she replied. "I was very jealous. I sat on the sofa and felt very sad." She didn't tell him about Irene's visit earlier that day to Lily's, or Sarah's subsequent reminder that we can never know another, that trust can often be misplaced. She didn't tell him she was sad because she hated when life changed.

He kissed her cheek, once, then twice.

And suddenly, standing there in the airless, buzzing lobby of the George Gershwin Theatre, with hundreds of patrons jockeying all around them, Sarah asked, "Do you remember Laura Carrington?"

Jason shrugged. "The actress? Sure."

Sarah touched his face. "Did you ever realize that Laura Carrington has a diamond-shaped birthmark on her left cheek?"

With a small scowl, Jason stared at Sarah, then his gaze moved back toward the inside of the theater, where they'd left their son. "Burch has one too."

Sarah nodded. "I've read that birthmarks are commonly identical in a parent, a grandparent, some kind of relative."

Jason turned his full body toward Sarah. "What are you saying?"

She bit her lower lip. "Sutter Jones told me Laura Carrington is my mother." She had said it out loud now, she had made it real beyond the edges of her conscience, the borders of her soul.

"You've got to be shitting me."

She assured him that no, she was not shitting him.

"Jesus," he said, and Sarah nodded in return. His eyes wandered around the crowd as if expecting something, someone to approach. "Did this guy ask for money?"

Sarah blinked. "What?"

"This guy, the lawyer. Did he ask you for money?"

She laughed. Unlike her, Jason was streetwise. She'd kept her life so closed from the rest of the world that she never had to worry about con men and their scams. "No, he didn't ask for money. What's wrong? You don't think I'm classy enough to be Laura Carrington's daughter?" She tried to sound as if she was teasing, but a small part of her hoped for assurance that, yes, she was classy enough to be the famous woman's child.

Jason pulled his eyes back to her. "I don't believe we're having this conversation here."

Well, neither did she.

"But do you believe this guy?"

"I had my doubts. Until I thought about the birthmark." She did not elaborate on how her parents met, what had happened then and now. She did not tell him about the education fund that Laura had established.

And then the lights flicked on and off, and Sarah squeezed Jason's hand and was glad to go back to her seat, where it was dark enough to mask the sorrow of her tears.

Imagine her, Jo Lyons, being foolish enough to let down her guard after all that she'd been through with men.

She'd retreated to the guest room after Irene left. She'd skipped dinner and had tried to ignore that Lily and Elaine tiptoed around the apartment long into the evening, as if the slightest noise might shatter Jo.

She was beyond shattering, she thought the next morning, as she sat by the window in the back of a taxi, with Lily next to her and Elaine next to Lily. She was beyond shattering because there had been far too much of that in her life. She would hold her head high, mourn in private, not complain in public. The way many women made it through many days, she supposed.

This day, Friday, Jo would make it "through" by doing as Lily and Elaine instructed. They had scheduled appointments with caterers who were the "chichiest of the chic" (Lily's term), hoping they might be able to steal some ideas, or at least adapt some. Lily had decided to pose as a bride, with Jo and Elaine acting as her attendants. They'd explain they were still in the decision-making process of the wedding plans, the whos, the whats, the wheres.

They'd made four appointments, a plot of Lily's no doubt to keep Jo occupied, to add a layer of Teflon merriment to soothe the exposed nerves.

Tomorrow they would ride to the airport in the limo Lily had managed to rent for their return trip to West Hope. They would pick up Elaine's father and his companion, Mrs. Tuttle, who were flying back from Miami, where they'd disembarked. Who wouldn't have fun when enveloped by happy vacationers clad in flowered shirts and sandals and sporting island tans?

Jo stared out at the traffic and high-rise buildings and the people-in-a-hurry. She thought about the cruise that she'd taken once. She'd negotiated a large amount of airtime on a Boston radio station on behalf of a client who was testing a new product. She hadn't known that the station was running a promotion for ad agencies and public-relations firms, awarding Caribbean cruises based on airtime advertising dollars spent. Jo had qualified for two trips but had gone only once, and then only because her assistant said she needed to relax, that maybe she'd meet a man. She hadn't accomplished either.

She didn't know if Andrew had ever gone on a cruise. Could he have gone with Irene?

Clenching her fist, she pushed her knuckles against her teeth.

Andrew.

Irene.

Had they really been lovers?

They had known each other for years.

Had their relationship soured?

Had someone found out?

Was that why he'd left New York City for West Hope?

Had it cost him his career—or had he relinquished it for her?

She closed her eyes and tried to force away the image of Andrew and Irene naked, kissing—oh, God—having sex, writhing and moaning and loving each other, his breath and his touch and his everything blending with Irene's the way it had blended with hers.

If she weren't in the cab, she would have cried out then.

Instead, Jo opened her eyes to the urban chaos outside the window, grateful she'd be home in thirty-six hours.

"Right here is fine," Lily directed the cab driver, and he steered over to the curb.

Jo got out without speaking, stood on the sidewalk, looked at the storefront whose sign read, ROB BARRETT CATERING.

Lily said with a giggle, "He'd better not think he's going to *Rob* us," and Elaine let out a laugh and Jo followed them in, because it was her job and she was a woman and was beyond shattering.

31

Foot-square slabs of ice, lit from the bottom, presenting chilled shrimp and cracked crab; summertime trays laden with thin, trimmed wheatgrass that served as a meadowlike bed for bright baby carrots and slices of sun-yellow squash; clear plastic trays embedded with tiny white lights, blanketed with a layer of aqua-colored sea glass, atop which sat delicate sushi selections.

"Fabuloso," Lily (who'd given her name as Louise Corning of Greenwich and Hamilton—Bermuda, of course) exclaimed. The too-black-haired, too-tattooed, black-leather-panted Rob Barrett had no idea that the hors d'oeuvre suggestions would end up in similar presentations on the menu of Second Chances.

They sat in a Spartan lounge where everything had been decorated in either pewter or black, from the low cocktail table to the abstract art on the wall. The chairs were made of some new high-grade plastic that looked futuristic but was uncomfortable. Rob Barrett offered champagne, but Lily twittered and said good heavens, it was only ten A.M. They settled on tea with spiced orange slices.

Jo wanted to ask the costs of the simple hors d'oeuvres, but Lily had warned her against talking money. "When you're dealing with Rob Barrett, it simply isn't done," she'd said in the ride over in the cab. Of course, Lily would know.

He asked what their thoughts were on Dover sole versus veal. "Tenderloins," he added, "with a light cranberry and walnut sauce."

If he hadn't said "cranberries," Jo wouldn't have been reminded of the berries Sarah arranged on the breakfast plates the morning after the Benson wedding, the morning after Jo and Andrew had finally made love. She sipped her tea, toyed with the orange slice.

"Well, my mother is a vegetarian," Lily said, perhaps referring to Sarah, perhaps meaning to give Elaine and Jo a reason to chuckle—as if they needed one beyond the entertainment of Rob Barrett, whose animated presence unwittingly was helping to lift Jo's mood.

"Mushroom phyllos!" Rob said. "But nothing like the phyllos you're used to seeing. Let me see if we have some in the kitchen." He pranced from the room.

"This is going well," Elaine whispered, but Lily just smiled. "But didn't you say he did your second wedding, Lily? When he was with a different caterer, before he was on his own?"

"I did. He did. But that was eons ago and my mother-in-law was the one who worked with him, not me."

It was hard to envision Lily in anyone's backseat, which might have been part of why the marriage did not work.

"Well, it doesn't look as if he remembers you, Lily," Elaine continued. "That doesn't upset you?"

Lily half-smiled. "Not at all," she said, straightening the hem of her Nina Ricci skirt. "Everything is going according to plan."

Jo had no idea what she meant. Then Rob returned with a small tray covered with delicate layers of phyllo dough and three tiny hors d'oeuvres resting on top.

"Try one," he said with a confident grin.

The room was hushed as Lily tasted. Her eyes fluttered to Rob, then she tasted again. "Hmm," she said, turning to Jo, turning to Elaine. "You know, girls, this is reminiscent of something we just had at the Bensons' affair."

Jo nearly gulped her tea.

"Girls?" Lily asked. "What do you think?"

Rob Barrett said nothing; he passed the tray to Jo, then Elaine.

"Well," Elaine said. "I don't think the phyllos at the Benson wedding were nearly as clever." She then turned to Jo and offered a wink, and suddenly Jo knew.

There it was, she thought. Lily's hidden purpose for this charade. She shifted on her chair and wondered what was coming next.

"So," Rob said smoothly, his voice lowering from its sales pitch to a curious grovel, "you were at the Benson wedding?"

"Why, yes," Lily replied. "You didn't do that one, did you?"

Rob set down the tray, cleared his throat. "Oh, my, no. It was New Year's, after all. We'd been booked for two years." He slipped his hands into the pockets of his leather pants. "We were asked, of course. But we had to decline."

And then Lily sighed sweetly and began shaking her head, and now Jo was certain, quite certain, that this whole scene had been planned by Lily, the ultimate scheming diva.

"It's such a shame about what happened," Lily said quietly.

"Oh?" Rob asked. "I heard the event was quite delicious."

"Oh, the wedding definitely was spectacular. But didn't you hear? What happened in Rio? What John Benson did to poor Irene?"

Jason insisted on going with Sarah. He suggested they call Sutter's office first; she refused. She wasn't sure that, once the moment arrived, she'd be able to enter, she'd be able to do this. At least this way Sutter wouldn't know that she was coming; at least this way she could change her mind and not feel foolish.

The cab let them off on the corner of Madison Avenue and East 67th. Sarah wanted to walk from there.

She would have liked to hold Jason's hand as they

ambled past a few boutique shops, a few discreet doorways, luxury apartments, or office suites. She wondered how long it had been since she and Jason had held hands, since she'd felt his long fingers tangled through hers. She would have liked to feel that strength now but felt too awkward to ask.

"Are you angry with her?" Jason asked, suddenly.

Sarah blinked. "Angry?"

"Well, haven't you wondered what it would have been like to be raised by her—by Laura Carrington? Growing up in Hollywood would have been a whole lot different than life on the reservation. If it were me, I think I'd be pissed."

Jason was a wonderful man who felt honesty was important, though sometimes he didn't understand tact. Or the Cherokee.

"The Rule of Acceptance," Sarah said. "To all things there is a time, a place, a purpose."

He laughed. "It's always that easy for you, isn't it? You retreat to your ancestors to explain everything."

It felt like a barb, a soft punch to her heart. Jason sounded as if Sarah thought life was blasé—hers, his, everyone's. She stopped walking; he did too. "I had a wonderful, full life with my father and Glisi," she told him. "Besides, who knows what I would have had with Laura Carrington? She might have been run out of Hollywood if she'd gone public about me. I might have been raised in a trailer outside of Yuma or some other remote place." She was attempting to make a joke, attempting to shift the discomfort she'd felt at his observation.

Jason merely shrugged.

As they began walking again, Sarah realized that if this situation had been his, if Laura had been his mother, he, indeed, would have been pissed. She wondered if something was wrong with her that she didn't feel that way too.

"Here it is," she said, stopping in front of a heavy oak outside door with a smoked-glass window on which was stenciled JONES AND ARCHAMBAULT, ATTORNEYS AT LAW. She drew in a long breath. Her knees grew weak.

Jason took her hand. He squeezed it and he smiled. "You don't have to do this, you know."

It was a small, loving gesture, and it helped buoy her strength. "Yes," she said. "Yes, I really do need to do this. I'd like to know what it is I've accepted."

"I'm sorry, but he's still tied up on the West Coast," a young man who introduced himself as Phillip Archambault said. "Maybe I can help, though. I'm familiar with...with the reasons Mr. Jones contacted you."

Sutter Jones's partner was not at all like him. For one thing he did not look even forty, and his light hair and green eyes indicated that he, unlike Sutter, did not have a drop of Indian blood, Cherokee or otherwise. He led them through the small reception area and into a dark-wood-lined conference room, which had a mural of a foxhunt through a thick green forest. "We've only recently moved our offices here from California," Archambault said. "We haven't had time to redecorate yet." He smiled and indicated they should sit down in the wine-colored leather chairs that surrounded a long, dark table.

"Do you know her?" Sarah asked once they were seated. "Do you know Laura Carrington?"

"Yes. Very well. My wife is an actress. Laura helped her get her start."

Sarah didn't ask who his wife was, though the name Archambault was not familiar.

"Laura is a very nice woman," the young man continued. "She's very kind. Generous."

Sarah nodded. "So I've heard."

From the corner of her eye she saw Jason shift on the chair. "What does she want?" Jason asked unexpectedly. "Does she want money or something?"

A few months ago, when the women first decided to open Second Chances, Jason had appeared at the shop one day. While Sarah was assembling her drawing table, Lily performed the honors of showing him around, describing the anticipated showroom renovations, being her delightful, enthusiastic self. When they returned to the area that would be Sarah's studio, he had laughed. "You don't really expect that the four of you have what it takes to run a business." It hadn't been as much a question as it had been a statement.

Sarah was as embarrassed now as she was back then.

She stopped herself from speaking up when she saw that Phillip smiled.

"From what I understand," the young lawyer said, "Laura only wants to meet her daughter. But I think Mr. Jones has already explained that."

"Yes," Sarah said, a little too loudly, as if her voice could smother Jason's insult. "And I've decided to meet her." She hadn't, of course, decided any such thing, not until that moment, not until right then. Besides, she reasoned, what if the woman did need money? If she were truly Sarah's mother...

"I think you'll be pleased," Phillip said, directing his comment to Sarah, not to Jason. "But I think it would be best if Sutter goes with you."

Jason sat up straight. "She needs an attorney to meet her mother?"

Phillip put his elbows on the long table and leaned forward. "It might make things more comfortable for Laura, and for you too, Sarah."

Jason narrowed his eyes. "I'm going too."

She shot him a stupefied look.

"Well," Jason said with a cavalier smirk, "if she doesn't want your money, maybe we can get some of hers. Studio time is getting more and more expensive. Maybe she'd like to become a patron of the arts. *My* arts." He slid one of his cards across the table toward the attorney. Sarah hadn't seen him take it out of his pocket.

The tall grandfather clock in the corner ticked off awkward seconds. Sarah thought she'd never been so mortified, not in front of Lily, not in front of anyone.

Then Phillip stood up. "Whatever you decide," he said, "just let us know. Sutter should be back in town over the weekend."

She found her legs; she found her voice. "Actually," she said, "I've got to get back to West Hope. I have three weddings to plan." She did not know what that had to do with anything, except that it seemed like a good exit line, a neutral way to pick up her embarrassment and get out of there.

"Get me a cab to Penn Station," she said once she and Jason were outside on Madison.

"Sarah, don't be angry."

"I'm not angry. I'm repulsed by your behavior. How could you do that, Jason? How could you turn this into something about money?" It was rearing its ugly, green, crinkled head again—that invisible battle line in their relationship: money, the quest for it, and the fact that it meant so much more to Jason than it did to Sarah. He wanted the trappings; she merely wanted the earth. As with the Rule of Acceptance, Jason thought her philosophy was foolish.

"I'm only trying to protect you," he insisted. "I don't want you to get hurt."

The sad part was, she knew it was true—his truth, anyway. "It also sounded as if you're hoping something might be in it for you. God, Jason, how could you?"

He shook his head. "I was trying to see if that lawyer would react. I don't want this woman to hurt you. I don't want her to hurt Burch."

She wondered if she could believe him and why, after all these years, she needed to wonder. She turned her eyes from him. "Did it sound as if she's trying to hurt anyone? I didn't tell you yet, but the woman established a scholarship fund for Indian kids. Even Sutter's partner mentioned she is generous. She helped his wife break into acting. She hardly sounds self-centered or needy."

His hand grasped her arm. "You're taking their word for it, Sarah. You don't even know them. You don't even know if one iota of the things they've said is true."

She shook off his touch and looked across Madison, because to look at Jason would only fuel more anger. "I know that my son has a birthmark just like Laura Carrington's. How does that play into your theory of a scam?"

To that, he said nothing.

"Besides," she added, "Sutter Jones is Cherokee. He knew me. He knew my buffalo-grass doll." She stepped off the curb and hailed her own cab, tears threatening to spill.

"Sarah, please—"

She opened the cab door. "I'll pick up my things the next time I'm in town. But there's a bag in the living room with a red dress inside. Please mail it to me, if you can afford the postage, what with the increase in studio time and all." Then she closed the taxi door and was too upset to look back.

32

"That will teach Irene Benson to mess with one of us," Lily said after they'd left their fourth appointment of the day, after she'd once again spread the word that Irene-the-Queen had officially been dumped.

Jo had said little, stuck as she was somewhere between being appalled at Lily's brazenness and thinking that she was a genius. Each of the caterers had been stunned at the news; each had displayed the same look of *wow* on his face (in one case, *her* face). Each most assuredly maintained calm and dignity until the women departed the premises, then probably pounced on their BlackBerries and alerted their associates, their friends, their media contacts. Within minutes the word would have spread from New York to L.A.

Ha-ha, Lily said was the word of the day, and Jo

could not say she'd feel sorry for Andrew if he became caught in the backlash.

"I think we should eat in tonight," Lily announced as Jo and Elaine followed her back into the apartment late in the afternoon. "We don't want to stir up any more commotion. We'll just let people think we've disappeared back to Bermuda or some other place." She flopped on the sofa and kicked off her shoes. "I'm exhausted."

Elaine said, "Me too," and sat down beside her. Jo remained standing, looking at the conspirators.

"Thank you," she said. "Thanks for being such good, loyal friends." Lily's antics and Elaine's backup had not removed the hurt Irene (or was it Andrew?) had caused, but they certainly had salved a great deal of the sting.

Lily patted the space on the sofa between Elaine and her, and Jo sat down. "We will always stick together," Lily said, taking Jo's left hand, Elaine taking her right. "I'm not sure Sarah would have approved of the way we handled things today, but she won't be able to argue with the well-deserved results."

Jo nodded, then said, "Speaking of Sarah, I wonder how she's doing. I wonder if she decided to meet her mother."

The three women went silent, then Lily said, "Well, if she needs our help, we'll be there for her too."

"The Four Musketeers," Elaine said, and they all laughed, then launched into a dialogue about picking Elaine's father (and Mrs. Tuttle) up the next day and wasn't it nice that the future can hold surprises and love at any age.

Barry Franklin was a small, quiet man whose computer-chip mind sorted and calculated with speed and precision that defied nature, though it might have been assisted by the double espressos he seemed to enjoy drinking.

Andrew had spent the past few days (and late nights) trying to keep up with Barry, reviewing page after page of John's business dealings, how they were structured, what were their missions, where they stood now. Terms like *leadership models* and *identifying benchmarks* and *sustained success* swirled in Andrew's mind when he crawled into bed long past midnight on Friday, worn out from the new responsibilities he seemed to have inherited but did not want.

He and Irene, however, had reached a compromise. Andrew would keep John's empire from being taken over until a proper consultant could be hired to prepare the package that would (hopefully) entice a buyer, or until John reclaimed his senses and returned to New York.

Andrew didn't care which of those events came first, though it would be nice if one happened soon.

The Benson Group had grown larger than Andrew knew. In addition to *Buzz*—the magazine in which John now had controlling interest—there were five radio stations sprinkled from Seattle to Charlotte; seven TV stations, mostly in the Midwest; and eleven daily newspapers, though three were in the process of being sold.

As compensation for his efforts, Andrew would receive John's stock in *Buzz* and his choice of a radio or TV station, though none was situated in West Hope. It was a very generous payment that made the hours with Barry more endurable. A financial future that might actually be secure grew more appealing each time Andrew thought about Jo.

Still, as he turned off the light over the headboard of the guest room's king-size bed, Andrew couldn't shake the feeling this was too good to be anything remotely like true.

Controlling interest in *Buzz* magazine.

A radio or TV station of his choice.

Just for being nice to Irene and seeing to it that she didn't lose everything her errant husband had amassed?

When Andrew was young, his mother often told him the story of a little boy named Gregory who wanted a bicycle very badly. Richard, the school bully, said he'd give him one. All Gregory had to do was run across the playground in his underwear.

"What would you do," his mother asked each time she told the story, "if you were Gregory and you wanted the bicycle?"

Irene was offering Andrew a big bicycle now, one that was bright and shiny and had bells and whistles that he alone could not afford.

Of course, he still could tell Irene, "Sorry, I'm going home." He could be content with what he had. Hell, he had been before this dropped into his lap.

But each evening when Irene stopped into John's study to say good night and thank you to Andrew and Barry; each morning when she appeared with her brave and still beautiful face, announcing the plans she'd made that day for herself and Cassie; each day that passed without another message from John, Andrew's intent to go home faded a little.

Irene, after all, was trying so hard to hold herself together.

Irene was trying so hard to carry on.

His role had nothing to do with a shiny bicycle. Did it?

He stared up at the dark ceiling and wondered if having lunch with Jo might help him put his own life back in order. He could not let his allegiance to Irene derail the love he felt with Jo. Tomorrow he would ask Irene for the card he'd given her with Lily's address and phone number so she could write a thank-you note for the nice flowers that she didn't like. Tomorrow he would call Jo and she would cheer him up. He closed his eyes and hoped the women hadn't left the city yet.

33

The Southfield Mountain wedding for the couple from Pittsfield and Julie and Helen's wedding-in-a-wheelchair were turning out to be easier to plan than Rhonda Blair's private Valentine's Day nuptials, especially after the famous bride had telephoned on Thursday afternoon and told Jo's mother she decided to invite two hundred guests after all.

"And she wants the guests in red," Marion told Sarah on Saturday morning when Sarah went to work, while the others were still in New York. "Dresses, tuxedoes, in red or white. She wants it to be as talked about as Truman Capote's famous black-and-white ball, only in red and white."

Even with her reclusive life, Sarah knew that Capote's black-and-white ball had been held in the sixties, probably around the time Rhonda Blair had been searching for husband number one. And while the late author's guest list had been comprised of society's finest, or presumed to be finest, the soap opera's attendees would no doubt be Hollywood. Flash, trash, glitz, tits, bling, bling, bling. The world over which Sarah's birth mother apparently once reigned.

After sharing the distressing news, Marion offered to stay and answer the phone—it rang so frequently these days.

Sarah slumped onto the stool at her drawing table, trying to focus on the work at hand and not on her life. She took a big gulp of herb tea; she tossed back her hair. She'd let it flow down her back today, not wanting to restrict it in a silver clip, not wanting to expose anything but her Cherokee blood, her Native American pride.

She had no idea why. Perhaps it was a way of tuning out the white side of her heritage; perhaps it was to serve as a reminder that there was a part of her that Jason would never reach, that he could never know.

Perhaps she was angry that Jason might be right, that Laura Carrington wanted to know Sarah for self-serving reasons. Or maybe she was simply hoping that Sutter Jones would call.

She stared at the drawings scattered on the table. The train ride back to West Hope from the city had been too long yesterday, too long and too lonely, with too much time to mull over what had happened, to wonder whether this incident with Jason would become another chasm in the growing void between them, to ponder when she'd meet the woman who claimed to be her mother.

The good-looking man-boy in the café car hadn't been on duty, or Sarah might have passed the time feeling more confident about herself, less like an insignificant lump of clay.

To all things there is a time, a place, a purpose.

She had stared out the window of the train at the gray strip of the Hudson and tried to understand what her purpose had become, now that she hardly was a lover, now that she hardly was a mother. She watched the slow-moving waters and thought about the Native Americans who'd once inhabited the area—the Mohawks, the Mohicans, the Iroquois—distant ancestors by the color of their skin, men and women who'd paddled their canoes on the quiet river, who'd known the often grim art of survival, at least for a while. They would not have been comfortable with flash and trash and bling.

Taking another drink, Sarah picked up a drawing and pretended to study it. It pictured her original concepts in red, black, and gold, the grand idea for Rhonda Blair. The look would no longer work. She'd need to transform it from broodingly seductive to jaunty, Hallmark-y, happy, a mood fit for two hundred red-and-white-clad guests. Exactly the mood that she did not feel.

"Andrea and Dave are here," Marion said from the doorway to the showroom.

"Who?" Sarah asked.

"The couple from Pittsfield. One of your Valentine's Day bride and grooms."

Bride and grooms. A happy, happy phrase for a happy, happy time.

It occurred to Sarah how strange it was that when some people were living out their happiest times, others were trudging through heartbroken, heartbreaking days, weeks, months. For every happy couple out there, Sarah wondered how many people were either unattached, unattached and miserable, or attached and wishing that they weren't.

She put down her red marker and said, "I'm on my way," because it was the time and place for Andrea and Dave, and their purpose, at least for now, seemed clear.

"You're married? Oh, my God!" Elaine shouted and Lily squealed and Jo smiled at the happy couple after they'd loaded their bags and themselves into the limo. The car was careening from the city and the traffic and the related noise.

Mrs. Tuttle—"Larry," for Laurene, now Mrs. Robert McNulty—sat in the backseat, holding out her hand, gently flaring her fingers so the women of Second Chances could see the shiny gold band that proved that she'd taken her second chance, and that Elaine's father had too.

In addition to their smiles, the bride and groom wore tans. Instead of finding the whole scene depressing, Jo felt oddly pleased at the reminder that love can work out anytime, at least for other people.

"I knew that ships' captains could marry couples," Lily said, "but I never knew anyone who actually did it."

Jo wondered if Lily was disappointed that Elaine's

father had married a woman his own age instead of falling for Lily. But Lily had Frank Forbes now, though their relationship sometimes seemed more like one of friends. She smiled at her arrogance to think she knew what constituted a loving relationship and what did not.

After patiently enduring the women-chatter about the ceremony (on the deck at sunset) and the flowers (white orchids from the islands) and the champagne (the cruise line provided a glass to every passenger who showed up to toast the "new" McNultys), Elaine's father said, "So how's the business going?"

"Men," Elaine retorted. "That's all they ever think about."

"Well, it's not everything," Lily added, then Elaine blushed and Mrs. McNulty blushed and Bob just laughed, and Jo thought maybe he and Lily would have been a decent couple after all.

"Business is great," Jo said. "Our only problem now is going to be how to know what we can handle and when we must say no."

Bob shook his head. "Never say no to good business. Say you'll check things out. Say you'll do your best. Never just say no."

Elaine sighed, then told them about the three Valentine's Day weddings. He laughed again and agreed they had a problem.

"I suppose I could lend a hand," he said, and winked at his bride. "If the new missus will allow it."

Larry, the new missus, smiled. Jo suspected they'd already discussed it.

"We want to start a new life together," Bob said.

"Our friends in Saratoga are either hers or mine. We want to have friends that we can say are ours." He took Mrs. McNulty's hand and said, "We've decided to leave Saratoga and move down to West Hope. I want to help out with the business. We've just learned that Larry's son is moving to Cincinnati with his company. Well, we sure as hell don't want to go to Cincinnati. But we do want family around. And, Elaine, honey, you and the grandkids sure are that." Then his smile drifted from Elaine to Jo to Lily. "And you girls too, of course."

"The Four Musketeers," Lily said. "Well, I'm not sure you're really ready to handle us, but you've surely got my vote."

Jo looked over at Elaine, but Elaine just sat there, smiling, tears running down her cheeks.

34

Sarah left the shop at seven o'clock. She hadn't eaten and she'd barely slept the night before; she needed food, she needed rest. After what seemed like too long a ride home, she pulled into her driveway, got out of her truck, and walked toward her front door, the weight of loneliness heavy on her footsteps. And then, at the front door, on the front steps, she saw a brown box, an overnight-delivery package, from *Donaldson, NYC.*

Hope rose. Had Jason sent a gift? A make-up present wrapped with love?

Then she remembered the red dress for Rhonda Blair.

With a deflated sigh, Sarah picked up the box, opened the door, and went inside. Elton was there, having opted to stay indoors when she'd left in the morning, apparently having had his recent fill of being spoiled by the neighbors. She fed the dog, then herself, then sat on the floor, where she was always the most comfortable. "Indian style," Lily had said when they were back in college, as she'd pointed out Sarah's penchant for curling her long legs around and tucking them under her butt.

She stared at the phone and considered that if she couldn't have a family one way, maybe she should try another. But first she should call Aunt Mae and ask point-blank if she'd known Laura Carrington and whether or not she'd ever heard that the woman was Sarah's mother.

Without hesitation, Sarah picked up the phone and dialed information in California; an operator gave her a phone number for the herb shop. Sarah checked her watch: it was only four-fifteen on the West Coast. Surely the shop would still be open.

She held her breath when a woman answered the phone.

"Mae?" Sarah asked, though the voice sounded neither old nor familiar.

"This is Belinda, Mae's daughter-in-law," a voice retorted. "Who is this?"

If Belinda really was Mae's daughter-in-law, that meant she was married to Douglas, Sarah's unfortunate cousin. Sarah considered mentioning that Douglas had spied on Sarah more than once when she was young—eleven or twelve—when she was swimming naked in the lake, washing her long hair in the mountain water. She considered telling the woman that Douglas was a pervert. Instead, she said, "I'm an old friend of Mae's. Actually, my Glisi was a friend of Mae's."

"Your what?" Belinda asked.

If the woman did not know the word *Glisi*, she must not be a Cherokee. Which probably meant Douglas had married a white woman. She wondered if they had any white Indian children and if he made fun of them the way he'd made fun of her.

Then she decided that none of it mattered. "Glisi was my grandmother," she said. "Please, could I speak to Mae?"

"Mae's dead," the woman said, so matter-of-factly that Sarah had no time to prepare, no time to react. "She's been dead five years. You want to speak to Douglas?"

Sarah said, no, she did not want to speak with him. She hung up the phone and stared at the receiver. Then she picked it up once again, this time dialing the cell number of Sutter Jones. When his voice mail kicked in, Sarah said, "Hey, this is Sarah Duncan. Whatever happened to you, anyway?"

Then she pulled herself up from the floor, went to the box where she had dropped it, and opened one brown-paper–wrapped end. She slid out the bag and removed the red dress. Now free from its confines, the red rose petals fluttered a soft, elegant dance. An envelope fell out: It was addressed to her. She recognized Jason's handwriting.

She picked up the envelope, considered throwing it out. Then there was a knock on her front door.

"You're here," she said to Sutter, who stood on her front steps. He looked younger when he wasn't in a business suit, more like a Cherokee in jeans and a North Face parka. "Mae's dead," she said to him.

"I know," he said.

She studied him a moment, looking into his black eyes, wondering how it was that she saw so much truth there when she still didn't always get that sense from Jason after so many years. It was the blood, she supposed, the connected link of DNA.

"May I come in?" he asked.

She stepped aside. "Of course. I'm sorry. Of course, come in." Closing the door behind him, she heard him speak to Elton.

"*Unalii,*" he said, and she knew that he was petting Elton, that he was telling him he was a friend. Sarah closed her eyes; tears quickly followed.

"*Unalii,*" she whispered.

He turned to her and held her shoulders. "Sarah," he said, "you've decided to meet your mother?"

"Yes, but not yet. Not now. First, I want to hear your voice. I want to sit and have you tell me stories of our childhood, of things I might have been too young to remember, of people like my aunt Mae and your mother, Little Tree, and what became of so many others. I want you to tell me about the reservation. Then I will meet my mother."

Since the first day that she'd seen him, the first day that she'd known who he was and why he'd come, those thoughts had taken root deep inside her heart. And now, standing there in her log cabin, with her tribal drums and woven blankets and furniture made of the forest's twigs, and the rented videos of Laura's films still strewn around the room, Sarah at last felt safe to share the things she felt.

Sutter placed his hand under her chin; she opened her eyes and looked into his again. Then he drew her close, taking her into his warmth, and he stroked her long, free-flowing hair, and he kissed the top of her head and said if she'd make tea that he would light a fire.

35

They sat at the long table in the Benson dining room eating veal marsala, wild rice, and steamed asparagus, a far cry from the pizza and hot dogs and beans that had become a staple in Andrew and Cassie's cottage. Sometimes he thought the change was nice, like wearing silk socks instead of cotton sport ones, and fine Italian leather boots instead of sneakers.

It was Saturday night, however, and they'd been at the Bensons' for a week. He'd tried calling Jo that morning, but there was no answer at Lily's apartment. The not knowing of whether or not the women had left, of whether or not they still were in the city or if they'd gone back to West Hope, had left Andrew with a hollow feeling all day while he and Barry worked, while he made sure Irene's life would be all right while his might be falling, piece by piece, apart. He hated that he hadn't made the time to call Jo at least once. He hated that he was such a man that he had easily compartmentalized his days and had not left room for her.

"Cassie and I went by Miss Claridge's this morning," Irene said now, smiling across the table at Andrew's daughter, who, he suddenly realized, looked more grown-up than she had a week ago. Was that a new shirt she wore tonight? A new pink sweater too? And where were the earrings from Eddie what's-his-name?

"Who's Miss Claridge?" Andrew asked.

Cassie rolled her eyes. "The school, Dad."

"The school?" He plunked his fork into his veal. "What school?"

"The school where Cassie and I have been thinking she might like to go." Irene made the announcement as if a deal were done, as if she were his wife and Cassie's mother and she was calling some shots he'd not known were even in the works.

"She goes to school in West Hope," Andrew said.

"The MacKenzie girls go to Miss Claridge's." That came from Cassie, who should have known better than to think he'd know who the hell she meant.

"Pop singers," Irene informed him. "They're twelve and fourteen and cute as buttons."

His eyes moved from Irene to Cassie then back to Irene. "Cassie goes to school in West Hope," he repeated. He stood up, put his napkin on the table.

"Oh, Andrew, do sit down," Irene said. "It's not as if I'm kidnapping your girl. But it appears as if, like it or not, you'll be here for some time. And Miss Claridge's offers a wonderful education. Far better than Cassie can get in that backwoods town where you've been living."

He moved to the tall windows, put his hands into the pockets of his wool-blend pleated pants, not jeans. On one hand, Irene was right. If they were going to stay in the city, Cassie should be in school. And he knew he couldn't do what needed doing if he was in West Hope, not here.

He turned around. "Cassie," he said, "is that what you want? To stay here in New York?"

Cassie picked up her water glass. She shrugged.

It wasn't right, he knew, to make this decision hers. She was only twelve, for God's sake; what was he thinking?

Irene stood up from the table and went to where he stood. "Andrew, dear," she said, "must we talk about this now?" Then she reached up and fixed his collar, the way he'd seen her fix John's collar on dozens, maybe hundreds, of occasions over the years, her trademark finishing touch, indicating that she had the last word in his appearance and that, finally, she approved.

And suddenly, from somewhere down inside his toes that were tucked in his silk socks, Andrew felt a chill start then travel through his bones. He grasped her hand, which had lingered on his throat, and said, "It's time for Cassie and me to leave, Irene." He would not be John's replacement, not in any way.

But Irene laughed. "Oh, you won't be going anywhere," she said, and walked back toward the table.

"Face it, Andrew, your future is right here." She sat down again, draped her napkin across her lap.

"No," he said. "I don't want John's shares in *Buzz* and I don't want a TV station. I'm sorry he did this to you, Irene, really I am. But I am going home. You're in good hands with Barry. He's perfectly capable of putting the Benson Group sales package together on his own."

She stared at the place setting in front of her. Then she said, "What is it, Andrew? Is it because of our past? Because we were lovers?"

Her words came out so quickly, so unexpectedly, Andrew almost didn't believe she'd said what she did, right there in front of Cassie. He almost didn't believe it, but then, this was Irene, a woman who controlled the things she had and got the things she wanted, hiding all the time behind manipulative smiles.

His stomach turned; the silk socks burned. Someday he might have needed to explain to Cassie about his teenage blunder with Irene—someday, but not here, not now, and never unless absolutely necessary.

"You and John meant so much to me," he said, trying to stand steady, choosing his words with care. "I'll always be grateful, but I'll no longer be indebted." Then he addressed his daughter. "Cassie, finish your dinner. Then you need to pack. We'll leave for West Hope in the morning."

He was afraid she'd come to him that night. He was afraid Irene would stand there in the doorway of the guest bedroom, wearing a sheer, very short chiffon robe and high-heeled slippers that matched. He was afraid her breasts would still look terrific, that they'd still be firm and high, still dark-nippled and inviting. The first breasts he'd ever seen.

He was afraid she would weaken his resolve through her touch, her scent, her needy state. He was afraid that somewhere in his gut, Andrew still was the young boy who once had needed her, had let himself be cradled by the love she had to give.

He was afraid, so Andrew fought off sleep that night, not daring to close his eyes until the sun began to rise, until the pink light crept around the edges of the penthouse blinds and sleep, at last, was there, and he, at last, gave in to it.

Not long after that, Andrew heard angry shouts.

"*Goddamn.*

"*Pissant.*

"*Bitches, bitches, bitches.*"

He shook the sleep from his eyes and from his brain and realized the words were coming from Irene, who indeed was standing in the doorway to the guest room, not in a sheer robe but in terry-cloth sweats, her cheeks aflame, her hair spiky with rage. She waved what looked like newspapers as if they were plump pom-poms and she a Dallas Cowboys cheerleader whose mouth had gone afoul.

BENSONS SPLIT.
JOHN ABANDONS IRENE FOR TAHITI.
WEDDING WAS A FARCE.

The headlines screamed from the pages, their decibels accelerated by the fattest, boldest type.

"Your friends, Andrew. Your friends did this!"

He sat up in the bed, pulled the blanket around his lower half, which was clad only in briefs. "Irene," he said, "calm down."

She stomped across the room and flung the papers on the bed. "No one knew," she said. "No one knew but the four of them. And you."

He stared at the newspapers. Could it be true? "And Senator Jervis," he quickly said, hoping that she'd read John's note to him, too. "And probably others, Irene. If you think about it."

"But no one else would throw it up in my face. No one else sashayed over here digging for more dirt. How much do you suppose they sold this story for?"

Andrew almost felt sorry for her as she stood in the bedroom looking very ordinary and not like Irene at all. "I can't believe they'd do this. Especially not Jo."

"JO!" Irene shouted again. "Get out of here!" she shrieked. "Go home to your small-town girl. But you'll be sorry someday, Andrew. You'll be sorry that you gave up all this—that you gave up ME—when you wake up one morning and wonder where your life went and why you wasted it on her."

With that, Irene spun around and stalked from the room.

Andrew sat there for a minute, trying to regain the bearings he truly might have lost this time, when Cassie poked her head around the corner. "Is she gone?" she asked.

"Hey, honey," he said, "come on in. You heard it all, I suppose."

"Jeez, who didn't, Dad? I think her voice echoed in New Jersey."

She plopped beside him and he tousled her hair. "We're on the East Side, Cassie. That's Long Island out there. New Jersey's on the other side."

She slumped against his side. "Dad," she asked, "can we go home now, please?"

Sometimes Andrew thought if his daughter ever left him he would crawl into a hole and let himself fade away. Thankfully, it did not seem that today would be that day. "You're okay about not going to Miss Claridge's?"

Cassie wrinkled her freckled nose. "You know I was just trying to make Irene happy, don't you? I mean, you didn't really think I wanted to go there, did you?"

Thank God she was as much his daughter as she had been Patty's. Still, there had been a moment...

Then Andrew smiled. "No, honey," he said. "I knew you wouldn't want to give up Eddie what's-his-name. Not even for the MacKenzie girls."

"Emmie and Mallory."

"The pop singers. Yes, I know that."

"They're not as cute as Eddie."

"No, I'm sure they're not."

"And I really want to do my spa day that Jo and everyone gave me for my birthday. I want to invite Marilla, okay?"

"Whatever you want, honey."

She paused, then said, "Dad? Is it true? Were you and Irene really lovers?"

"Not exactly, honey," he said, his heart moving up to his throat. "But I'll explain it to you if you want."

She thought for a moment. "No," she replied. "I think I'm too young to understand."

He laughed and she poked him. "Hey, can we go home now, Dad? Please?"

He nodded and said, "Wait here while I take a shower." He stepped out of bed, dragging the blanket with him.

"Hurry up," Cassie said. "I'll be waiting right here, reading the newspapers."

He stopped a second, wanting to turn and ask his daughter if she thought that Jo or Lily, Sarah or Elaine would have done that, if they would have sold Irene Benson's story for money or for fame. But then he shook his head, deciding it was one of those things he should not be analyzing with his daughter. He uttered a small chuckle, then headed for the shower, feeling lighter than he'd felt since they'd arrived last week.

36

Sutter Jones spent the night. They sat on the floor in front of the glowing fireplace and reminisced about their childhoods, about the mountains and the streams and the lake where they both swam at different times, in different years. Each of them, however, had believed it was the magic lake.

"When you look into the waters and witness your reflection, you will find harmony and balance and all things good in life." Sutter said the words that they both knew, one of the many legends they'd both been raised to understand.

"Do you suppose it's true?" Sarah dared to ask.

He shrugged and said, "Do you suppose it's not?"

Sutter talked about his mother and father, about his only brother, who'd abandoned the Cherokee. He talked about his son, who'd sought what he referred to as the truthful ways. Sarah talked about Glisi and her father and how much she missed them both. She told him about the summer triangle of stars and how she thought they were there. "With my mother," she added. "My mother, who I thought was gone."

Then Sutter took her hand and called her "Silent One," and Sarah's eyes filled with lost and lonely tears, for Silent One had been her name, her legacy in Cherokee.

"You know my name," she said.

"I always have."

"What is yours?" she asked. "I don't remember."

"Standing Wolf."

She liked the sound of his name, the serenity of the picture it made in her thoughts. "Does Laura know our names?" Sarah asked.

"Yes. Of course. She knows many things."

Sarah smiled. "Not everything, I hope." She took his hand in hers; she studied the smooth bronze skin, the strength within his long, sturdy fingers. With his other hand he stroked her silky, raven hair. Then he held her close and she held him too, and they watched the fire and talked about their Circle of Life and how nice it felt to have found each other.

At two A.M. Sarah made breakfast of eggs and day-old bread and fruit that she found in the freezer. Sutter laughed and suggested her culinary abilities were a unique art form. She swore she was a better cook before Burch went away.

Which moved the conversation from California back to her log cabin in the Berkshires, back to the present and all the things she would rather have ignored, but there was Sutter, willing to listen, and there was Sarah, at last able to talk.

With Elton tucked beside them, they fell asleep just before dawn, on the floor before the fireplace, covered by the woven blanket Little Tree had made.

Not many miles away, two or maybe three, Laura Carrington watched the sun rise over the mountains in her room at the Hilltop Bed and Breakfast. She waited and she hoped Sutter would come back soon with the news that Sarah had at last agreed to meet her.

She hoped it would happen soon, before her illness progressed further, before her time here was done.

37

Andrew couldn't wait to see Jo. He thought of little else as he drove up the New York Thruway, where his old Volvo crossed the Hudson in Newburgh, moved into Connecticut, then trekked north to West Hope. It was a route that he and Cassie had traveled often in those first months on their own, when Andrew had been unsure what to do in West Hope on weekends, so he'd packed up his young daughter and brought her back to the familiar: the museums, the theater, the park.

It wasn't until he realized Cassie loved riding horses that Andrew decided to trust the stable in the Berkshires to do Cassie no more harm than the one in Central Park.

Such had been the belated start of his attempt to fully commit to the country and the quiet country life.

He might have done it sooner if he'd thought he'd meet Jo.

Relaxing his grip on the steering wheel, Andrew looked over at Cassie, who dozed quietly beside him. His daughter was content, they were returning to their world.

He smiled with anticipation.

He'd been surprised when Jo and the others showed up at Irene's—he'd been disoriented, actually, seeing them at the penthouse, out of context. It had been like seeing a doctor or dentist in the produce department of the market: You know that you know them, but it takes a second, a minute, to put the person in the place where you know them, to meld one world into another, to get your awareness legs.

His legs, of all kinds, had been thrown off by Jo. It seemed clumsy when today's lover showed up at the door of yesterday's. He'd been *discomfited*, Lily might have said if she'd known the whole story.

He needed to forgive himself for not trying to call Jo sooner; he hoped that she'd forgive him too.

Soon he would know, because he was headed back to West Hope, and he had a plan. He'd make up for his discomfiture (if that was a word) with whatever it took. He'd let her know the Bensons were far behind him now, that his priority was in West Hope, that his priority was her.

He nodded his affirmation and kept his foot pressed on the accelerator, each passing mile bringing him closer to the wonderful woman he loved.

"We're going to cancel her," Lily announced at the emergency meeting she'd called late Sunday morning.

"Cancel who?" asked Elaine, who'd been the last one to get there, later even than Sarah, who'd arrived only moments before.

"Rhonda Blair."

Sarah looked at Lily, Jo, and Elaine, then at Elaine's father and the woman Sarah had been told married Bob McNulty on the cruise ship. Though Elaine still called her Mrs. Tuttle, Mrs. McNulty laughed and said it was all right. Change, Sarah mused, sometimes happens quickly. She thought of Sutter Jones, how disappointed he had seemed when she said she had to go to work. How he had made her promise to meet him that night for dinner at the Hilltop Bed and Breakfast, which served private meals on weekends to their special guests.

"Before you cancel Ms. Blair, remember that I'm here to help," Elaine's father said. "We can do it together."

Apparently Marion had told Jo who'd then telephoned Elaine and Lily to tell them Rhonda Blair now wanted a red-and-white wedding ball. Sarah didn't know why the drama couldn't have waited until Monday.

"And I already have the gown," Sarah said. She reached into the box she'd brought—the one Jason had sent. She pulled out the red rose-petallike dress.

"Wow," Elaine said.

"It's gorgeous," Jo added.

"It's going back," Lily announced.

"It can't," Sarah said. "I bought it from a vendor on the street."

Jo was sitting by the computer. "How much?" she asked.

"It doesn't matter," Lily interrupted. "We're going to cancel her." She bent down and lifted up a tote bag that Sarah hadn't noticed. She took out one, then two, then three newspapers. She displayed the headlines. "The Sunday editions say it all," she said, a smirky grin creeping across her face.

"Oh, no," Jo said.

"Hooray," Elaine commented.

But Sarah didn't get it. So what if the media learned the real story about Irene and John? What the heck did that have to do with Rhonda Blair? Or with Second Chances? It's not as if the headlines read "Irene Benson slept with Andrew Kennedy of Second Chances, the second-wedding planners."

Lily set down the papers. "For those of you here who feel you're in the dark, let me explain." She launched into a diatribe about the visit to Irene, then Irene's visit to them, then the vengeful plan Lily had concocted. "If you want to keep a secret," she said, "never tell a social-climbing caterer. Present company excepted."

Bob McNulty said he'd never climbed any ladder, social or otherwise.

"And I'll bet my next paycheck," Lily said, "if we have next paychecks, that Rhonda Blair had no intention of going through with a big wedding. I think Irene set it up to watch us fail, to have us go to great time and expense only to have Ms. Blair cancel at the last minute. They're friends, remember. Rhonda and Irene."

Sarah remembered that Rhonda had originally requested *lavish*, the same way Irene had done. "Maybe she's just getting back at you for those," she said, gesturing to the newspapers.

"Not possible. Jo's mother said Rhonda called Thursday afternoon. We didn't leak the story until Friday. Irene must have called Rhonda after she'd dropped her bomb at my apartment. She was so afraid we'd stolen her little Andrew. She found a way to keep him, then she thought of a way to screw us too. Hey, if we're out of business, he's out of a job, right?"

Elaine said Lily must be right because she knew how Irene thought. Lily was, after all, a lot like the woman.

"I beg your pardon?" Lily asked.

Elaine said she meant no offense, "It's just that with all that high-society stuff, Lily knows the dance. And at least she waited until we had the check."

With that, Sarah smiled.

Jo smiled.

Bob and Mrs. Tuttle smiled too.

Lily didn't seem to know if she should laugh or cry. "Well, think about it," she said. "Does anyone in this room honestly think the media never would have found out what happened between John and Irene?"

One after another, they all stopped smiling.

"There's one more thing," Lily said. "We probably can forget about being asked to plan any big-time weddings now. At least for a while, Irene will still have clout in the social register. So the question is, can

Second Chances survive with the likes of Allison and Dave? And Julie and Helen, if they were paying?"

"We'll have to try," Elaine said. "We've come too far. Besides, we have lots of other bookings."

"Not quite as many once we weed out the 'Irene-prompted' ones," Jo added.

"But we'll have our integrity," Lily said. Sarah wasn't quite sure how that was connected, but everyone else agreed, so she decided she simply was too anxious, with Sutter and Laura on her mind.

Andrew hadn't expected that Jo wouldn't be home in the middle of a Sunday afternoon. But her car wasn't in the driveway, and the house wore the blank face that said no one was home.

He stood at her back door, peered in the window, and wondered if he should just break in.

Then he decided he must be overtired for thinking such a thought. His lack of sleep last night, his Irene confrontation(s), the long drive home, had surely addled his brain.

As soon as he and Cassie had arrived back in West Hope, he'd turned her over to their neighbor, Mrs. Connor, who babysat for Cassie, though his daughter was too old for them to call it that. "I'm going to be tied up with some business maybe overnight," he'd said, using a *lame* (Cassie's word) excuse when he'd dropped her off.

"Monkey business," Cassie said, with a quick roll of her eyes, and Andrew said, "Behave." Cassie wanted to comment, he could tell she did, but she seemed to think better of it and simply said, "Good luck." He wondered if hearing Irene's tirade had made Cassie realize how fragile life and friends and friendships can be, even when you don't want them to turn out that way.

He'd quick-kissed her good-bye, thanked Mrs. Connor, and sped off toward Jo's, where he was now, standing on the damn back steps, not knowing what to do.

If he broke in, it might piss her off.

He thought about the snow day when he'd been here, when they'd spent hours in bed together, stranded under the covers, thanks be to Mother Nature.

He wondered what she would do if he broke in, then sneaked up to her bedroom and waited for her there.

Surely the idea was a brilliant one. How could she be pissed at that?

With a huge, exultant smile, Andrew skipped down the stairs, then moved around the house to the porch on the other side.

A window was unlocked, though he might have broken the glass to get in anyway. He pushed it up—thinking he'd have replacement windows installed once he and Cassie lived there. Then he started climbing into the dining room, hoping no one noticed from the street. If someone did, he supposed he could wave and say, *Jo forgot her key*, then they would know that he belonged here.

And he did belong here, didn't he?

Just when he thought he had his balance, his body

thunked onto the floor; he whacked his knee on the corner of the sideboard.

Ouch.

Shit.

He lay there a few seconds, waiting for the stars to fade and the jolt of pain to lessen. When it did, Andrew struggled to his feet, brushed off his butt, and looked around the room.

The first thing that he noticed was the scent, Jo's scent, light honey and vanilla, not fruity or flowery, but a real, welcoming scent that lingered like lace and moved over him like love.

With a smile that struggled to rise above his pain, Andrew walked—no, limped—toward the staircase that led up to her bedroom. He slowly ascended, wishing she were there. On the top step he paused. What if she was? What if Jo already was there, already in bed, with another man?

He laughed. He reminded himself that this was not New York, and Jo was not Irene or Patty, or any of those women who seemed to think Andrew was there just to be used. He also reminded himself that her car—or a car that might belong to an unknown, clandestine lover—was not in the driveway.

He pushed himself forward and limped into her room.

She was not there. He stood for a moment, studying the scene, the neat white bedspread tucked perfectly beneath peach-colored toss pillows that she'd clustered together like decorator accents. On the nightstand stood several peach candles that looked as if they'd never been lit; on the bureau was a cache of more candles, those in brass holders of varying sizes. He had not realized that Jo loved candles. He had not noticed them on the two glorious occasions when he'd been in the room. He'd had other things on his mind, he guessed. Other things to look at.

Andrew took off his jacket, hung it on the back of a cane-seated chair that sat in front of what looked like an old sewing machine. He unbuckled his belt, then looked down at his feet: he still wore his city boots, not his West Hope sneakers. He would never need the boots again, or the silk socks he wore inside them.

Once Andrew had disrobed, except for his Calvin briefs, he turned back the bedspread and slid between the sheets.

And he began to wait. He would wait, he knew, as long as it took. If it meant waiting for the sun to set then rise again over the town that was now home, Andrew would wait for the woman he loved to come back to his arms.

38

What the hell are you doing here?"

He had fallen asleep. It took Andrew a second to realize that he had fallen asleep, that he was now awake, that he was in Jo's bed, that Jo stood over him, her frame silhouetted by the light in the hall, her body as rigid as if she were Red Riding Hood and he the big, bad wolf.

"Surprise," he said, sobered by the fact he'd been woken up by the sound of a woman shrieking twice now in the same day.

Was this the same day?

He propped himself up on one elbow, wishing that he'd stayed awake, wishing he'd thought to light the peach-colored candles and look like an eager lover instead of a guy who was worn out from too much talk and too much stress and too much driving and too much Irene.

Jo did a one-eighty and exited the room.

"Jo?" he called after her, but the only reply was the sound of her footsteps tromping down the stairs. He flopped back against the pillow that smelled like honey and vanilla. "Shit," he said. "Shit."

Hauling himself from the bed, Andrew slipped into his socks, his pants, his city boots. He pulled on his shirt but left it unbuttoned. He slung his jacket over his shoulder. As he started to move, pain sliced through his knee. "Shit," he said again, and wondered, not for the first time, what he had done in a past life to deserve such crappy luck.

She was standing at the kitchen sink, her back to the stairs. She didn't seem to be doing anything; she didn't seem to be moving, and the water wasn't running.

"Jo?" Andrew asked quietly. "I'm sorry I scared you. I thought it would be fun to surprise you."

She didn't respond. He set down his jacket and began buttoning his shirt.

"I thought you'd be glad to see me," he added. He didn't say that he could have predicted this, that he'd never done very well when it came to women, that he'd never figured out why. Patty had once told him that he tried too hard, that women liked their men rough around the edges, unpredictable, undependable, bad boys, if not to the bone, then at least under the surface of the skin. He wondered if forty-three was too late to turn bad.

"I knew you were here," she said to the window, to

the indoor/outdoor thermometer, the birdhouse, and the big backyard. "You left your car in the driveway."

He tucked in his shirt. "Well, yeah. I didn't want to shock you. Just surprise you. Upstairs."

She didn't answer again. Her silence warned him not to move too close. Ten, twelve feet seemed a safe distance.

"Jo," he said, "I'm sorry if I overstepped my bounds. I thought it would be fun."

"How did you get in?"

He felt ridiculous now, having to admit what he'd done. "The dining-room window," he confessed. "I wrecked the shit out of my knee." He thought that she might laugh, but she did not. Instead, she turned around.

"How dare you," she said. Her beautiful green eyes had become dark, unpretty.

He stepped forward. "Okay. It was a lousy idea. I said I'm sorry."

But she was shaking her head, her thick, silky taupe hair swishing one way then the other, making him wish he could lose himself in it and forget about the rest. "How dare you come back to me," Jo said, "as if... as if nothing has happened."

He had no idea what she meant. God, sometimes he wished he really was gay, the way that he'd pretended for so many months, when he'd written the column for *Buzz* magazine, when he'd been working for John because he was Andrew's mentor and Andrew felt he owed him and... oh, God, it seemed a lifetime ago now.

"Irene Benson," Jo suddenly blurted. Then she turned

back to the sink, poured a glass of water. "You can't sleep with both of us, Andrew. I'm not going to be your plaything while you're out here in the country. Go back to the city, where you can sleep as often as you want with poor, abandoned Irene. God, Andrew, the woman is so old, it really is embarrassing. But she has plenty of money, so I guess that makes up for a lot of things." Then she flipped around and looked him in the eyes. "Get out of my house," she said. "Get out of my house before I call the police."

If Jo was surprised when she saw Andrew's car in her driveway and his near-naked self in her bed, he had to believe she wasn't nearly as stunned as he was by what she'd just said about Irene.

There was another moment where time stood achingly still before Andrew walked out the back door without putting on his jacket, wondering how long it would take for his knee to feel better and his brain to function again.

39

Sarah dressed slowly for dinner with Sutter. She chose a long, straight, pewter-colored wool dress that she had worn to Burch's band concert in the fall, because he'd said that she looked pretty in it. She added a loose-fitting black leather belt and a black leather necklace with a silver pendant she'd created, an abstract of two eagles flying side by side, soaring in the wind.

She hadn't known until today who it was she was thinking of when she first sketched the design. She'd only known it wasn't symbolic of Jason and her. It was as if she'd always known their souls were never meant to be. Not for forever, anyway.

A time, a place, a purpose, she thought as she adjusted the necklace in the mirror and brushed her hair again.

Jo would urge her to beware that she was not just

reacting to the rift with Jason, that she was not attracted to Sutter because she was on the rebound.

Elaine would not offer advice, because she was better at taking it than giving it.

Lily would applaud, because she believed man and woman should be together, no matter what, no matter who.

Sarah smiled into the mirror, knowing that, in part, each of her friends would always be right, because they had their own perspectives, their own truths. Still, she could not ignore the irony that all along she'd thought she'd be the one to lose Jason to another woman. It had not occurred to her that, instead, he might lose her to another man.

She slid into her coat, said good night to Elton, then started for the door just as the telephone rang.

She hesitated. What if it were Jason? What if it were Burch?

What if it were Sutter canceling their dinner plans?

It rang again.

She wanted to disregard it, to walk out the door as if she'd left five minutes earlier and had never heard the ring.

Maybe it was Laura Carrington.

She dropped her purse and picked up the receiver.

"We've got to help," said the person, Lily, on the other end of the line.

Sarah glanced at her watch. She had ten minutes to get to the Hilltop Bed and Breakfast; on a good day, it took eight. "What's wrong?" she asked.

"Well, it's Andrew, of course. This is such a beastly mess. Andrew called Elaine and said Jo threw him out and Elaine called me and, oh, it's hideous. He knows she knows about Irene. She—Jo—never dreamed he'd come back from New York. She must be very angry—"

"Lily," Sarah interrupted, "just because we've been friends for years doesn't mean we have to share every single aspect of our lives." She was thinking more of Sutter and of Laura. She was wondering if she broke things off with Jason, where that would leave her with her son.

"Oh, pooh, Sarah, stop being so closed up. Stop being so . . . so *you*."

Sarah wanted to think that Lily might not have meant that, but she knew differently. Of all the roommates, they were the two most extreme, the difference between a new moon and a full one.

"All right," she responded with controlled irritation. "What shall we do?"

"We must go talk to Andrew. The three of us: me, you, Elaine. We have to convince him how nasty Irene was when she confronted Jo. Then he'll know how to talk to her, what to say. *If* she'll listen to him."

"So we'll go tomorrow."

"No. We have to go tonight. Tomorrow Jo and I are taking Julie and Helen to check out reception venues. We have to do this tonight, or there simply won't be time."

Her friends were so important. But yet . . .

"I can't," she said.

"What on earth do you mean?"

"I mean I can't, Lily. I can talk to him tomorrow,

but I can't tonight. I have dinner plans with the man who wants me to meet my mother."

There was a short pause while Lily took a breath. "That Indian, Sutter Jones?"

Sarah smiled. "Yes, Lily. That Indian. I'm sorry. Really I am. But good luck to everyone." She hung up quickly, before her allegiance to her friends usurped the new feelings that were in her heart.

Andrew had gone home and kept the lights turned off. He figured he might go down in history as the worst father in the world, but he wanted to leave Cassie at Mrs. Connor's. Sometimes the hardest part about being a parent was trying to find some time to be alone, to get drunk if you wanted to, or to just sit there in the dark and cry as if you were a kid.

At least it didn't take a rocket-freaking-scientist to examine Andrew's life: He had no job—he'd for sure wrecked his chances of going back to Winston College once their most famous alumnus, John Benson, the man who'd finagled Andrew's teaching post in the first place, learned that Andrew, too, had walked out on Irene.

So he had no job and he had no woman—Jo would never speak to him again. Why would she? The thought of her picturing him making love to Irene was as repulsive to him as it must be to Jo.

If he weren't careful, he supposed he could lose Cassie the way Sarah had lost Burch: the second parent, a more alluring lifestyle. Hell, it had almost happened once.

He didn't have a dog or a cat or a dead goldfish he could talk to. He didn't even have any real friends left, because the two he'd always counted on had both lost their minds, one to Tahiti, the other to God-knew-what, maybe the guru in Dallas. She never had explained what that was about.

So Andrew sat there in the dark, too empty and depressed to worry about what he should do next, when a loud, insistent banging threatened to break down his door.

"Andrew Kennedy, open the goddamn door." It was Lily, because it wouldn't have been Jo.

He shuffled across the floor. "Okay," he said. "The goddamn door is open."

Lily pushed past him and marched into the cottage, snapping on lights as she made her way into the living room. Elaine followed more quietly behind, patting his shoulder, telling him that everything would be fine.

"Sit down," Lily commanded, and so they did. "Look, Andrew," she began. "I know this is absolutely, positively none of our business, but you must tell Elaine and me what happened between you and Irene. Is it the truth? That you were lovers? And, what's more, are you still?"

Suddenly he knew that the tabloid headlines about Tahiti had come from the women, well, from Lily, anyway. He smiled at the way his world had become all-consumed by women. He smiled at the ways in which life had become more interesting because of it.

"This isn't funny, Andrew," Lily continued.

He shook his head. "I know," he said. "I'm not

laughing. Believe me." Then he stood up and Lily sat and he paced around the small room, from the doors that led out to the garden to the stone fireplace he loved, all the while reciting the story of Andrew and Irene.

That he'd been seventeen.

That the Bensons had been separated.

That it had lasted just one week.

And then he realized that the secret he'd once thought he'd take to his grave had now been spilled out onto the braided rug for all to hear and know.

"Dear God," Elaine said when Andrew finished and sat down across from them.

"She raped you," Lily said. "She took advantage of a minor child and she broke the law."

Andrew blinked. He'd never thought of that. He'd thought first that he was lucky, then later came the guilt. But he'd never thought Irene was at fault.

"She was the adult," Lily continued, her anger tempered now by what sounded like sadness. Sorrow for the innocent child. Him.

"Lily," he said, "I was a teenage boy. Do you know what teenage boys are like?"

"How noble of you to defend her, Andrew. But she sure has known what she's been doing all these years. Hanging it over your unsuspecting head. Getting you to be the Bensons' showpiece, the hugely successful man for whom they took all the credit. 'He's like a son to us,' John said how many times? You made them look good, Andrew. But the truth is, you were the only one with a conscience. The only one who cared."

It would take a while, Andrew knew, before the

impact of Lily's words would sink in. It might take days or weeks or months before he would acknowledge that she was right, though in his heart right now, he knew what she said made sense: Irene had used him from day one to satisfy her perverse, self-centered self.

He wondered if Jo would see it that way too.

40

♥

I think I'm in love with you."

It didn't matter which of them had been the one to say it; the energy that radiated between their black and silver eyes had welded their hearts together.

"And I'm in love with you too."

It was Sutter who spoke the second time, so Sarah must have been the first to say the words.

"It makes no sense," she said. "We've only just met."

"And yet we've known each other forever."

"But—" she began, and he put his finger to her lips to shush her. "I know." She smiled. "Rule of Acceptance."

He looked so handsome tonight, in a white turtleneck that set off his dark hair and eyes.

They sat at a cozy corner table that Grace Koehler had set just for them, with burgundy flowered linens and deep wine-colored candles. Grace had made vegetarian lasagna and small crusty French breads. But neither Sarah nor Sutter was interested in eating much.

"I want to get my son back," she said so softly, she had not realized it was on her mind.

"I'll help you," Sutter said.

They held hands across the table, their knees touched underneath. Sarah never wanted this night, this moment to end.

And then she said, "I want to meet my mother, Sutter."

"I know," he said, then added, "when?"

She felt his energy, his warmth, go from his hands to hers. "As soon as possible," she said. "Before I lose my nerve, I guess."

He smiled. "How about tonight?"

She blinked. "Tonight?"

"Laura came with me, Sarah. She's upstairs waiting in her room."

"Jo," said Andrew, standing at her back door again, seeing her face to face but not having been invited in.

She folded her arms.

"Jo," he said, "will you please let me explain?" He didn't know if Lily was right, that what had happened with Irene was totally her fault. He only knew that it was long ago, and it was time to be done with the past.

"Lily called," Jo said. "She told me I was fired if I didn't hear your side of the story."

Less than an hour earlier Andrew felt as if he had

no friends, no life. He'd made the small mistake of looking in the wrong direction.

"Did she say anything about letting me into the house?" he asked. "It's kind of cold out here."

She hesitated—well, hell, who could blame her?—then she finally stepped aside and let him back into her life. This time, Andrew promised himself, promised Cassie, promised Jo, he would not screw things up.

41

This was the night she never thought would happen. This was the night she'd prayed for but had never really thought would happen.

Sutter had come up to her room; he had knocked softly; he had said that Sarah was downstairs, that she would like to come up.

Laura took a drink of water, put on fresh lipstick, straightened her hair, which was white now, no longer auburn. She added the silver hair clip, the one Sarah had made. Then she turned to the small table by the chintz-covered wing chairs in the corner. She was glad she'd brought the photo album. Sarah might like to see how much Laura had loved her father, and how much he had loved her.

She was too nervous to sit down, so Laura stood and waited.

This was the night she never thought would happen. This was the night she'd wished for on a thousand stars.

Sarah followed Sutter slowly up the winding stairs, each step a little steeper, each a little braver.

When they reached the top, Sutter stopped and turned to her. "I do love you, Sarah Duncan, Silent One," he said. Then he kissed her on the cheek and brought her to the door marked number three, and he gently knocked.

"You're beautiful," Laura said.

"You said that to me once."

"And I frightened you away."

"I wasn't ready to meet you then."

"Nor I you, I suppose."

"So it's true. You are my mother."

"So it's true."

"My son has your birthmark."

Laura smiled. "My grandson," she said.

Then Sarah heard a soft click of the door latch behind her and she knew that Sutter had left them to be alone.

EPILOGUE

Julie and Helen looked positively fabulous in matching ivory satin tuxedoes as they—and the minister—sat in white velvet chairs.

The media was grateful for the impressive guest list: politicians from near and far, Republicans and Democrats. Sarah supposed if they had thought to ask, Julie would have told them that she was a Washington lobbyist for the disabled, had been for many years. Helen might have added that Julie was enormously respected, but that was apparent by the senators and representatives who showed up on Valentine's Day.

"Who needs Irene Benson?" Lily said with a smile. "We'll be booking second weddings for the Beltway people now."

"Speaking of Irene," Elaine said, "Andrew told me she and John are back together. It's hard to know which of them is more of a masochist."

"After all that nonsense," Lily said, and Sarah agreed because no one knew nonsense better than their Lily, except maybe Rhonda Blair, who'd threatened to sue Second Chances, until Sutter intervened and said Rhonda had never signed a contract. Two days later they heard Rhonda had broken her engagement, that she was being consoled by a New Age guru in Dallas, the same one Irene had turned to in her short-lived grief.

"Dad just called," Elaine said. "Things are going smoothly up on Southfield Mountain."

They'd split the duties between the two weddings: Andrew and Jo had gone with the McNultys to tend to the nuptials of Allison and Dave. Lily, Elaine, and Sarah took care of things down on the ground, which was more convenient for Sarah, because as soon as this was over, she was leaving for New York.

So far, the plan was working. Every other weekend she brought Burch to stay with his father—the rest of the time Burch lived with her in the log cabin. She wasn't sure whether or not he was thrilled about the arrangement (though Melissa had found an older, full-time boyfriend, thanks to Sarah's prayers to Glisi, Sarah was certain). Burch agreed to do this until school was finished in June; he also agreed to try to accept Sutter. Sarah didn't tell Burch about the note Jason had sent with the red dress; she'd read it the day after she met Laura.

Sarah, Jason had written, *I know you know we've grown apart. I've tried to find my heart's way back to you, but after all these years, I realize we are so different. I think we stayed together because of Burch. I think we stayed together because we always were apart.*

She'd read the words and had felt oddly relieved.

Part of me will always love you. You have given me our wonderful son, and for that I will be forever grateful. But I think the time has come for both of us to go our separate ways.

He had been right, of course.

So now she and Burch spent every other weekend in New York. Burch stayed with his dad; Sarah stayed with Laura in the fourth-floor apartment on 82nd Street and Central Park West. Burch joined them for Saturday dinner or Sunday brunch, the small family linked by two diamond-shaped birthmarks... and by time, and by place, and by purpose.

The weekends in between, Sutter traveled to the Berkshires. Sometimes he stayed for four days, sometimes five. Lately he'd been talking about the old town hall in West Hope, where Frank Forbes now had his antiques shop, and how the second floor would make a nice attorney's office.

She decided not to try to talk him out of it. He was Standing Wolf; he would only bring peace.

Up on Southfield Mountain it was god-awful freezing. A light, snowy mist had coated Sarah's cupids with heavenly glow and would look wonderful in the photographs in Allison and Dave's wedding album.

Jo and Andrew ended up helping the McNultys serve hot chocolate with cinnamon and the heart-shaped, red-frosted cake that the bride had requested.

It wouldn't have been Jo's choice, but she was learning that the best thing about planning weddings was listening to what the brides and grooms really wanted and providing it in the loveliest, most romantic way.

As the sun began to set and most folks scurried to the lifts to take them off the mountain, Andrew cornered Jo in the back of the makeshift kitchen under the big white tent. "It's not so bad, is it," he asked, "this wedding thing?"

"It's not so bad," she said. It had been a wonderful few weeks, making up with Andrew, finding their ground again, reinventing their new love.

He slipped his arm around her, pulled her to the corner of the tent. "I think I'll try to get my job back at Winston College," he said. "Stick around West Hope for a while."

She smiled. "That's wonderful. But you'll be deserting Second Chances?"

"I'm a guy. I can handle two jobs if I'm needed."

"Oh, believe me, Mr. Kennedy, you're needed."

They stood that way a moment, then Jo heard Cassie whisper, "Hurry up and ask her, Dad. I'm freezing." Cassie was crouched on the other side of the tent wall, her ear pressed to the canvas.

Jo laughed and Andrew shrugged.

"She wants me to hurry up and ask you to marry me," he said.

"Marry you?" Jo asked.

"Please say yes," Cassie whispered from outside. "So we can all go home."

And Jo said "*Yes*," how could she not, because this

journey they'd been on together had already taken way too long.

From her apartment window in New York, Laura Carrington looked out onto the street, hoping Sarah would arrive soon.

She hadn't had a good day. The doctors told her there would be bad days and good. She supposed when the bad outweighed the good, the end might not be far away.

But she had Sarah now, and she knew Sarah would carry on. Sutter had rewritten Laura's will, which now left Sarah in charge of the education fund for the children of the reservation. With Sutter's help, Sarah would carry on Laura's legacy, her penance for her life, for the wrongs that she had done.

But she had loved Joe Duncan, and he had loved her too. And they had made a sweet child who had become a kind, loving woman and who, one day soon, would look to the heavens and see her mother with her father and her grandmother riding up there on the stars.

About the Author

Jean Stone is the author of more than a dozen novels from Bantam Books, many of which have been translated into several languages. A native of Western Massachusetts, she is a former copywriter and owner of an advertising agency.

THREE TIMES A CHARM is the third book in her "Second Chances" series, and is featured along with Jo, Lily, Sarah, Elaine, and Andrew—and their "second weddings" blog—at *www.secondchancesweddings.com*.

For more information on Ms. Stone and her other books, visit *www.jeanstone.com*.

DON'T MISS

Four Steps to the Altar

by

Jean Stone

Coming in August 2006

Read on for a preview . . .

BANTAM BOOKS

Four Steps to the Altar

Four best friends,
four second chances at
happily ever after . . .

JEAN STONE

Author of *Three Times a Charm*

FOUR STEPS TO THE ALTAR

ON SALE AUGUST 2006

"Marry me, Lily."

It was early in May, a year when spring had come deliciously early to the Berkshire hills of Massachusetts, teasing the landscape with purple crocus and yellow daffodils, plumping tree branches with expectant buds, warming the earth with the promise of a new season, another chance at another beginning.

It was early in May, and it was the end of the day, the end of another wedding that Lily and her second-wedding–planning partners had created, this one a Sunday evening event between a nurse and a carpenter who lived in Albany and had met at a school play when their kids were in first grade. It was a second wedding for the nurse, a third for the carpenter.

If Lily Beckwith married Frank Forbes, it would

be his second, her fourth, which wouldn't matter, because hardly anyone got married only once anymore.

Still, she would have to say no.

She zipped the quilted case that held the silver hors d'oeuvre trays they'd used for the crab cakes and spinach quiches. She moved it to the stack of things that Frank had offered to load into his truck and return from the reception at the country club to the rental store. He was generous like that. Always around to help the small bunch of enthusiastic women who took on too much work because it was such fun.

"Frank," Lily said softly, "I don't know what to say." She'd known him a year, well, less than that, actually, since she'd come back to West Hope, where she and her old college roommates had opened Second Chances, proclaiming themselves the be-all, end-all, know-it-all experts for second-time brides. They'd leased a shop in Frank's building on Main Street, and Lily had moved into the apartment upstairs. Because Frank was a man, and because he was single, it was inevitable that Lily quickly had snared him. It was also inevitable, she supposed, that he now felt secure in popping the question. She should have expected it, should have been prepared. Instead, she lowered her eyes. "Will you let me think about it?"

He laughed good-naturedly. "We can do a prenup. I'll keep my meager antiques business, you keep your late husband's vast fortune."

He was trying to lighten the mood, Lily thought.

He had no idea things would not be that easy. She shook her head. "But I've already been married a few times."

"I don't care if you've had a few hundred husbands. I'd like to be the few hundred and first."

He was a dear man, Frank Forbes. He was gentle, kind, steady, and strong. He was good-enough-looking, not too short or too tall, not dashingly handsome, but he had sturdy, broad shoulders and sincere brown eyes and a sweet, receding hairline. He'd make a great husband, partner, mate. And he loved her! Lily had felt sure of that from the start.

"You do love me, Lily," he said, taking her hand, his callused, workingman fingers threading around her soft, delicate ones, smothering her large pear-shaped pink diamond, the ring she'd bought one day on a whim.

It was the pink diamond—not the previous marriages—that was the real problem.

If Lily married Frank—or anyone—she would lose her inheritance from poor, dead Reginald Beckwith, her most recent husband. As much as Lily cared about Frank, would he—would any man—really be worth fifty million? Not that she'd ever see the cash, certainly not the way Reginald's beastly sister, Antonia, rationed Lily's allowance as if it were chocolate and Lily, a diabetic.

Fluffing her wispy blond curls, Lily resumed her role as a coquette. "Don't be a goose, darling. I simply need a bit of time. You understand, don't you?"

She stood on her tiptoes and kissed his forehead. "Now I must go check on the girls." Then she flitted away, butterfly that she was, too embarrassed to admit to Frank that, short of going to Antonia and distastefully groveling, Lily simply couldn't marry him. It just wouldn't work, economically speaking.

She sucked in her cheeks and tried to tell herself that was okay.

2

♥

"If the old bastard asks about John Benson, I'll say we haven't spoken for a while, that I've been busy with friends, launching their new business." Andrew stood at the mirror that hung over the bureau in the bedroom of his small cottage. He straightened the open shirt collar and adjusted the shoulders of his khaki twill blazer. He hoped it was okay not to wear a tie.

"The Dean of Academics at Winston College—the 'old bastard,' as you call him—might not even know John," Jo replied.

He turned to look at her, the vision of loveliness camped out in his bed, where she regularly was whenever Cassie slept over at her friend Marilla's. (Though Andrew had tried to tell Jo that Cassie was very hip for twelve years old and would be cool about them sleeping together, Jo had insisted, for propriety's sake, on not giving his daughter "too loose" a message about love and sex.) Sometimes Jo and Andrew stayed here, sometimes at Jo's house, where they would all live once he and Jo finally were married, which was just weeks away, though it seemed like decades. He leaned down and kissed her full, sexy mouth and wondered not for the first time how he had gotten so lucky. "Thanks for the encouragement, but even the new pope knows John Benson."

When Jo laughed, her green eyes crinkled and her whole high-cheekboned face glowed. She tucked her taupe-colored, slept-on hair behind her ears, then kissed Andrew's cheek. "Winston College was lucky to have you as a professor once. They will be lucky again."

Andrew groaned, sat on the side of the bed, and tugged on his right sneaker, then his left. "Are the sneakers too..."

"Too what? Too you? No. They're perfect."

He felt her gaze on him as he began tying the shoelaces.

"You really are nervous, aren't you?" she asked.

He double-knotted each lace, the way he'd taught Cassie to do for good luck. "I want to be able to support my new wife in the style to which she has become accustomed."

She said that wouldn't take much, then they both laughed and he took her hand.

"Yes," he said. "I'm nervous. I need my old job

back. Call it a man-thing about having a decent paycheck. But I'm afraid John has cut the strings that got me there the first time." The first time had been nearly six years ago, when he'd moved from New York City to West Hope, when he'd gone from being an international television journalist to a small-town college professor so he could raise his young daughter in the peace of the country. John—media mogul, Winston College alum, and hefty benefactor—had been a mentor to Andrew back then, had wanted to help him heal the wounds of a ripping divorce. Time, however, had changed a few things, and John was no longer an Andrew Kennedy fan, and vice versa.

Jo covered his hand with her other one. "You will be fine. You don't need John Benson. And if the college doesn't want you, you can still be a wedding planner. Maybe I can talk to the others about giving you a raise."

He reached for a pillow—his pillow that was next to her—and bounced it off the side of her head. She grabbed it and pretended to throw it back at him, just as he shouted "Uncle!" and leapt from the bed. He returned to the mirror, squared his shoulders again, and combed his tawny, never-in-place hair with his fingers.

"You'll come to the shop when you're done?" Jo asked.

"No."

Jo raised her lovely, lean, naked body up on one elbow. His heart did the little dance that it did whenever she revealed that she had her clothes off, the same little dance that made him feel like a teenager with just one thing on his mind.

"No?" she asked.

He shook his head, tucked his car keys into his pocket. "I'm going to stop at the hardware store and check out the plans for our new house." The new house was not exactly a new house, but a family room and a first-floor master bedroom suite that they were going to add on to Jo's house so it would be big enough for the three of them—Andrew, Cassie, and Jo.

"And then you'll come to the shop?"

He leaned down and kissed her. "And then I'll come to the shop. In the meantime, please stay right here in bed. It will help me relax to think that while I'm in the old bastard's office, your beautiful body will be rolling around in my sheets."

Jo decided to wait there an hour. Not that Andrew would know if she'd showered and dressed and gone off to work, but the thought of him sitting in the dean's stuffy office, smiling because he was thinking of her in his bed, was part of Andrew's charm that she could not resist. Playing along with it made her smile too.

But instead of "rolling around" or being tempted to go back to sleep, Jo slid into that heavenly state where you can make dreams happen, where you can always get the endings that you want.

She pictured Andrew, coming home from the college, tossing his briefcase into the corner of their new family room, meandering toward the fireplace, telling her about his wonderful day, that his most difficult student had mastered writing a press release, that the year's first edition of the school newspaper was on deadline and awesome, that the old bastard dean had said Andrew was doing a fine job and the college was fortunate to have him on their roster.

She saw Cassie, watching *American Idol* tapes in the "old" living room—the original room of the original house that Jo's grandfather had built for his bride seven decades ago—giggling with her best friend, Marilla, as the girls tried on makeup and revamped each other's hair with braids and extensions and who knew what else.

And Jo felt her spirit, floating contentedly on her happiness cloud, drifting around the warm, cozy kitchen (it would be her turn to be the domestic goddess for dinner), making healthy chicken soup for her family because last night had been Andrew's turn and he'd cheated by ordering pizza.

She smiled and wrapped Andrew's covers more closely around her, warmed by the scent of their lovemaking last night, eager to start their great life together. Only three more weeks until May 27, the date they had chosen for their wedding, for Jo Lyons, 43, to wed Andrew David Kennedy, 43, both of West Hope, Massachusetts, or so the local newspaper notice would read.

One day at the shop, Lily had suggested they have the article published in *The New York Times*, what with Andrew, once known as Andrew David, a recognized face in many living rooms during the evening news, and Jo one of the partners in Second Chances, an up-and-coming business in a field where glamour and hype definitely mattered.

But Andrew and Jo had said, "No way," simultaneously, that this was their marriage, not a publicity stunt.

Lily had been annoyed. It was bad enough, she'd complained, that Jo was going to wear a petal-pink shantung suit, a Chanel knockoff. It was bad enough that there would be only two attendants, Jo's mother to stand up for her, and Cassie for Andrew in lieu of a "best man." It was bad enough they had invited only sixty or so people and that the reception would be on the lawn of the Stone Castle, down by the lake and the dock and the rickety rowboat where they'd apparently fallen in love.

These things were bad enough, according to Lily, for the marriage of two wedding planners. But no publicity? Positive horrors.

Elaine, however, had understood, and Sarah had commented on the ridiculous tradition of publicly announcing the bonding of love, as if the bride and groom were the winners of the July 4 town raffle or the grand opening of an appliance store out on Route 7.

Jo turned onto her side and thought about how

happy she was. For so long she had been so aimless, so empty, living in Boston, her career-driven days a sad substitute for her lonely nights. If it hadn't been for Brian—for the fact that he had come back to her, for the fact that, once again, she succumbed to his magic elixir that he dared to call "love"—Jo would not have lost everything, would not have returned to West Hope, would not have built a new business with her old friends, would not have met Andrew. It occurred to her that if Brian's trial ever got under way, if she had the chance to face him in the courtroom, she should thank him for jump-starting her life.

Her cell phone rang, snapping her back to the present. Could Andrew's interview be over so soon?

But the caller wasn't Andrew, it was Sarah.

"I wondered what time you're coming to work."

Jo looked at the clock. "Sorry. I'm running late. I should have called." As with Cassie, there was no need for the others to know that Andrew and Jo sometimes slept together all night. Luckily, cell phones still provided an anonymous "cover" as to the whereabouts of the persons on each end of the line.

"No problem. But I'm already here and I forgot to pick up daisies at Dennis's Flower Shop. I need to figure out how many will fit into the backdrop for the Gilberts' wedding." The wedding was going to be yellow and white and would be outside in a meadow. Sarah had designed a lattice wall that would frame the wedding party and would be adorned with as many daisies as she could weave through it.

"I'll pick up a few dozen. Will that be enough?"

"It should be. Thanks. And tell Andrew I'm sorry if I interrupted anything." She said good-bye and hung up before it registered with Jo that Sarah had surmised exactly where Jo was and, apparently, the reason she was late.

So much for the anonymity of cell phones.

She clicked off the phone, pulled herself out from under the covers, sat on the edge of the bed, and laughed at her old-fashioned self.

"What's so funny?" Cassie suddenly asked from the hall and appeared at the open doorway of Andrew's bedroom before Jo realized that she wasn't alone after all, or before her reflexes were quick enough to cover her nakedness.